5

ELLIE HENSHAW

The Earl's Dangerous Secret

First published by Blakesley Press 2024

First edition

ISBN: 978-1-917278-00-3

This book was professionally typeset on Reedsy.
Find out more at reedsy.com

Chapter One

ENGLAND 1805

A caller after midnight could only mean bad news.

Emily Ellerton rammed her arms into the sleeves of her dressing gown as she raced to the landing. Her heart pounding in her chest. She prayed tonight's visitor would not bring more heartache, like the night long ago when she had hidden in the shadows, crouching down and peeping through the banister rails, the sharp edges of the spindles digging into her small hands. She had fled to her room then, diving beneath the covers while trying to convince herself that what she had heard wasn't true.

Well, tonight she would not hide away. She would face what the night brought. Coming to a hurried stop, she leaned over the banister. The flickering light from the wall sconce cast sinister prancing shadows across the black and white tiled floor. As the butler opened the door, a sharp blast of frigid night air swirled around her.

On the doorstep below lay her brother.

"George!" Why was her brother slumped in the doorway?

He was supposed to be in Austria as part of the diplomatic service. He wasn't moving. An icy dread spread through her as she gripped the banister rail. "What's wrong with him, Hodgson?"

The butler lifted George up and assisted him inside. "He's wounded, miss."

"Wounded!" Emily flew down the oak staircase. After her aunt and uncle, George was the only family she had left. She couldn't lose him.

Her brother's mop of thick black hair was plastered to his head. He wasn't wearing a hat. Why would he be without a hat on a night like this?

Kneeling beside the butler, she helped him to sit her brother on the hall chair. An ominous dark stain marred his grey coat. "He's bleeding. Fetch some bandages and warm water. Then send someone for the doctor."

"No, no doctor," George rasped.

"You're hurt. You need a doctor." Her heart beat a terrified tattoo as she took in his gaunt face and deathly white skin. He'd lost weight since she had last seen him. He'd always taken good care of himself. What had happened to him?

George shook his head and clutched her arm. "Too dangerous, sis." His voice was rough and cracked; his desperation slithered into her bones. "Promise me you won't call a doctor."

Under her trembling fingers, the rough wool of his coat felt cold and damp. She lifted her hand to his forehead; he was burning up. He needed a doctor and soon, but how could she defy him?

The portrait of their parents hung above them, she raised her gaze to their beloved faces, gripping the silver heart-shaped pendant they had given her as a tenth birthday present. She couldn't lose another loved one. What was she to do? George had always looked out for her, especially after their parents had failed to return home. She clenched her jaw; at least George had come home to her. She gave a firm nod. If this was what George wanted, then that's what she would do. "Very well, no doctor, but you must let me dress your wound." When he didn't argue, she peeled back his bloodied shirt and winced at the hole in his shoulder.

The butler returned and passed her a cloth and a bowl of warm water. With shaking hands, she cleaned George's wound and wrapped a bandage around him. She then sat back on her heels. How was she going to explain this to her aunt?

A sharp knock on the front door made her jump. George grabbed her hands in an agonisingly desperate grasp. "Oh God, Em, I'm sorry. I didn't think he'd get here so soon." He dropped his head before lifting his wide, fearful blue gaze to her. "Please, you mustn't let him know I'm here."

She'd never seen him like this. "Why? Who is it?"

He shook his head. "If you don't know anything, you can't give anything away."

"But..." She didn't want to be left in the dark again, kept from the truth like before. But he was right. His safety was paramount. Answers would have to come later. At least this time, she would get answers. "I'll get rid of whoever it is. Hodgson, take George and hide him in the priest hole." George had made it here, he would make it along the corridor and through the study with Hodgson's help.

The butler nodded and helped an unsteady George to his feet.

Satisfied no one would find him there, she looked down at

her dressing robe; it was smeared with George's blood. She couldn't answer the door like that. Picking up the bowl in one hand and her skirts in the other, she raced back upstairs, emptying the bloodied water into a plant pot as she passed. She reached her bedroom, grateful that she kept a small candle alight at night in case her aunt had need of her. With shaking hands, she placed the bowl next to her jug on the washstand.

The sharp knock came again. An authoritative knock that made it clear they would not give up.

There wasn't anybody else she could send to answer the door because her aunt had already sent the footmen on to her uncle's town house, and waking her aunt was not an option as it could trigger an attack of her ailment. She didn't have time to wake her maid, so she needed something she could put on by herself. Opening her wardrobe, she pulled out her cornflower blue riding habit along with a petticoat and blouse. After slipping off her bloodied dressing robe and nightdress, she hid them in the back of her wardrobe where she kept a small pistol. With no time to arrange her hair, she left it unbound and hurried to put on her riding habit.

Emily reached the front door whilst still doing up the last button. She paused and took a deep breath to fortify herself. George had always looked after her; now it was her turn to look after him. He was her brother, and he was counting on her. She would do everything possible to protect him. With that firm resolve in mind, she clamped down on her rioting nerves and opened the door.

A tall, well-dressed gentleman stood in the doorway wearing a long caped coat and a tricorne hat. The shadows hid his face, but even so, her every nerve vibrated with an innate familiarity as though she'd known him her whole life.

Surprised, she inhaled deeply and was assailed by the aroma of wet woollen clothes, horses and a hint of cologne made from sandalwood and bergamot, an expensive concoction that gave him a tangy sense of self-assurance and condescending arrogance. The combination prickled along her tongue and she clenched her jaw to combat the effect. She didn't like it one bit, and that was before the stomach-churning realisation that this could be the man who had shot her brother. Her heart did a triple beat.

"Why are you calling at Oakleaf Manor at this ungodly hour?" Her voice rasped against the hatred constricting her throat.

"I'm here to arrest Mr George Ellerton."

Arrest George? No, she would not let that happen. "George isn't here." She gave him a haughty stare, hoping it would be enough to send him on his way.

"I beg to differ, Miss...?"

"Miss Emily Ellerton. I'm George Ellerton's sister. And you are?"

"Lord Nathaniel Renwick, Earl of Thornburn. At your service." He gave a curt bow. "Now stand aside and let me enter."

The Earl of Thornburn! She'd heard of him. He worked as an attaché to the British consulate along with her brother, who had always spoken highly of him. But why would he want to arrest George? She gave her head a determined shake. She had promised George she would get rid of this man and she would not break her promise to him. "My lord, it is the middle of the night. You can hardly expect me to let you enter."

As he lifted his face, the light from the hall lantern illuminated his stubble-hewn jaw, his lean aristocratic nose and wide cheekbones, a glint catching the resolute steel gaze levelled on her. "Do you usually wear a riding habit when you answer the door in the middle of the night?" His glittering gaze flicked from the top of her loose hair to the tips of her boots and back up again.

"Do you usually wear cologne when you knock on doors in the middle of the night?" She raised her chin, glaring down her nose at him.

The slow, sensual quirk of his firm lips gave her his answer. A deep flush heated her cheeks at the implication of his normal nocturnal visits. Had he been on his way to such an encounter when he'd been interrupted by the pursuit of her brother? Inexplicably, the thought annoyed her and her blush changed from embarrassment to anger.

He took a step closer and leaned conspiratorially into her ear. "That would depend upon whose door I was intending to knock. If I'd known you were going to open this door, I would have dabbed on a little more cologne for your pleasure."

"I wish you had." She waved her hand in front of her nose as she leaned away from him. "Goodness knows you could do with it."

He gave a husky laugh.

Her jaw dropped. How dare he have the temerity to chuckle? To stand on her doorstep after demanding to arrest her brother and chuckle at her. She let out a long, slow breath.

He sobered immediately, and Emily got the disconcerting impression he would not be side-tracked for long.

"Well, perhaps in future you ought to let your butler open the door." He rested his shoulder nonchalantly against the door frame, ensuring she could no longer shut the door. "For that matter, where is your butler?" He gave her an enquiring stare, but the corner of his lip lifted.

This was a man who thrived on investigation and getting to the truth. He would not be thwarted easily.

Emily folded her arms across her chest. "Away."

"May I ask where?"

"No, you may not."

In a casual, deceptive move he shifted forwards, his bulk filling the doorway, his body an immovable force filling the whole of her vision. "Are you alone, then?"

His tone slithered down her spine like a caress, but in her agitated state, it only served to raise her ire. "Most certainly not. My aunt is residing with me."

His swift steel gaze searched the inside of the hall before dipping down to capture her eyes, causing a tingle in the pit of her stomach. "So, why did your aunt not open the door?"

Emily blew out a slow breath, as though the need to explain everything to him was a bothersome inconvenience, but there was more to her need for composure. "She is a trifle deaf and did not hear your incessant knocking."

"Then why did you not rouse her and allow her to open the door instead of yourself?"

"If you must know," she said, releasing her breath again in a heavy sigh, "she is unwell at present, and I did not wish to distress her. So you will understand why I cannot let you enter."

He shook his head with implacable resolve. "If she is a trifle deaf, then she is unlikely to hear me if I do come in." He moved forwards again and forced Emily to take a step back.

She allowed him that one step, but then stopped and stood defiantly before him. "On the contrary." She lifted her pistol out of her reticule and pointed it at his chest. "A pistol shot is sure to raise her."

Lord Thornburn's left eyebrow rose a fraction. "Miss Ellerton, I am here on His Majesty's instruction to arrest your brother, and I intend to do exactly that. As for your aunt, I am quite certain a pistol shot is sure to severely distress her." He rested his fingertips on the barrel of the pistol and nudged it so it was no longer pointing at him.

Hating the fact that she could not shoot him when he was here on His Majesty's instruction, she stepped back. "Very well, but I can assure you that George is not here."

He did not deign to respond as he strode past her and glanced at the hall chair. Emily held her breath, fearful he would know for certain that something had taken place there, but if he suspected anything, he gave no indication. With a flick of his coat, he dismissed the chair and headed back to the door.

She only had a second to gather her wits as he signalled to someone. A moment later, another man entered the house. He had a wide, crooked nose created by a fist or two and not by nature, and his eyes were too close-set. Emily took an instant aversion to him.

"Miss Ellerton, may I present my assistant, Mr Pykett? Simon, this is George Ellerton's sister."

Mr Pykett gave a crude attempt of a bow. "Mightily pleased to make your acquaintance, Miss Ellerton," he drawled as his eyes travelled lazily up and down her length.

Emily fingered the trigger of her pistol, sorely tempted to shoot him in his foot for his repugnant ogling.

Lord Thornburn stepped between them. "Pykett, search the house. I'll stay here and keep an eye on Miss Ellerton."

His gallant behaviour threw Emily, aware he'd stepped between them to protect her from Mr Pykett's leering, but she couldn't help glaring at Mr Pykett with loathing.

"Don't look at him like that. He's one of our best operatives."

"Doesn't say much for the rest of you," Emily said in a scathing tone.

"Your brother included," Lord Thornburn retorted with a tilt of his head.

Her jaw clenched at the way he'd deflected her barbed remark straight back at her own brother. How could George have esteemed this man?

Mr Pykett threw her a disgruntled look as he headed off towards the kitchens and servants' quarters.

Panic thudded through her. Should she follow Mr Pykett to ensure the servants did not mention Hodgson was here? Or should she stay where she was in order to prevent Lord Thornburn from arresting George in the very unlikely event of him detecting the entrance to the priest hole? Fearing her greatest threat lay with the servants saying something they shouldn't, she turned to follow Mr Pykett.

"No, wait here." Lord Thornburn twisted to face her, his greatcoat swinging out in a menacing arc. His words were an order spoken by a man with the total confidence that he would be obeyed.

Emily studied the tall, arrogant man stood before her still wearing his hat and greatcoat inside, showing this was no social call; he meant business. The temptation to disobey him to prove her superiority over him was strong, but not as strong as what she owed her brother.

She swayed on the spot and decided her best course of action was to behave as though she had nothing to hide, although she was quite certain he could hear the pounding of her heart echoing around the cavernous hall.

Linking her hands behind her back, she tried to appear nonchalant as she gave him a curious glance. "You're wasting your time. You know that, don't you?"

"I never waste my time," he replied in a tone of absolute certainty.

Unperturbed, she persisted. "George is in Austria."

"That is one place I know for definite he is not."

"How?" Emily said, unable to keep the accusing tone out of her voice. His slow, evaluating gaze reminded her that she needed to be more circumspect with her responses: George's life depended on it.

"Because I've spent the better part of a fortnight following his trail."

"Then you've been following the wrong one." She used the haughty lift of her chin as an excuse to look away from his discerning gaze.

Instead of responding, he turned and surveyed the hall. "How old is this house?"

Her stomach clenched; she suspected where this line of questioning was headed. She gave a shrug of her shoulders. "I don't know – I'm not interested in history."

Not true. She knew each of her ancestors who had lived here over the centuries, all the stories and follies of every member of her family tree.

Lord Thornburn walked over to the far wall and ran his gloved fingers along the wainscoting. His gaze following the wooden beams that intersected the wall and arched across the ceiling. "I reckon this house dates back to around Tudor times."

"You think so?" Emily turned as though to observe the building herself while she fought the impulse to swallow. He was referring to the dissolution of the monasteries and the subsequent need for secret places to hide priests. The same place she was now using to hide her brother. It took all her strength not to glance along the corridor to the study and the hidden door to the priest hole.

"Are you not cold standing here without a fire?" His heel squeaked on the tiled floor as he spun around to face her.

A jingle of trepidation skittered through her. His presence threatened more than her brother's freedom; it pricked at a primal intuition that he could be far more dangerous to her.

Digging her nails into her palm, she fought the overwhelming desire to shiver for it would only confirm his intimation. "I'm perfectly fine. I shall be returning to bed the moment you have finished your pointless search of my home."

But a lot of priest holes were built behind fireplaces and one way to find them was to light a big fire and hope the heat forced the occupant out of their hiding place. Something – she'd learned through researching her family history – that had been tried here in the past and had led to an alternative place being built. One that would not be affected by the heat from the fires.

"Oh, we shall be here a while yet, I assure you. Why not let me light a fire for you as you have no butler to arrange that at present?" He raised his eyebrow, daring her to deny it.

She gave a shrug of her shoulders. "There really is no need. My aunt and I are heading to London on the morrow."

"You'll still need a fire for in the morning."

The verbal volley of pretence and his effect on her senses finally got to her. There was no risk to George, but Lord Thornburn's constant goading made her forget her resolve not to let him get the better of her. "My lord, if you wish to make a fool of yourself by wasting wood in a futile attempt to locate priest holes that do not exist and in the process warn George – whom you believe to be in the area – of your presence via a very large smoke signal, then please, by all means, be my guest." Finished, she took the seat she'd sat George in not ten minutes ago, and waited for him to make a cake of himself.

"Seems you do know your history, after all."

She scowled at him. "I never said I did not know my history, just that I was not interested in it."

"Touché," he said with a sweeping bow.

She gave him a curt nod in acknowledgement of his acceptance of her winning return volley. It was refreshing to find a gentleman who would concede victory to a lady so willingly. If she hadn't been so worried about George, she would have enjoyed the moment fully, but for now she was more concerned with returning to George's side, before she was too late. She cast a surreptitious glance at the grandfather clock. "Shouldn't Mr Pykett have finished his search of the kitchen and servants' quarters by now?" she asked, trying to make her voice sound unconcerned.

"I expect so. He's probably searching the upper rooms via the servants' stairs."

Emily leapt up from the chair.

"Is something amiss?" He strode towards her, the hopeful expectation that she'd given away George's hiding place showing on his face.

"My aunt, she's still asleep upstairs. I cannot have him burst in on her."

"Then we had better go and wake her."

Emily led the way upstairs and left him outside while she roused her aunt, Lady Amelia Drayford, and gave a whispered explanation that Lord Thornburn had come to arrest George. Her silent response to her aunt's questioning look was enough for Lady Drayford to understand that George was hiding in the house.

She assisted her aunt into a black bombazine dress and placed a wool shawl around her shoulders.

Emily carried a lighted candle as they joined Lord Thornburn, who was standing in the corridor outside her aunt's room.

He removed his hat and gave her aunt a quick bow before tucking his hat under his arm.

Her aunt took matters into her own hands. Leaning on her cane, she grasped Emily's free arm and led them into her withdrawing room. "This way, if you would be so good."

Emily placed the candle on a small table next to a pale pink striped settee as she helped her aunt to sit. She pursed her lips as Lord Thornburn surveyed the room, obviously trying to ascertain if there were any hidden passages leading off where George could be secreted. It riled her that he was so determined to arrest her brother that he'd take any opportunity to attain his goal, even to the extent of foregoing politeness and manners. "He's not hiding in here, I can assure you," she said in an icy tone. She was mollified when he appeared to take her tone for genuine verisimilitude and stepped away from the panelled walls he'd looked on the verge of tapping to see if they echoed.

"I apologise. I did not mean to abuse yours and Lady Drayford's hospitality."

"I am glad to hear it." Emily lowered herself onto the settee opposite the empty fireplace. "In fact, if you're still so eager to light a fire, you may do so. I'm sure my aunt would appreciate it."

"By all means," he drawled through gritted teeth. "It would be my pleasure."

"A nice, large fire," Emily goaded, with the smallest smile tugging at her lips.

He pulled off his gloves and bent to his task, his coat stretching against the long muscular lines of his body. He stood up once finished. "Is this to your liking?"

"Perfectly," she said, reaching her fingers out to the fire. "We shall be toasty warm in no time."

A muscle flickered in his sensual jaw as he paced the room.

"My lord," Lady Drayford said as she watched him wearing a path in her carpet, "perhaps you could take a seat while you wait. It is most vexing to watch your impatience when it is our home being searched and not your own."

He brought himself to an abrupt halt. "My apologies. I'm just anxious to locate and apprehend George."

He sat next to Emily; heat sizzled between them as his thigh grazed hers. Emily threw him a sideways glance before shifting, unable to endure the confusing sensations coursing through her at this brief but intimate contact.

"May I ask on what charge?" Lady Drayford asked.

"Treason, ma'am."

"Oh, utter nonsense. I know my nephew well enough to know he is not capable of that." Her voice carried the confidence of her words.

"I thought so, too, once." Bitterness darkened his words.

He had doubted George's guilt in the past. Emily had to convince him that he was wrong now. "You know for yourself George is incapable of committing treason." She twisted in her seat to face him.

Lord Thornburn's steel-grey eyes held her gaze. "I've seen

the evidence," he said with gentle finality.

She shook her head. "No, it's not possible."

His gaze never left hers.

His belief in George's complicity was absolute. He believed George was guilty, so he would never give up until he arrested him. She had to convince him of the error of his belief. She reached out and placed an urgent hand on his arm, grasping the damp wool of his coat sleeve.

His eyes turned dark and questioning.

Realising what a breach of propriety she was committing, she withdrew her hand, but her faith and trust in George had been communicated to him in that moment. That, and something else which had passed between them.

"Emily, do not alarm yourself, my dear," her aunt said. "Lord Thornburn has a job to do, and you know George will prove his innocence, even to the satisfaction of his lordship."

He turned away and broke the spell Emily had been under and looked instead at Lady Drayford. "I hope so, too – but first we must find him."

"I'm sure he will turn up when he is ready," Lady Drayford said, grabbing her handkerchief as a bout of coughing consumed her.

"Aunt, are you all right?" Emily sprang to her feet and rushed to her aunt's side. "Do you want me to fetch your medicine?"

"No...I'm...fine," she tried to say between coughs.

"You are not fine, and your health is not being helped by this man's intrusion." Emily pulled her aunt's shawl tighter around her shoulders.

"I'm sure Mr Pykett will be finished soon," Lord Thornburn said.

"Then I suggest you go and assist him, as the sooner you are finished, the sooner my aunt can return to the warmth of her bed. We do have an early start tomorrow."

"In as much as it is your brother's misbehaviour that brought us here, I feel the blame lies with him."

"You dare to blame my brother when it is you who has intruded on a fool's errand?"

"It is no fool's errand," he snapped back.

Emily surged to her feet, but was spared from replying by Mr Pykett's arrival.

"Well?" Lord Thornburn rose from his seat and strode across the room as though putting as much distance between himself and Miss Ellerton as he could.

Mr Pykett shook his head. "He's not here. I've searched everywhere."

"Feel foolish yet?" Emily asked.

Lord Thornburn's jaw hardened, and a muscle throbbed at his temple. "No. But it is imperative we find George. The future of the Kingdom rests on finding out how badly he has betrayed us. If he turns up, please insist he hand himself in instantly. For King and country."

Emily pursed her lips at his insistence that George was a traitor and implying she was also if she didn't make him hand himself in.

Receiving no reply, he bid them goodbye and strode from the room with Mr Pykett in tow.

Emily released a long breath, raced to the window, watching them collect their horses and ride away. "They're gone." She whirled from the window and snatched up a candlestick.

"I take it he's in the priest hole?"

"Yes, he's in the dark and he's wounded."

"Wounded! You didn't tell me that," her aunt said as she picked up her skirts and followed in Emily's wake.

"No, I feared you'd have tossed Lord Thornburn out on his ear and he'd know for certain George was here."

"I don't think I would have been as obvious as that."

Emily turned to her aunt as she helped her down the stairs. "I know, but I couldn't risk it."

Aunt Amelia nodded. "You did the right thing."

"I hope so," Emily said, biting her lip to stop it trembling as she remembered George's fevered brow and his deathly pale skin.

* * *

Nathan galloped a short distance away. He reined his horse to a halt behind a copse of trees and studied the house through the branches. It was difficult to make out the three-storey Tudor mansion as heavy clouds hid the moon, leaving the house in deep shadows.

"Miss Ellerton was a surprise," Pykett said as he reined his horse alongside.

Nathan gave him a warning look, but he had to agree that Miss Ellerton was not what he'd expected. Instead of a shy, country-bred young lady, she was a feisty, stubborn, protective and glorious young woman, who could fill out a riding habit in the middle of the night to make a man's ardour throb. She was a surprise indeed; an irritating, vexing surprise and one he'd like to get to know better, a lot better. But that wasn't an option, for many reasons. He was glad to be leaving her and her haughty attitude behind. "Yes, and just as devious as her brother," Nathan said as his horse snorted impatiently.

"You think George is there?"

"Until yesterday, we were two days behind him. He slowed down for a reason. He must be around here somewhere."

"You believe she's hiding him?"

"Wherever he is, Miss Ellerton is hiding more than she's letting on." Nathan ignored the slow drips from the branches above. "How many servants were there?"

"Ten. In the house were a housekeeper, cook, three housemaids, two ladies' maids and one hall boy. In the stables, I found a coachman and stable boy."

"Were any of the horses missing?"

"No, there were no recently vacated stalls and none of the horses had been ridden lately."

Nathan shifted in his saddle. "Two women living alone and no menservants in the house. Didn't that strike you as odd?"

"It did. I asked the housekeeper about the butler."

"And her response?"

"She told me if I had anything to discuss regarding the staff, I was to take it up with her ladyship."

"Damn it. George has schooled his staff well – I wouldn't have expected more from my own servants."

"So, what now?"

Nathan let out a deep sigh and shook his head to clear the images of Miss Emily Ellerton, her Titian hair left unbound to cascade over her shoulders and coming to rest above the shapely silhouette of her breast, a hint of silky white blouse peeking out from under her tightly fitted riding habit. Her chin lifted in defiance of him, ready to protect her lying, conniving brother to the hilt.

He knew the price of putting your trust in the wrong person, and he prayed Miss Ellerton would not pay the same devastating price he had. "I need to return to London before Lord Brakenhale has to leave. He'll need to know what we've found out so far."

"He will not like the news," Pykett said, shaking his head.

"No, but if he's going to turn this crisis around, he'll need all the information we can get."

"So, what do you want me to do?"

"Stay here and keep a watch on the house."

"How long for?"

"As long as it takes. Keep me informed." Nathan squeezed his horse's flanks and galloped away from the house and away from the distracting Miss Emily Ellerton. Something told him she was rare, but the last thing he needed now was a distraction like that, especially after his last distraction and the lives it had cost.

* * *

Behind the disused servant's door in the study, Emily located the complicated opening switch for the secret entrance to the priest hole that was hidden in the oak panelling. As the door swung open, she swept down the stone steps and ducked into the cramped room. Her aunt followed her, the clip of her walking stick sounding like a death knell.

The damp, narrow, low-roofed cave chiselled out of the house's solid rock foundations felt like a tomb; finding George laid out on a bench that ran the length of the wall only added to the ominous effect.

The light from her candle flickered over him as her hand shook. "Hodgson, is he..?" Her breath locked painfully in her lungs and she couldn't finish the question.

"He's alive," Hodgson assured her. "But he's not good – he needs a doctor, and soon."

Heat flooded back into her cheeks. "Thank the good Lord."

Her aunt pushed past her and touched George's forehead. "He's got a temperature. We must call the doctor at once."

"No doctor," George rasped.

"It's all right, George." Emily bent down and took his clammy hand in hers. "They've gone. We've got rid of them."

"They'll be watching the house." He squeezed her hand in return.

Emily caught her aunt's worried glance, but her aunt was not one for standing around.

"Well, in that case, I had better take a look at you. Hodgson, fetch some brandy, fresh bandages, my red sewing basket and some warm, dry clothes – these are drenched through. Emily, I'll need you to hold the lantern for me. Can you do that?"

"Of course, anything to help George," she said as Hodgson squeezed past on his way to collect the requested items.

"Good, because this will not be pleasant." Her aunt peeled back George's blood-soaked bandages. She pursed her lips on seeing the bullet-hole, and bent to examine it. "When did this happen? It's not fresh."

"Monday evening," George said, his gaze dropping.

Emily knew he spoke the truth; it wasn't worth lying to their aunt about things like this.

"That's nearly two days ago," her aunt reprimanded him. "And you continued travelling here even though you'd been shot?"

"Had to, needed to get to safety, before they caught me."

Emily gasped. "Did Lord Thornburn or Mr Pykett do this to you?"

George rocked his head from side to side.

"Are you certain?"

"I think I'd remember something like that," he said between clenched teeth.

A wave of relief washed through Emily at the knowledge that Lord Thornburn was not the one who had shot her brother, but it was such a disloyal thought under the circumstances that she pushed it away as she took in George's current perilous condition. "Then who did this?"

"I don't know, but I do know whoever it was they were lying in wait for me."

"They knew you were coming?"

"Yes."

"How? You weren't scheduled to return to England for months."

"That's one question I wish I knew the answer to."

Her aunt laid a hand on her shoulder. "Leave him be. Questioning him further will only agitate him, and he's going to need all the strength he's got for the next few minutes."

Emily saw her aunt's determined expression and tried to calm the trembling coursing through her. She moved around to the other side of the bench as Hodgson returned. Taking the lantern, Emily used her candle to light it and lifted it high.

Her aunt gave George a long drink of the brandy before pouring some onto the wound. He cried out in pain. She took a piece of dowel out of her basket. "Bite onto this," she said to George as she set to work trying to locate the ball.

Emily winced as her aunt struggled to extract the bullet using a surprisingly large variety of implements from her sewing basket. Emily suspected that her aunt had done this on many occasions, but right now she was more grateful than curious as to when and where her aunt had learned such things.

"Hold him still, Hodgson," her aunt said whilst pushing a pair of small tongs into the wound.

George grunted in pain and tried to rear up, but Hodgson threw his whole weight across him and pressed him back down.

"Nearly there, George, steady now." Her aunt took a deep breath and slowly pulled the tongs back out. "Got it."

The tight knot in Emily's stomach unfurled, and a tear trickled down her cheek. She gave her aunt a thankful smile.

"He's not out of the woods yet," she said, wiping away the fresh blood that the bullet's removal had caused to escape. "I still need to stitch him up, and to do that, I'm going to need you to hold the lantern steady. You've been shaking it like autumn leaves in a thunderstorm."

"Sorry," Emily said in response to her reprimand.

Her aunt shook her head. "I'm sorry as well. I'm too old for patching people up; it's not good on my nerves."

Emily saw that her aunt's hands were also shaking. This entire experience was taking its toll on her. "Do you want me to stitch him up?" She wasn't sure she could do it, but it was the only option if it was too much for her aunt.

"No, Emily, I'll manage. Trust me, you don't want the first person you sew up to be someone you care about – it's difficult enough without that extra pressure." She examined the bullet she had extracted. "Oh dear Lord, no."

A horrible fear spread through Emily. "What's wrong?"

"The bullet has cracked! I didn't get all of it out!"

Emily's world tilted on its side. This could not be happening. She couldn't lose George. "What do we do now?" she asked in a choked whisper.

As her aunt ran her fingers along George's collarbone, he reared up in pain. "I'm not able to remove it. He's going to need a surgeon."

A surgeon! George must be truly bad if he now needed a surgeon. Emily squeezed the brass handle of the lantern, twisting her fingers around the hard metal, trying to cling onto something solid and tangible in her suddenly changing world. "But how?" She looked at George. His sweat-soaked was hair plastered to his creased forehead, his chest marked by the dark red blood surrounding the bullet hole. He would never forgive them if they disobeyed his instructions, but what choice did they have?

"If we can't call a surgeon to the house, then we need to get him out of the house." Aunt Amelia pushed herself stiffly to her feet. "We shall set off for London on the morrow as planned, but George will go in my place, dressed as me. They will be expecting two ladies to leave, so that is what they will see."

"I don't think he is well enough to travel." Emily glanced at her brother's pale complexion.

"We need to get him to a surgeon. We can't keep him hidden in here. There's no place for a fire. It'll be dawn soon and we're only a few hours from London. My brother will know what to do once you arrive."

"Too dangerous," interrupted George, trying to sit up.

Emily pushed him back down. "You're in no fit state to argue." She touched his heated brow and exchanged a worried look with her aunt. George needed more than a doctor now. He needed a surgeon – and if this was the only way they could arrange it, then so be it. She gave her aunt a nod of agreement.

Chapter Two

Lord Thornburn's boots clicked loudly on the orange and ivory tiled floor in the cavernous, empty halls of the foreign office. It was late – or, more to the point, it was early – but Lord Robert Darnell, Viscount Brakenhale, would still be at work.

He took the stairs two at a time, then marched past the marble columns and elaborate decorations that adorned the corridor before signalling to a footman to open the door. The high-vaulted office was in gloomy darkness. A fire burned low in the grate, casting a feeble light onto the white fire surround inlaid with Sienna marble. On a large oak desk, two candle stubs guttered their death throes over a stack of open correspondence — a testimony to the long hours Robert had been working.

Nathan shook his head, knowing better than to suggest his friend go home and get some sleep. Instead, he turned his attention to the heavy drapes covering the windows. He strode over and threw them open without asking for permission. The reward for his efforts was a weak, fog-shrouded dawn that failed to emit any further light into the room.

"And that, my friend, is why I did not bother." Robert finished writing his sentence before putting down his quill and coming around his desk. He clasped Nathan firmly by the hand. "But you are a welcome sight for my sore eyes."

Releasing Robert's hand, Nathan indicated the sideboard with a tilt of his head. "And your decanter is a welcome sight for my parched throat."

"By all means." Robert walked over and filled two glasses.

Nathan took a seat and swirled the amber liquid around his glass before knocking back the contents.

"Is it bad news that brings you to my office this early?"

"I hardly like to think I would be tardy in bringing you good news." He waited until Robert conceded his point with a nod. "But you are correct. The news I bring is not good."

Robert leaned back in his chair, rolling his quill between his hands. "Either you have not discovered the identity of the traitor, or it is the traitor's identity that I will not like."

"I know who the traitor is."

Robert took a deep breath and braced himself. "Ah. Who?"

"George Ellerton."

"You're positive?" His voice showing his disbelief that George Ellerton, of all people, could have betrayed them.

"Trust me. I'm not going to make a mistake like that again."

"I would have bet money on it not being George."

"So would I, down to my last penny." Nathan put his empty glass on the desk. George had been their most reliable operative, someone any one of them would have been eminently pleased to have by their side on an assignment, especially himself. He had trusted George like a brother, but now he had betrayed them, along with their King and country. Worse than that, his actions threatened to destroy everything Nathan had worked tirelessly towards to atone for his past mistake. He couldn't let that happen. He owed too much to allow that.

"You have evidence?"

"Nothing I can show, but I have my testament and that of Mr Pykett and my brother, Peter, as witnesses to George behaving subversively, meeting with a known French collaborator and deliberately failing to carry out your last assignment."

"Damn it." Robert surged to his feet and strode to the window. "He was supposed to be delivering confirmation to the Russian ambassador in France that the promised six thousand British troops had been agreed to. Without that, the tentative coalition we have formed will collapse, along with everything else we have worked for." Turning around, he rubbed his forehead. "I thought at least that had been settled prior to my summons back to England. Now could not be a worse time for this to happen."

"What about the negotiations in the Prussian court? How are they progressing?" Nathan hoped their hard work had not come to naught.

"Not good. King Frederick III is worried enough about Napoleon's retribution should he discover what we have been arranging together. The last thing I need is for him to discover one of my retinue may have jeopardised those arrangements."

"When do you plan to return?"

"Yesterday would have been my preference. However, a sennight, two weeks at the most, is all I can spare before I must return. This is one goal Britain cannot afford to lose. But first we need to catch George. Where is he now?"

"We traced him a few miles from Oakleaf Manor, where we lost his trail. Suspecting that was his destination, we searched the house but were unable to locate him."

"Were any of his family at home?"

"Yes, his aunt, Lady Amelia Drayford, and his sister, Miss Emily Ellerton. Have you met them?"

"I've met Lady Drayford on a few occasions, but I've never met Miss Ellerton. What was she like?"

Nathan knew this line of questioning was Robert's way of distancing himself from the hurt of George's betrayal, yet the image of Emily in a riding habit and her long Titian tresses gliding over her shoulders flittered across his mind, but his most vivid memory was that of the stubborn jut of her chin and her flagrant defiance of his authority. "Not very co-operative," he said in an aggrieved tone. "She pulled a gun on me when I tried to enter the house."

Robert raised his eyebrows and managed a smile. "How did you handle that?"

"Easily enough when I made it clear that she didn't have a choice."

Robert nodded. "It may be a good idea to keep a close eye on Miss Ellerton. If George cares about anyone other than himself, it will be his sister."

"I've left Mr Pykett to watch over the house."

"What about your brother? Was he not with you?"

"No. I left Peter in Brussels, following up a possible lead while Pykett and I set off in pursuit of George. I expect Peter back any day now."

"Good, I need George Ellerton apprehended. I have to know what damage he has caused."

"Very well. I will head back to Oakleaf Manor. Lady Drayford and her niece were planning to come to London for the season, but I doubt they'll come now if George is there or likely to turn up."

"Oh, they'll come. There's one thing I do know about Lady Drayford; she's not one to miss a party." His tone conveyed his certainty.

"I hardly imagine her to be one for dancing."

Robert chuckled. "You're right there, but she likes to preside over the proceedings and observe everything that is going on."

"I still say they won't come under the circumstances."

"Willing to bet your last penny on it?"

"No. Where that family is concerned, all bets are off."

Chapter Three

Grey mist clung to the early dawn streets of London, condensing on the flanks of the sweating horses pulling a smart black coach at a hurried pace.

Inside the plush interior, Emily cradled her brother's head on her lap, wiping the sweat from his brow as their carriage rocked along the cobbled streets. George groaned in pain as the coach jolted.

"Shh," she soothed, stroking his dark curls off his face. "We're nearly there."

George tried to smile, but only managed a grimace.

She'd suggested he take laudanum to ease the pain of the journey, but he'd refused, claiming the need to keep his wits about him. However, he'd deteriorated during the journey, his temperature rising, and she feared it would soon be the fever that would deprive him of his wits.

A double thump sounded from above. That was the signal from Hodgson that they had reached her uncle's town house in Upper Brook Street.

She helped George into a sitting position, tied her aunt's bonnet under his chin and handed him her walking stick.

"Come on, George. We need to make it up the steps." When he didn't respond, she shook him.

"Argh. What did you do that for?" he asked, giving her an accusing look.

"I need you to wake up, just for a little while. We need your co-operation if we're going to get you up those steps without causing curiosity. Can you manage that?" She looked into his unfocused, round blue eyes.

"Yes," he said as he swayed backwards and slumped against the squabs.

Hodgson opened the door. "Are you ready, miss?"

"I'm not sure he'll make it."

"He'll manage, miss. He's strong." Hodgson leaned in and grabbed George around the waist. "Time to go."

George tried to push his hands away while muttering something inaudible.

"You can moan all you like when you're in the house." Hodgson pulled the unresisting George out of the coach.

Emily followed behind, grateful few people were about at this early hour of the morning. Taking the opposite side to Hodgson, she supported George up the short flight of steps.

Hodgson had already knocked on the door and the butler was waiting to assist them, along with two footmen. Once inside, they part dragged, part carried him upstairs, laying him carefully on her aunt's bed. Emily removed the bonnet and George's boots, then she helped Hodgson undo her aunt's borrowed dress.

"I'll take care of the rest, miss," Hodgson said.

Emily left him to it and went in search of her uncle. She met him hurrying up the stairs. "Uncle Charles, I am so glad to see you."

"The footman informed me that Amelia is not well."

"Not exactly." Emily led her uncle to George as she pulled off her gloves. She knocked on the door. "Can I come in?"

"Yes, he's decent, miss."

Emily entered, followed by her uncle.

"My God, George!" Uncle Charles pushed past her. "What's happened to him?"

"He's been shot. Aunt Amelia removed most of the ball, but a small piece is still lodged in his shoulder that she couldn't get to. We need to call a surgeon, but one we can trust, who is willing to say he has been treating Aunt Amelia."

"I know of someone. Leave it to me."

"Good." Emily sagged with relief into a chair next to the bed.

"But where is my sister?"

"We dropped Aunt Amelia off at the corner of Baker Street. She said she would arrange for somewhere safe to hide George when he's better. We disguised George as her so we could get him into here without anyone suspecting who he is. Last night, two men called, wanting to arrest him."

"On what charge?"

"Treason."

"That's absurd."

"We know. I don't know how long we can safely keep him here. But I'm unwilling to let him out of my sight whilst he is so ill."

"I understand. I'll send for the surgeon. Once he's seen him, we can make plans."

"Thank you." Emily took George's heated hand and pressed it to her lips. "We'll soon have you better again."

A groan was all the response she got.

* * *

The surgeon came and managed to remove the remainder of the ball. He prescribed remedies to fight the fever and laudanum for the pain.

When Emily asked what George's chances of recovery were, the surgeon replied that he was strong and young and was being well looked after. It was just a matter of hoping the fever broke soon.

Emily stayed at George's bedside, wiping his forehead and praying for the rest of the day and night. His fever got worse, and he muttered in his sleep, garbled sentences mixed with the names of places and people she had never heard of.

By the early morning, she was worn out. Her fears and worry taking its toll, her body gave in and she fell asleep in her chair.

On finding her thus, her uncle ordered her to her own bed. He did not relent, even though she argued. Too weary to fight, she left her uncle to continue her vigil.

She awoke mid-morning, the sun filling her room. She dressed and hurried to check on George. "How is he?"

"Still the same," her uncle said.

"I'll take over now."

"Have you had any breakfast?"

She shook her head.

"Then you'll do no such thing. I can stay with him a while longer. You can come back in one hour's time, not a moment sooner."

Emily started to argue, but her uncle stood up and ushered her from the room. "You may return in one hour."

Seeing that it was pointless to argue, she did as ordered and headed to the breakfast room, where a light repast awaited her. Her uncle meant well, but she couldn't eat anything, not with George so ill. However, out of respect for her uncle, she diligently buttered a slice of toast and forced herself to take a bite; but even that was too much for her worried stomach to accept. She pushed her plate away.

She decided to defy her uncle's edict and return to George. Her uncle could be obstinate, but then, so could she.

Hearing male voices as she passed her aunt's withdrawing room, she pushed open the door to find Hodgson talking to her uncle. "What is it?"

Her uncle waved her inside and shut the door. "Lord Thornburn has called."

Did the man never give up? "What did he want?"

"To ask after your aunt," Hodgson said. "I told him you were not receiving visitors, but he insisted I inform your uncle that he was here."

"Has my aunt returned yet?"

Hodgson shook his head.

Emily bit her lip. Her aunt had said she would return as soon as she had made plans for George. Well, if she wasn't back, they would have to deal with Lord Thornburn's visit themselves. "Is he on his own?"

"Yes, miss."

The last thing she needed today was to deal with Lord Thornburn, but what choice did they have? "We'll have to see him. If we send him away, he may return with a retinue of men to search the house – and we can't risk that."

Her uncle straightened his cuffs. "I'll speak to him."

"No. Let me go."

"You can't. The impropriety." Her uncle gave her a stern

look.

"I'll leave the door open. Hodgson can wait outside." If anyone was going to get rid of him, it would be her. She had promised George and she would not let him down. She would convince Lord Thornburn to leave them alone.

After a long pause, her uncle nodded. "Very well."

She turned to the butler. "Send him to the green salon." It was the smallest receiving room. She would tolerate him, but she would not accommodate him.

Walking to the room, she smoothed down her yellow morning dress in an attempt to quieten her rioting nerves. She entered to find Lord Thornburn standing by the empty fireplace. She sucked in a deep breath at the sight of him. His figure was imposing. He was tall, broad shouldered. His wide chest tapering down to a lean waist and sculpted muscular legs. He exuded strength and determination. Something fluttered within her, settling in the pit of her stomach.

He turned, acknowledged her, and bowed.

Emily bobbed a curtsey, feeling unsettled by his use of propriety after his arbitrary manner of their first meeting. She reminded herself that George wouldn't have ridden for two days in the pouring rain with a bullet in his shoulder if it hadn't been for Lord Thornburn's pursuit of him. So, whilst Lord Thornburn may not have shot him, he'd still caused George's current illness.

She raised her chin; she did not want to spend time with him. She decided to get this ordeal over with as quickly as possible, for more than just George's sake. "My lord, I apologise that my uncle is unable to see you. But as you seemed quite insistent, I hope you do not mind that I have taken his place." Her legs began to shake, and she sank onto the green striped settee, instantly regretting using this room when he took the chair opposite her; the small proportions necessitating the close proximity of the furniture, making his nearness crowd her.

"No, indeed. I am sorry for my intrusion, but I heard your aunt was unwell and wished to offer my services."

His tone was genuinely concerned, but she wasn't fooled for a moment.

"That is most kind of you, but not at all necessary." Emily swallowed as the distinctive scent of his cologne muddled her sleep-deprived mind. The last few days had taken their toll. It was as though she was being stretched out on a rack and reaching breaking point. Now Lord Thornburn was here, and she had to fight the warring emotions of excitement and fear his presence caused to surge through her. She needed to watch every word she spoke and every gesture she made, or else she would give away more than even he suspected. But she couldn't let herself snap. She had to stay calm and focused. For George.

"You look tired," Lord Thornburn said as his perceptive gaze roved over her, "if you don't mind my saying."

Oh, she minded, she minded very much, but stopped short of telling him so in no uncertain terms. "My uncle, Lord Tysling, and I have everything under control," she assured him instead. "My aunt is a fighter. She is determined to be well enough to attend Lady Eubank's soiree."

"I am glad to hear it. However, I would still like to speak to her today."

Emily's heart thumped in her chest, but in her tired, stressed state, anger superseded her fear. She pushed herself up from her seat and glared down at him. "You seem awfully eager to disturb my ailing aunt."

"You can have no misunderstanding of the importance of my request." He came to his feet and loomed over her.

Important it may be, but it was also impossible. She needed to persuade him to give up on his determination to visit her aunt. "You wish to harass an old lady who is ill?"

"No, I merely wish to ascertain that it *is* an old lady who is ill."

"You question my word?"

"I question everything." He took a step towards her.

"Everything except George's guilt!" Emily threw back at him.

His jaw hardened and his flint grey eyes glittered like a lightning storm. He said in a harsh, clipped tone, "Is it your aunt who lies ill?"

Lifting her chin, she stepped forwards and looked him full in his eyes as she uttered one word: "Yes."

"Then you won't mind proving it to me."

"By all means. When she is well enough, I shall send word and you may visit her then."

"I wish to see her now." His determination carved along the hard line of his jaw.

"So, you're willing to make a fool of yourself a second time and insult the sensibilities of two ladies into the bargain?" Emily balled her fists at her sides. "As an attaché to the diplomatic service, I would've thought they'd have taught you some manners."

Nathan's blood boiled. How dare she cast a slur against his gentlemanly conduct when it was her brother who was the traitor? "Well, it seems they failed to teach me manners the same as they failed to teach your brother patriotic loyalty." He realised the error of his words the moment he had spoken them.

"Get out," she said, pointing at the door. "And when my aunt is well enough to receive visitors, you will offer your apology for ever doubting my word, but that apology will be nothing compared to the one I will demand when George's innocence is proven. Then, my lord, I expect you to grovel."

As Nathan furiously pushed past her, the air crackled between them. He looked down at her. His tall, overbearing form did nothing to frighten the brave, enraged young woman in front of him. He watched her chest rise and fall in angry, self-righteous gasps.

Her loyalty to her brother, although misplaced, showed her to be an exceptional woman. It was refreshing to see such unswerving loyalty; in his world, it had been all too lacking as of late. "If only your brother had a quarter of the loyalty you have shown here today, we wouldn't be in this quandary," he said, surprising himself with his words.

Emily's mouth dropped open. Here she was standing in the way of his search for her brother, whom he desperately needed to arrest, yet instead of making threats to her, he was complimenting her loyalty to that same brother. Her breathing slowed, quietening the pounding that had been filling her ears. She took a moment to fully assess him.

His stance emphasised the strength in his muscular body. She should feel small and in danger next to him, but he'd reined in his rage and held it in check, which demonstrated his inner strength. His ebony hair, while giving his face a dark and devilish halo, had a tendency to curl around his collar. An unruly lock fell across his brow, hinting to a gentleness within him. His eyes were an ominous thunderstorm grey; perceptive, vibrant, yet etched with pain.

Beyond the outward display of indomitability, she sensed the vulnerable boy inside, and her innate caring instinct wanted to reach out and comfort him, to comfort the man who wanted her brother wrongly hanged for treason. She instantly stilled the impulse. But compliment or not, he was still wrong about one thing. "Loyalty runs in my family."

He glared at her for a moment. "Every family tree has one bad apple."

"Not mine."

"We'll see." His steel gaze swept over her before he turned on his heel and strode from the room.

Emily stared at the empty doorway. She could not make him out. He'd put his feelings towards George aside long enough to recognise her familial loyalty and was gentleman enough to compliment her for it. She regretted her slight against him, for she could understand why he had been chosen to work for the diplomatic service.

If only he could see the truth where George was concerned. But until then, she would do everything she could to protect George from him.

* * *

Stepping onto the pavement, Nathan waved his coachman away; he was in no mood to sit in the confines of a coach at present. He needed the exercise of walking to help clear his head of Miss Ellerton. She was clouding his judgement and his behaviour.

On discovering that she had come to London against all

his expectations, he'd had an overwhelming need to call and ascertain whether George was there. But that wasn't his only motive for calling. He'd been so preoccupied with seeing her that he hadn't thought through the impracticalities of attending alone should he discover George. He'd realised the folly of his actions the moment he was shown in, but he was determined to see it through. Instead, he'd been captivated by her defiant air, her stalwart loyalty and her gorgeous petal-pink lips. He heaved a heavy sigh; this would not do. He needed to be clear-headed. He couldn't risk destroying his and Lord Brakenhale's hard work, all because he was distracted by the sister of a traitor. And that's all she could ever be to him; a traitor's sister.

* * *

Leaving all thoughts of the puzzling Lord Thornburn behind, Emily hurried to George's bedside. There had been no improvement. His fever still raged and he slept fitfully. Since he'd joined the diplomatic service, she had spent her days and nights worrying about where he was and if he was safe. Now he was here, with her, and she'd never been so scared.

Unable to leave him, she spent the rest of the day mopping his brow and praying. Her uncle offered to take over as the evening drew on, but she shook her head. If this was going to be George's last night, then she would spend it here with him. Her naïve belief that he would recover from his ordeal in a day or two squashed by the terrifying fear that he may not survive the night.

Her uncle offered to sit with her awhile, but she waved him off to bed saying she'd need him to be fresh to sit with George in the morning – if he lived that long.

He squeezed her shoulder as he left. "If you need anything, just call."

She nodded, unable to talk through the knot of fear coiled in her throat. Picking up George's hand, she pressed it to her lips. She didn't want to let him go, but she could feel him slipping away from her. She grasped his hand tight in hers. "Don't leave me, George. Please don't leave me. Not after you came home to me."

As the hours drew on, George thrashed about in the bed and his muttering became more agitated. She whispered soothing words whilst mopping his brow, but nothing comforted him. She closed her eyes, trying to keep the torrent of tears at bay.

Beside her, George's body went rigid, and he shouted, "Nathan! Look out!"

Her eyes snapped open. The urgency and fear in George's voice cut through her. She grabbed his hand and squeezed it. "It's all right, George. Nathan is safe, he's safe." But now her own heart pounded and her mind raced. George had been fearful for Lord Thornburn's safety. He must have been close to him once. He must have cared enough to shout out such a heartfelt warning, and even now in the throes of a fever, be terrified for his safety. Was this a memory he had been reliving? If so, then his warning had worked; for Nathan was alive. Did Lord Thornburn owe George his life? But if that was true, why was he so hell-bent on arresting his saviour for treason?

Emily sat back in her seat, still holding his hand. "George, please get better soon. I love you. I need you," she said, rubbing his hand.

George muttered something incoherent in response, but Emily noted that while she didn't understand the words, his tone was more relaxed and he was no longer agitated. She was hopeful for the first time in days that her prayers may be answered.

A few hours later, they were as George's fever broke. He turned and looked at her. She saw his confusion replaced by recognition.

"My God, Emily, you look awful," he said, before he slipped back to sleep.

They were the best words she'd ever heard spoken.

Chapter Four

Nathan strode into his study, his hair still damp from his long soak in the bath. The warm water soothing the aching bones from his arduous travels in search of the traitor, but his mind still tormented him about where his search had led.

To a man he would have gladly given his own life to protect. A man who had stood by his side as they faced dangers and celebrated with him when they'd triumphed. Yet now he was working against them to destroy everything they'd worked together to achieve. It seemed incredulous to believe, but believe it he must otherwise the screaming denial of his heart would annihilate him.

Dropping into his dark green leather chair, he rested his head back as he thought of what George's betrayal would do to George's sister, Emily, who still believed in him. Believed he would prove his innocence and vindicate himself. He wished he had the luxury of trusting his heart where George was concerned, but he had to accept the truth and ensure he brought George to justice — a justice Emily would never accept, and he hated the fact that he was going to cause pain and anguish to a devoted and loyal young lady. He'd caused enough pain in the past, pain that plagued him every day, and it grieved him greatly that this time he didn't have a choice in the matter.

The butler entered and announced his brother's arrival.

Nathan stood up and walked around his desk to greet Peter. "It's good to see you." Dark circles lay beneath his brother's eyes. It hurt Nathan to see them. Peter had always been quick to laugh and find the funny side during their missions when all seemed lost. One quick remark and they'd all laugh. Morale returned, resolution restored. His well-quipped jibe had saved many a mission. His humour, so typical of him, now lost to them. George's betrayal had done more than endanger England's future; it had taken its toll on the men who once stood by his side.

"You too." Peter rubbed the stubble on his cheek. "Sorry about my appearance, but I didn't want to waste time getting cleaned up before I reported to you."

Another sign of the toll taken by his usually pristine brother. Nathan's hands curled into fists. What more would be taken from them before they caught the traitor? "What news from the continent?"

Peter sank into a high wingback chair, next to the fire burning low in the grate. He shook his head. "Nothing good. Rumours of Lord Brakenhale's supposed dealings have reached fever pitch and his return to England now is causing heightened speculation about every conceivable plot our enemies can think of to bandy about."

Nathan leaned his hip against his desk, his shoulders taut as he fought the overwhelming fury to strangle George, not only for his treachery to his country but for the harm he was causing to Robert Darnell. A man of such great conviction and integrity reduced to defending himself to the very people he served so diligently — all because of the greed of one of his own men. One they had all trusted. "Please tell me you have uncovered something that can help Robert turn this mess around."

Peter lifted his hands in a hopeless gesture, the snap and crackle of the fire filling the silence. "With so much uncertainty surrounding Robert's true allegiance, very few of the dignitaries were prepared to be seen conversing with anyone associated with him. What little I did learn is of no use and most probably false."

"What about Dubeck? Surely he still has contacts who could succeed where our presence would fail?"

Sighing, Peter ran his hand through his hair, dislodging a lock which fell across his brow. "I had hoped to delay telling you this news."

Pinpricks of trepidation prickled over Nathan's skin. In a ragged voice, he said, "Go on."

Leaning forwards, Peter placed his arms on his knees and said in a dejected tone, "Dubeck is missing."

"Missing! If George has done anything to him, I'll..." Nathan stood, flexing his hands as though ready to do battle. "Dubeck has given enough for our country."

"And what has England given him?"

Nathan didn't answer; he didn't need to.

"Heartbreak and grief," Peter said, looking past Nathan. "After the loss of his wife and daughter, what could England have possibly given him?"

Nathan walked to the window, trying to see something that would take away the memory of what had happened that night long ago. But no fancy houses or immaculate gardens could wipe away such vivid images or the guilt that lodged in his chest. He rested his head against the cool pane. "I tried so hard to protect them, but I was too late."

"I know. There was nothing you or any of us could have done."

That wasn't completely true; Nathan rued his mistake every day. "Please do not let us have failed Dubeck again."

"You mustn't blame yourself for what happened."

How could he not? But for now, he needed to focus on the present more than ever. He thumped the window frame. "Dubeck is at the heart of our network. With him gone, there is no one to protect Robert's reputation. No wonder the poison about him spread so quickly."

"We'll find him," Peter said.

"We'd better. I owe him too much to let anything happen to him."

"I know." Peter came and stood by his brother and rested a hand on his shoulder.

They stood in silence, side by side.

Lifting his hand, Peter said, "By the way, I followed your search of George to Oakleaf Manor and, on finding Simon Pykett on watch, I relieved him of his post. I hope you don't mind?"

"He found no trace of George, then?"

"You can ask him yourself," Peter said, as they heard a knock on the front door. "I requested he join us here. I suspect that's him now."

Nathan went to the sideboard and poured three glasses of his best brandy. Simon Pykett may be a common thug born in the gutter, but he knew a good glass of brandy when he tasted one and expected not to be fobbed off with inferior brands when reporting to his superiors.

On entering the room, Simon accepted the proffered brandy. He took a sip and rolled it around his tongue before downing the rest and passing the empty glass back to Nathan for a top up, which he dutifully complied with. Then, as one, they all sat. Nathan behind his desk with Peter and Simon opposite in the dark green wingback chairs.

"I take it from Peter that George never made an appearance?" Nathan asked Simon.

"No, I found nothing unusual. The only incident was when Lady Drayford and Miss Ellerton left the following morning. As they were leaving, I saw someone running through the woods. I went in pursuit and found out it was the young hall boy. On questioning him, he said he was taking advantage of his mistress being away to visit his family. Suspecting this was a diversion, I headed back to the house and surrounding area but couldn't see anything untoward. I waited until Peter arrived and ordered me back to London. Although, I suspect the ladies know something and have headed to London for more than just the Season."

"They did. Lady Drayford is ill, and they came to see the doctor."

"She didn't seem that ill when I saw her in the carriage."

"They called the doctor out to her as soon as they got here. I was informed that she had not seemed at all well when she was assisted from the coach. She had to be practically carried into the house."

"She could walk perfectly well when she left Oakleaf Manor, a little slow perhaps, but nothing that would suggest she needed to be carried."

Nathan surged to his feet. "Damn that conniving little minx."

"You think Miss Ellerton's done a switch and hidden George in her uncle's town house?" Peter said, with a shake of his head.

"No wonder she was so determined not to let me visit her aunt. I should have trusted my instincts, but I made the mistake of going alone. To be honest, I wouldn't have put it past her to cave my head in if I'd found her brother." Nathan pulled open his desk drawer and grabbed his pistol.

"Do you want me to round up the boys?" Simon asked.

"No, I want to keep this low-key."

"Just the three of us? Are you sure that will be enough?" Peter came to his feet and placed his glass down on the desk with a loud clunk.

"Yes, if my hunch is correct, it was George who needed the doctor. As the only way he'd have stayed in such a conspicuous place was if he wasn't in a fit state to argue." Nathan glanced at the ormolu clock on the mantel as it struck 2 o'clock. "And I don't think we can afford to waste any more time."

But that wasn't his only reason for taking just the three of them, as what he was about to do would be hard enough on Miss Ellerton without turning up with an army of men to arrest George and causing all the speculation and rumour that would accompany such a spectacle, not to mention the family shame. If George had any sense of family feeling, he would come quietly and avoid any unnecessary distress to his aunt and sister. As for himself, it was the least he could do for Miss Ellerton, considering what he was about to do to her brother.

Chapter Five

Emily entered her aunt's room with a smile on her lips. George was sitting up in bed, his arm in a sling. An empty bowl of soup sat on the tray in front of him. "I'm glad to see you've eaten it all." She lifted the tray off the bed and placed it on a small table, taking care not to knock over the candle in the centre.

"How could I not? It's cook's favourite recipe for when one of us is ill."

The shiny sheen to his skin was gone, his pallor of the last few days now replaced with colour.

"Indeed. Just the aroma makes me feel better. Reminds me of being warm and cared for, with everyone fussing over me, especially you." She sat gently on the bed so as not to cause him any pain.

"Yes, well, I had no one to tease and plague when you were ill. I just wanted you to get better so I could annoy you again."

Emily smiled at him. It was more than that; he'd always been a caring older brother. When she'd got stung by a bee whilst they were playing cricket in the garden, he'd raced over to her and pulled the sting out of her hand. He then carried her to the kitchen where the cook gave her a damson jam tart still warm from the oven. He'd sung silly songs to her and told her jokes, some of which she didn't understand, but he'd learnt them at boarding school and they were the only ones he knew. She had giggled mainly from the way he told them rather than the jokes themselves. He'd done whatever he could to make her smile and had been overjoyed with his success.

When their parents died, George had come home from boarding school shocked and pale, but he'd taken one look at her and instantly tried to cajole her. He hadn't been very successful, but knowing that he was hurting as much as her and yet still trying to cheer her up, she didn't have the heart to let him believe he'd failed, so she'd given him a smile, for trying, for caring, for being him. Now it felt good to be the one giving him the comfort and care. A way of thanking him for all he'd done for her.

She reached up and pushed a lock of hair from his brow. "We certainly had some fun times."

"We did," George said.

They were quiet for a while, both lost in their own reveries of past times.

George recovered first and reached out and took Emily's hand in his. "I can't stay here. I must find somewhere else to hide."

Lord Thornburn's words about how desperately they needed to hear from George echoed through Emily's mind. Although he was not strong enough, she had to at least broach the subject with him. "Should you not report to Lord Brakenhale?"

"I'm not well enough to travel to Austria."

"But Lord Brakenhale is in London."

"What's he doing here?" George pushed himself upright

with his one good arm.

She placed a pillow behind him. "According to the papers, the government summoned him back due to some information falling into the wrong hands."

"That's not good. His removal from Austria could ruin everything."

"Then you see how important it is that you report to him."

George pursed his lips. "I cannot."

"Do you not want to clear your name?" Emily slid off the bed. There was no way her brother could ever betray his country, but to stay hidden when they desperately needed to find him was hardly patriotic.

"Of course I do," George said, grabbing her hand, "but I am without the capacity to do so at present." He gave her a desperate, pleading look.

"What do you mean, without capacity?" She pulled free of his grasp.

"If I walk into Lord Brakenhale's office, they will arrest me on suspicion of treason. Lord Thornburn will give testimony that I failed to carry out my mission, and that I colluded with known French conspirators."

"But you'll have an opportunity to defend yourself."

"I cannot defend myself from those accusations."

"But...? No, you must be able to." Emily sank back onto the bed. She couldn't believe for one moment that her brother could have betrayed his country.

He shook his head. "I was in the process of carrying out Lord Brakenhale's last mission when I found evidence that we had been betrayed. I took it upon myself to discover more. I arranged a meeting with a known French conspirator to gain further information. Lord Thornburn and his brother witnessed this meeting and a subsequent encounter. That alone is enough to see me swinging from the gallows."

"But what about the evidence you discovered? Surely that would prove your innocence?"

"Indeed, it would."

"Then, where is it?" Emily stood up, prepared to fetch the evidence herself.

"I gave it to a trusted colleague."

"But why?"

"Because I was being watched, and I had to get those papers to Lord Brakenhale. So I became the decoy, leading my pursuers on a wild goose chase to allow my colleague to continue on with the mission in safety. That's when I got this bullet in my shoulder, and that's why I cannot let anyone find me. They will retrace my steps and start searching for my colleague as soon as they realise I do not have the papers. I have to stay hidden to keep him safe."

Emily's mouth dropped open into an "O" of understanding. He needed to stay hidden; not because he was a traitor, but because his discovery would put his colleague in danger.

She remembered how close Lord Thornburn had come to finding him and shuddered. George was right, he couldn't stay here.

They had to move him. And fast.

Chapter Six

The coach bearing the crest of the Earl of Thornburn careened through the London streets, swerving around carriages and bullying carts out of its way.

Inside, Nathan pulled his pocket watch from his waistcoat. He flipped open the lid and rubbed the leather of his gloved thumb across the glass. Every lost second was another lost chance to catch George. He let out a slow breath; his need to catch George growing with each tick of his watch.

His brother tapped him on the arm. "We're here."

Nathan slid his watch back into his pocket and hopped out before the coach came to a full stop. "Simon, you take the back. Peter, you're with me." He ran up the short flight of steps that led to Lord Tysling's town house and hammered on the door.

A few impatient moments later, the door opened. Together, he and Peter barged their way into the house.

"Don't trouble yourself to announce us. We'll do it ourselves."

They pushed past the butler and headed up to the first floor. At the top of the stairs, two burly footmen blocked their way.

The butler arrived, huffing behind them. "Let them pass.

They're here on official business."

"Sensible decision. You two stay where you are," Nathan said to the footmen before turning to the butler. "Where is Lady Drayford's sitting room?"

"This way, my lord."

Nathan allowed the butler to lead them to the room, but once there, he stepped in front of him and pushed open the door. "I'll make the introductions while you wait outside until I give you permission to move."

Miss Ellerton and her uncle were already on their feet. Lord Tysling took his eyes off Nathan and his brother long enough to nod a dismissal to the butler, who then hurried out of the room.

"Miss Ellerton, Lord Tysling," Nathan said by way of greeting and forsaking the dictates of etiquette by not bowing, "May I present my brother, The Right Honourable Peter Renwick. Peter, this is Miss Emily Ellerton, George's sister, and Lord Tysling, his uncle. Civilities over, I request you lead us to George Ellerton."

Miss Ellerton folded her arms across her chest. "I take it you've not brought Mr Pykett with you today?"

"He's about."

"Harassing the household staff again?"

"No, he's more occupied with ensuring no one tries to escape from the house." Nathan did not miss the quick glance between Miss Ellerton and her uncle. The exchange gave him confidence and a sense of overwhelming relief that he was finally closing in on George.

She turned her attention back to him. He waited. Sometimes the best course of action was to do nothing and wait for your opponent to reveal their intentions. Her eyes alighted on his damp hair curling on his collar – he'd have known it even if his eyes were shut because the hairs on his nape vibrated in vivid awareness of her intense scrutiny. Again, he waited.

"At least you had the good manners to bathe this time," she said.

Ah, diversion. Well, let's see where this leads. He raised the corner of his lip in the merest mockery of a smile. My move: goading. "Anything to please you."

"You know what would please me." The terseness of her tone showed his tactic was working.

Remembering his goal, he brought his jubilant emotions under control. He must not overplay his hand. He gave a conciliatory tilt of his head. "George proving his innocence would please me, too, but that's rather difficult for him to do when he's hiding behind your skirts."

She spread her hands wide and twirled in a slow circle. "There, you see, there's no one hiding behind my skirts."

His gaze skimmed over her slim form as she turned, her curves emphasised by the simple outline of her pale cream patterned day dress. "True, but perhaps today he has taken to hiding behind doors." His gaze lifted to the only other door in the room.

She glanced from him to the door and back again, as though measuring the distance between each of them to the door.

Nathan's lip twitched in triumph as they both raced across the room.

She beat him to it and stretched out her hands to bar him from entering. "I beg of you not to disturb my aunt."

Too buoyed up with the prospect of capturing the traitor, Nathan ignored her and tried to push past, but she stubbornly refused to budge. "Do not make this harder than it needs to be," he said, trying to convey the futility of her actions.

"Me make it harder than it needs to be? You're the one trying to arrest my brother and hang him for a crime he is innocent of. All I am doing is trying to stop you from disturbing my ailing aunt."

Her cream fichu filled the space above her bodice, the lace edge separating at the hollow of her throat with every breath. Not the rapid gasps of the frightened, but the deep, sharp gasp of the righteous.

Could he be wrong about who lay beyond this door? "Prove to me that it is your aunt in there, and I will gladly leave you alone."

"And how do you propose I do that without disturbing her?" She gave him a curt look.

She had a point, but he would not concede it to her. "You know full well you cannot. You're only delaying the inevitable."

She placed her dainty hand against his chest. Heat flared through his body, his pulse thundered in his ears. He tipped his head down and took in the Titian goddess before him. A mere wisp of a girl defiantly defending her family from him, while he was fighting the swirl of ardour surging through him from her innocent touch.

His eyes caught and searched hers. The relentless determination in them gave way to surprise and shock. She, too, felt this swell of desire that passed between them. But this was not the time to be distracted by his body's responses. No, he could never allow himself to be distracted, for he did not deserve to feel this way. Not after what he owed to others. He had to get away from her, but first he needed to discover who was behind this door.

He took a deep breath and considered the possibility that if he was wrong about George – although he doubted it – and it really was an ailing Lady Drayford beyond, then he should at least attempt some form of gentlemanly conduct. "Perhaps, under the circumstances, we should enter quietly, so as not to distress your aunt."

Emily, enthralled by the thumping of his heart beneath her fingers, took a moment before his words sank in, as she revelled in the magnetic pull between them. She'd experienced the sudden increase in tempo her touch had ignited, as her own heart echoed his every beat. She lifted questioning eyes to him, but he seemed to be searching her face for an answer to the same question.

The instant he regained control over himself, her own heart rate slowed and her senses returned. It was then his words penetrated her mind, and she comprehended his thoughtfulness regarding her aunt's supposed delicate health.

She could hardly berate him for his consideration without piquing his curiosity as to why she would risk her aunt's health when he had so magnanimously offered to enter her room calmly – especially given the fact that he believed it was George in the room and not her aunt.

Having no other choice, she removed her hand from his chest, fighting the urge to examine her fingers where a raw heat radiated from them, and reached behind to grasp the soothing coldness of the door handle. She gripped it like a lifeline. "Thank you, that's most considerate." Unable to delay the inevitable anymore, she twisted the handle and opened the door.

She hid her smile as Lord Thornburn's jaw tightened at the sight of Lady Drayford fast asleep in her bed.

"I'll wake her," Emily said. "I don't want her to be startled. It sets off her ailment." She gently shook her aunt awake and explained that they had guests, indicating Lord Thornburn, who was checking behind the door, under the bed, and the servant's entrance.

He turned to Peter, who was standing in the doorway. "He's not here. Search the house."

Emily's heart constricted at the sight of him having to make sure that a man he once revered was not lurking in wait for him. She wondered again what could have happened between them. But she refused to let him forget what she had told him the last time he was here. Straightening, she folded her arms across her chest. "Am I going to get the apology you owe me?"

Ignoring her, Nathan took in the array of medicine bottles on the bedside table, the fire low in the grate, the ornate dressing table full of ladies' paraphernalia; there was nothing of a masculine nature here. He touched the wax dribbling down the candle. It was warm and soft. An empty bowl of soup stood by the candle, the contents dried, attesting the length of time it had been there. Nothing had been prepared in a hurry. If George had been here; it was too long ago for them to catch up to him now. However, he was not yet ready to concede this round to her.

"Still doubt me?" she asked as she walked to the window. "Or are you waiting for Mr Pykett to capture George as he comes running from the house? If so, then you're sadly going to be disappointed, for I can clearly see him awaiting George's arrival. And you know he can't be in the house, otherwise your brother would have found him. So," she said, spinning on her heel to face him, "am I going to receive your apology or not?"

Nathan took in her smug expression. She was enjoying

this. Well, he'd wipe that smile off her face soon enough, but for now, she had won. "Until I can fully ascertain that you've had no part in George's disappearance, there will be no forthcoming apology from me." His voice was steel-edged. "I reiterate again the national importance of your brother's apprehension. Please see to it that he hand himself in forthwith."

"If it was in my power to do so, I would."

He clenched his jaw, gave a stiff bow to Lady Drayford and walked out of the room, calling Peter to follow him.

Lady Drayford waited until the front door slammed. "Well, that was a close thing."

"Yes, indeed." Emily sank onto the bed and put her head in her shaking hands. "I do not know what we would have done if you had not arrived when you did." However, her shattered calm had more than just the stress of George's timely escape to disturb her. Her mind whirled with the implications of her body's reaction to Lord Thornburn. Even now, heat infused her fingers where they had touched his chest. She squeezed her tingling hand closed, trying to combat the effect he had on her. That was one complication she could do without.

Chapter Seven

Walking side by side in perfect unison, Nathan and Peter entered Lord Brakenhale's office and took the seats he indicated. The deep red velvet curtains were tied back, allowing the late afternoon sun to fill the room. Two stacks of correspondence sat on the desk, one pile spread open and the other pile neatly folded, sealed and addressed to various foreign dignitaries in Robert's distinctive handwriting.

Robert finished the sentence he was writing before laying down his quill and looking up at them. "Pray tell, to what do I owe for this visit?"

"We've just come from Lord Tysling's town house," Nathan said. "I was convinced that George was hiding there. However, if he was, we were too late. But we do have other news."

Peter cleared his throat. "Dubeck has gone missing. The last person known to have been with him is George."

Robert lifted his pen and trimmed the nib with a knife. "You think he's come to harm?" His voice was gruff. Dubeck meant a great deal to Robert. To all of them.

"Either that or he is in hiding for his own safety. I pray it is the latter."

Robert nodded. "So do I."

Peter plucked at the brass stud pinning the brown leather to the arm of his chair. "With Dubeck missing, setting up a new network that does not include anyone George may have corrupted will be expensive, and the coffers in the Austrian account are already running low."

"So soon?" Robert asked in a disinterested voice.

"I'm afraid so."

Nathan came to his feet and paced about the office. "I'll see that they are replenished. We cannot afford for our operations to be without funds at such a delicate time."

"Thank you." Robert gave a frustrated sigh. "I feel so damned useless stuck here when I should be back on the continent ensuring England's future."

Nathan had never seen his friend so dejected. The impotency of sitting around doing nothing was an unbearable torture for such an active, involved man. He was always hatching some new venture, often taking letters in person so he could have an instant answer and be straight onto his next mission without delay. In politics, time was of the essence. "Is there anything we can do?"

"Yes, I want you to keep a close eye on Miss Ellerton. With Dubeck's disappearance, she is the best chance we have of capturing George."

Oh no. The last thing Nathan needed was the complication of dealing with Miss Ellerton. "Perhaps it would be better if Peter kept an eye on her instead."

"No. You're the one who's already had contact with her. I want her to know you are watching her. If she's going to make a mistake, she's more likely to do it if she's under pressure.

And I want her to feel under pressure. She is not to go anywhere without you turning up. Am I making myself clear?"

"Very." Nathan greatly respected his boss, but this was one assignment he'd rather not have. But he'd never disobeyed Robert before and he would not start now.

"Good, now off with you. I have things to do, as do you."

Nathan and Peter bid goodbye and headed out of the office.

As they walked down the stairs, Peter said, "You always get the best assignments. Miss Ellerton is certainly worth a toss in the hay."

"Don't be so crude."

"Hey, she's the sister of a traitor, so she doesn't deserve any special consideration from us."

"She's not the one who has betrayed us."

"Is that so? Then what do you call harbouring a traitor?"

"We don't know that she has." But Nathan couldn't help considering his brother's words. He was right. However much he admired Miss Ellerton for her loyalty to her brother, he had to accept that her actions themselves had been traitorous. Regardless of what effect she had on him, he needed to put that aside and remember that while she protected George, she betrayed her country and everything he stood for. "I call her a young lady who will wish she'd never been born after I have finished with her."

"That's more like it," Peter said, slapping his brother on his back.

Chapter Eight

Emily twisted away from her mahogany dressing table to face her aunt. "Aunt Amelia, I do not want to go to a party tonight."

"You told Lord Thornburn I was determined to go to Lady Eubank's soiree. What will he think if we do not go?"

"He's not invited." But the mere thought of bumping into him sent tingles through her stomach. She glanced at her aunt and gave a shrug of her shoulders, pretending indifference. "So how would he know?"

"You think he does not have someone watching?"

Emily glanced at the windows. Was he outside even now? She rubbed her arms to calm the goose bumps that puckered her skin as fear and excitement skittered through her. "Then isn't that more of a reason not to go?" It certainly was for her. It was one thing to act with bravado when he was near, for his presence riled her. It was another to keep up such a charade when she thought she was safe from him. But if he was lurking in the shadows - watching. She suppressed a shiver - she wouldn't be able to relax. She'd be forever on edge and she needed to stay in control. George was depending on her.

Her aunt tapped her walking stick on the polished floor-boards. "We must act as though we have nothing to hide and go on about our activities as usual. Tonight's soiree is only a small get together. So it will not seem odd that I am attending so soon after my bout of illness. Plus, it will distract you from worrying about George for a while."

"Hardly." Emily traced the swirling lace pattern of the mat on her dressing table with her finger. The swirls echoing her own turbulent thoughts.

Her aunt heaved herself to her feet and came over to her, giving her shoulder a squeeze. "I appreciate this is difficult, but if we stay closeted in here going nowhere and then suddenly head off somewhere, then they will know exactly where we are headed and why. The only way to protect George and ensure that we can still visit him is to keep our schedule full of events, so that the only conclusion they can draw is that we are here for the Season only."

What she said made sense. Yet Lord Thornburn was out there. She couldn't do it. "I'm sorry, but I'm not in the mood for socialising."

"Just try to remember you are doing this for George."

Emily squeezed her eyes shut. After George had travelled for two days with a bullet in his shoulder to get back home to her, she could not let him down now. "Very well. I'll do it for George."

"That's my girl."

* * *

"Lady Drayford, how wonderful to see you," Lady Eubank said, as she received Emily and her aunt to her party. "You are fully recovered, I hope?"

"Indeed, although my niece would have found it difficult to keep me away from one of your parties, even if I had still been unwell."

"I am gratified to hear it. But come, let me find you a seat by the fire. I would not like you to become ill again."

"Thank you." Aunt Amelia allowed Lady Eubank to lead her and Emily to the fireplace, where a spare seat was to be found. She sat down, resting her outstretched hands on the handle of her walking stick, and surveyed the room while Emily stood by her side.

They spent the next hour greeting her aunt's acquaintances, who asked after her health and wished her well.

Emily understood the wisdom of attending the party, but the repetitive nature of the conversations began to drain on her. She was on the verge of asking her aunt if they could leave when a hush descended on the crowd to be replaced with excited chatter. Someone interesting had joined the party. She glanced at the doorway and her heart lodged in her throat. Lord Thornburn was making his bow to their host.

"What is he doing here? He wasn't invited," Emily hissed.

"Men like him are always accepted anywhere, even without an invitation."

"We must leave. Now!" Panic throbbed through her as she cast about for an escape route.

"No, Emily, he will think we are running away. We have every right to be here. We have done nothing wrong, remember that. And most importantly, we must act as though we haven't. The more we can throw him off the scent, the safer George is."

Well, they'd done nothing wrong except harbour a man wanted for treason. But then he was innocent. So, by her aunt's reckoning, they had done nothing wrong. But she sure felt as guilty as hell.

She stood and waited, expecting him to come straight over to them, but no, not him. Instead, he took a slow, deliberate stroll around the room. It reminded her of being a naughty child, waiting to be told off. Whilst she dreaded the inevitable scolding, at least once it was over you could relax again. Instead, the waiting intensified her trepidation. He was doing this deliberately. She tried to ignore his tactic, but her legs were like melted wax and her hands were too warm inside her gloves. She fidgeted with the buttons, wishing she could remove them. Unable to endure watching his lazy journey towards her, she turned away, but she was acutely aware of where he was in the crowded room. As he drew near her, the hairs on her nape quivered. He stepped in front of them and bowed.

"Lady Drayford, it is good to see you looking so well." His arrogant grey eyes flicked to Emily, and he raised an enquiring brow at her.

She pretended not to have noticed. She didn't need to explain herself to him.

"Thank you, Lord Thornburn," Aunt Amelia said. "I trust you are well also?"

"Yes, indeed. And you, Miss Ellerton?" He turned and took Emily's gloved hand, raising it to his lips. "I hope your aunt's illness has not taken too much out of you."

"No, I am well." She gave him a smile that belied her politeness as she pulled her hand free of his grasp. "But I am glad she is better, as it does not give rise to any doubts or suspicions."

He pursed his lips but did not respond. The fact that he would not answer her jibe piqued her ire and, remembering the way he had left two days before, she decided she would get an apology out of him tonight at this very party. Plastering on her brightest smile, she raised her face to him.

"I believe you still owe me an apology." She gave him a challenging quirk of her brow, daring him to deny it. She waited as emotions played across his lean face. He was debating whether to play the hand she'd dealt him. Satisfaction tugged at her lips when she saw he had made up his mind.

He held his arm out to her. "Perhaps you will permit me to make my apology during a turn around the room?"

She glanced at her aunt, not willing to leave her alone. But her aunt waved her off. "I'll be fine, and you could use the exercise."

"Lead the way." Emily placed her hand in the crook of his arm, ignoring the shiver of excitement that skittered through her.

They meandered between the guests for a while before he dropped his granite gaze to hers. "It is a pleasant evening; would you prefer to stroll in the garden?"

Deciding an audience would be a hindrance to the amount of grovelling she intended to put him through, she nodded and allowed him to guide her outside, along one of the lantern lit paths, until they came to a small secluded Grecian styled stone gazebo.

They walked up the steps and were greeted by a cool breeze whispering through the open arches, rustling the leaves of the ivy that clung to it.

"This is a pleasant spot." Emily rested her arms on the

wooden sill and enjoyed the feel of the cool air on her cheeks. It was a welcome balm to the stress of George's predicament and Lord Thornburn's nearness.

"Yes," he said in a tone that suggested he had no idea what he was agreeing with.

She glanced at him. His chiselled face was in quiet repose. Did nothing disturb him? She'd see about that. "My lord, we came out here so you could make your apology to me in private. If, however, you would prefer an audience..." She stepped towards the entrance of the gazebo.

With catlike deftness, he grasped her arm and tugged her back inside, giving her a calculating look. "No, in here is perfectly acceptable. Although, I must say, your aunt looks exceedingly well considering."

How dare he cast aspersions on her, true though they may be? It was most ungallant of him. "That's a poor start to your apology, assuming you have any intention of giving the apology that is very much deserved."

"Is it deserved?"

"You know full well it is."

Nathan sucked air over his teeth while he considered the benefits of continuing to argue with her about who was truly ill. He decided that it gave no tactical advantage to do so.

"Very well, I will concede to you on this point." He'd concede her one victory and that only to gain her trust and the lowering of her guard. When her lips curved in triumph, he continued, "But on this point only."

Her green eyes formed tight slits at his unconcealed mistrust of her. "I'm still waiting for your apology."

He raised his hands in acquiesce. "I apologise for harassing you and your aunt when she was ill. There, will that do?"

"I suppose it will have to. But my previous demand still stands. The apology you will give me when George's innocence is proven will be a great deal better and more humbling than this last one."

Nathan remained quiet for a moment, weighing his next words carefully. "If it should turn out that you are correct in this matter, then I will gladly bow to your edict."

"You'll do more than bow, I can assure you." Emily searched his gaze, trying to determine if his words bordered on insult or honesty, but deciding that as he still believed George guilty, it had cost him a lot to offer his concession. As for George, he still needed to stay hidden to protect his colleague, and she needed to deflect Nathan's suspicions about her knowledge of his whereabouts, and she realised there was a way to do that. Immoral it may be, but it was for a worthy cause. She slid her gloved hand idly along the top of the bench that ran around the inside of the gazebo. "My lord, I have something I would ask you."

Her coyness put Nathan instantly on the alert. It was a marked change in the way she had behaved toward him and hinted at duplicity, but his curiosity was piqued. "What is it you wish to ask?"

Emily turned to face him, the hem of her pale green sarsnet dress brushing his boots. "I understand that you may not be at liberty to answer me, but please, for my own peace of mind, I must have an answer." His expression was inscrutable, and she feared she may have overplayed her hand. Her breath locked in her chest.

It was a nerve-wracking moment before he spoke. "If it is in my power to grant you an answer, I will do so," he said, with slow deliberation.

"Have you arrested George?"

His normally stalwart expression showed his surprise, and it pleased her that she could get under his impenetrable facade.

"What makes you ask that?"

"Why must you answer my questions with questions?" she said, stamping her foot.

"Why must you?"

"Don't play games with me. I am sick with worry."

"Why? What has happened?" He stepped forwards, closing the gap between them.

She reined in her temper, but tears pricked the corners of her eyes. She twisted from him, dashing her tears away.

His hands grasped her shoulders in a firm grip and turned her to face him. Even hidden by the moonless night sky, she could see uncertainty but also concern in his dark gaze.

"Please Miss Ellerton, tell me what has upset you so."

Emily bit her lip as a tear escaped to roll down her cheek. Five days of pent up worry for George's health broke free, and she used it to mislead him. To commit a wrong to achieve a right? Surely that was commendable? She hoped God would forgive her for the lies she was about to tell. Taking a deep breath, she said, "Nothing, nothing has happened, and that is what is worrying me."

"How so?" he asked with a sceptical crease of his brow.

She sucked in a shattered breath. "When you arrived at Oakleaf Manor, you said George was back in England. Ever since I've been expecting to hear from him either in person or by letter, but I've heard nothing." She swiped a loose strand of hair from in front of her eyes. "And while I hope and pray that George has not been caught, at the moment, that seems the best alternative. For I cannot imagine him returning without informing us somehow. Which must mean he is too ill or, or..."

"Too ashamed to show his face."

"No, George is no traitor." Her spine straightening with the strength of her conviction.

"Then why has he not shown his face to either you or me?"

"Because," her bottom lip trembled, "he's hurt or worse." Her whole body shook in remembered fear for George's life and how close she had come to losing him, the pain and fear too raw to contain.

The depth of her distress penetrated Nathan's scepticism as her tears rolled unbidden down her cheeks. He reached into his pocket and pulled out his handkerchief, and began gently wiping away the tears that streaked her soft skin. He didn't know what to make of her words. The tears were real. Born out of worry for George. He instinctively knew they were real. Was it possible he was wrong about her? Either way, he would still have the house watched.

He grasped her chin and raised it so he could watch her reaction to his words. "No, Miss Ellerton, we have not arrested George."

Her eyes widened and her sharp intake of breath caught in her throat. Unable to bear seeing her so devastated, he wrapped his arms around her. It felt so natural for her to be in his embrace. He pulled her against his chest and rubbed her back with soothing strokes. He hated George for what he was putting his sister through. For all the comfort he was giving Emily, he wanted to punish George in equal measure. He became even more determined to capture him, not just for King and Country but so Emily's misery and uncertainty could end.

He gave a rueful laugh, as his capture would only end in his death by hanging, and that was hardly going to bring comfort and release to Emily. Sadly, where George and Emily were concerned, there was no good outcome. She was going to be adversely affected by whatever happened, and for that, he was truly sorry.

Unable to move, Emily stood motionless in his embrace, letting him hold her. Shocked and somewhat numbed by his tenderness, her guilt at knowing he was showing this tender side of himself as a result of her lies stopped her from being able to push away. She allowed him to stroke and soothe her as a myriad of emotions swirled around her. She was still overwrought with worry for George, but Nathan's ministrations began to relieve her of her stress and anxiety and a sense of calm and renewed strength filled her. For that, she was grateful to him. She lifted her head, sliding her hands up his chest as it swelled with his deep intake of breath. The span of his well-muscled body increasing. It was a reassuring, comforting sensation.

Nathan dipped his head to look at her. A halo of fiery hair surrounded her tear-streaked face and over-bright malachite eyes. But even in her delicate state, her chin held a stubborn tilt, and he fought to hide a smile of admiration for the principled, spirited young woman in his arms.

"Can you promise me something?" she whispered.

Her breath mingled with his and hot blood pounded through his veins. "That depends on what it is you want?" His voice was a husky rasp.

"If you capture George, will you inform me immediately?"

Capture George! Nathan was more interested in capturing her tear swollen rosy lips that he'd been absorbed in watching as they shaped her words. His head bent forwards of its own volition, but he caught himself before his lips touched hers, stopping a hair's breadth away.

"I promise," he breathed, although at that moment, his body and his mind were making two different promises. He gave himself a mental shake. This was madness. He stepped back, releasing her. He couldn't get involved with her. He'd made an oath and he wasn't going to break it.

Emily was momentarily lost — bereft with the loss of his arms and chest that had been encompassing her so completely. For in those few moments, she had known what it was like to feel safe, secure, protected. And if she was honest – wanted. She'd not missed the dip of his eyes to her lips, and had resisted the magnetic force urging her onto her tiptoes to close the distance between them. Whilst it was a struggle for her to fight this new sensation, she still resented the unceremonious way he set her apart from him.

"Here." He shoved his handkerchief at her. "You had better dry your eyes. It's high time I returned you to your aunt. She'll be wondering where you are."

She flinched at his words as though he'd slapped her, but she took the proffered handkerchief and with a regal lift of her chin dried her eyes with a quick swipe of her cheeks, then held the handkerchief back out to him.

"No, you keep it," he said in a gruff voice.

With a sharp flick of her wrist, she said, "I'd rather not," and dropped it into his hand.

Nathan ground his teeth at her rejection of his handkerchief. He couldn't understand why it should bother him so much. It was only a scrap of material; rather wet material, he noted, as his fingers closed around it. But nothing of import, the same as Miss Ellerton. "May I offer you my arm, or will you reject that as well?"

Emily noted his terse tone and wasn't sure why he should be so offended. "No, the offer of your arm is acceptable. After all, you will hardly offer to let me keep it."

"Oh, so you only wish to use my person and my belongings so long as it's only temporary?" Nathan was mystified as to how they had come to this inimical predicament.

Her expression showed her surprise at the force of his seething reply. "Indeed, as your interest in me will only last until George is caught."

Well, she was right in that respect, but then he hadn't done anything unpardonable. "In as much as I have not abused our situation, you can have nothing to rebuke me for."

"Maybe not in action, but your every thought has been the capture of my brother."

"Not every thought," Nathan said with a growl.

The shock of his admission caused her to gasp in affronted outrage and look away.

"Oh, so that is what this is about?"

"Whatever do you mean?" Her head snapped round, her eyes glinting like wet leaves after a summer storm.

He stepped forwards in a predatory manner. "You're having a missy sulk because I didn't kiss you."

Her chest rose in indignation. "You are mistaken if you think I would encourage the attentions of the man who would hang my brother for a crime he is innocent of."

"Perhaps. But maybe you were curious to know the feel of a man's lips on yours?" His voice was deep and husky.

"You presume too much if you think I have never been kissed before."

"*Have* you ever been kissed before?" Nathan placed his left arm beside her head, cutting off her only way of escape.

"Have you ever been slapped before?" she retorted, her eyes forming tight slits.

He fought to hide the smile that tugged at his lips as he let his fingers trail through a loose tendril of her hair laying against her neck. "Only by the inexperienced."

Emily's hand twitched to slap him, but her outrage overrode her impulse. "You have too high an opinion of yourself."

He leaned conspiratorially closer and whispered in her ear. "It's an opinion shared by many a lady."

She twisted away as his breath caressed her sensitive earlobe. "I don't doubt that the ladies you frequent are easily swayed, in many ways."

"I'm afraid ladies of ill repute are not what interest me." He ran the tip of his finger down the length of her alabaster neck and along the neckline of her dress, brushing the sensitive tops of her breasts. "I prefer my conquests to be a little more refined."

Ripples of sensation thrummed through Emily's whole body. Her eyelids slid shut against the onslaught of excitement that surged through her. How could this man evoke such feelings within her? She had to get away; she couldn't let him get the better of her.

Forcing herself to ignore what his fingers were doing to her body, she brought her face back to his, noting his eyes had dipped to her décolletage. "At least give me the respect of looking at my face."

He lazily lifted his smoky grey eyes to hers. Desire swirled in their fathomless depths, and her stomach tingled. She sucked in a deep breath. "I thought you said you did not intend to abuse our situation?"

"No, I believe I said you had nothing to rebuke me for as I had not abused it."

"Well, you are nearing that point."

"Oh, so I haven't crossed it yet?" His breath disturbed the feathery wisps of her hair laying against her cheek as he trailed his fingers back up the neckline of her dress and traced a line across her shoulder, stopping on her sensitive nape.

She fought to keep her knees from buckling under her. "For the sake of our fragile understanding, I will forget your trespasses so far, but I will not allow any further indulgences from you." She wrenched herself away from his caresses. "As we may need to communicate with each other in the near future, I suggest we part before one of us renders that impossible."

He shoved away from the wall.

She did not waste a moment as she pushed past him and headed back to the house. Back to safety and back to sanity.

Nathan let her go, trying to regain some equilibrium to his rioting emotions. Robert had ordered him to make Miss Ellerton feel under pressure, well he had certainly achieved that, but right now he was the one caught in a physical maelstrom of his own making. Instead of luring her into his trap, she had ensnared him instead. He watched as she walked calmly towards the house.

Emily was anything but calm. Her hands shook as she tried to open the French doors leading to the side of the house, not yet ready to face the guests inside and certainly not her aunt who would take one look at her and demand to know what had happened between her and Lord Thornburn.

What *had* happened between them? One moment he was comforting her. The next he was being positively rude and then, well, he was all but seducing her – and with barely a touch. A mere stroke of his fingers and she had practically melted into a puddle at his feet. She'd only just escaped with her dignity in place.

She glanced back at the gazebo and saw Lord Thornburn watching her. Yanking the door open, she hurried inside and out of sight.

This was not the end of the matter. He'd changed the rules of their game. She may have convinced him she was innocent of knowing George's whereabouts, but she was still a connection to him and he intended to ensure he had power over her. If he thought that, then he didn't know her very well, because this was one battle she was determined not to lose. George's life depended on it.

* * *

Handing his hat and coat to his butler, Nathan headed to his study. He walked to the fireplace and picked up the poker, prodding the dying embers, trying to ignite warmth from them.

He replaced the poker on its stand and began flexing his stiff shoulders as Peter entered.

Peter dropped onto one of the green leather wing-backed chairs and propped his ankle atop his other knee. "Did you get what you wanted from Miss Ellerton?" He gave an enquiring raise of his brow.

Nathan let out a ragged sigh. The heat from her skin still burned under his fingertips. "Not quite. She asked me if we had arrested George. She was worried as she'd not heard anything from him."

"And you believed her?"

"I saw no reason to disbelieve her." He was not in the mood to explain himself. Especially to Peter.

"Did she put on the waterworks for your benefit?"

"She was upset, yes. But the tears were real."

"Good God, Nathan. It's the Comtesse de Alessandro all over again."

"Do not speak her name to me."

"I feel that I must. You know full well the result of your involvement with her; I will not let you make that mistake again."

"I do not need reminding." Nathan tore the words out, trying valiantly to bite back the anger and pain that twisted inside him. "I never go a day without remembering."

Peter pushed himself up. "I'm sorry. I did not mean to distress you. I just don't want you paying such a heavy price for a woman's deception again."

"Nor I."

Peter gave his brother a long look. "But you do have a tendre for her?"

"No, of course not."

"You admire her then?"

Nathan stared into the fire, watching the flames contort and writhe. So beautiful, so mesmerising. He reached his hand out towards the flames and the heat burned him. Yet so dangerous. He'd been burned before. Yet he was not the one who had been scarred.

"You're using your attraction to her as an excuse to doubt George's complicity," Peter said.

"Don't be absurd."

"I wish that I were." Peter strode over and prodded his brother in his chest. "I know it pains you to hear this, as George was your close friend, but you have to put that aside. We've both seen the evidence, and it's not just you he has betrayed, but all of us. You cannot let the rest of us down now because of your past association with him."

Nathan closed his eyes. Peter was right. He couldn't let Miss Ellerton cloud his judgement of George.

Folding his arms, Peter said, "The same goes for Miss Ellerton. She's planted her flag firmly on George's side and you will never sway her from that."

"I'm not trying to," Nathan said between clenched teeth.

"Then what have you being trying to do all evening with her?"

Nathan pushed away from the fire and strode over to the sideboard, pulled the stopper out of the nearest decanter and poured himself a liberal glass. Taking a swig, he grimaced as the liquid burned a hot path down his throat. This was not his normal tipple, but right now, he didn't care.

He leaned his hip against the sideboard and considered his brother's words. What had he been trying to do with her? Get her to admit the truth about George's location had been his intention. But she'd put a stop to that line of questioning when she'd raised those heartbroken peridot eyes to him. Swimming with pain and fear and the uncertainty about her loved one's safety. A pain which he understood only too well. All he'd done was the same as any true gentleman and comforted her and offered her a shoulder to cry on. Which she had readily accepted. But his thoughts had moved on to other things; her rosy lips, her rounded breasts, the feel of her body pressed against his.

He rested his head back and shut his eyes as he remembered cornering her, teasing and seducing her. He'd frightened her but still her courage had risen to the surface and she'd faced him as an equal adversary and walked away from him the victor.

He let out a derisive laugh. No, he needn't worry about his feelings for her anymore, as no doubt after tonight she despised him. All things considered, it was for the best.

He placed his glass down, walked to the door, and said, "My job."

He closed the door behind him, but he did wonder who he was trying to convince.

Chapter Nine

Emily peeked from behind the coach blind, her gaze sweeping the length of the London street. She ignored the elegantly dressed lords and ladies strolling along, relishing the sunshine. Instead, she glanced at the shadows, trying to see if someone was hiding there; watching. A gentleman stepped from a doorway and looked up at her coach before carrying on his way. She didn't recognise him. Probably some innocent, carefree man with nothing on his mind except the pursuit of enjoyment. She released the blind with a snap. If she continued like this, she would drive herself mad.

Over breakfast, her aunt had insisted that they make up for the time lost due to her *illness* and acquire all the items they should have purchased before now. Emily had not wanted to go shopping. Not today. Not after last night. And not after knowing Lord Thornburn could be out here, even now, watching her. She shuddered. This was a bad idea.

She turned to her aunt as the coach rumbled over the cobblestones. "I still say this is unwise. Especially after I convinced Lord Thornburn I was concerned about George. How is our shopping trip going to convince him of the sincerity of my words?"

"By all means, you should look preoccupied by something that is worrying you. In fact, I suspect you will be unable to act otherwise." Her aunt gave her an assessing stare, which Emily instantly looked away from. "If we should encounter any of Lord Thornburn's men, you are quite at liberty to lament the fact that I have ordered you to accompany me. Anything that will increase their sympathy for you will be of benefit to our cause."

"Aunt Amelia. How can you say such things?" Heat flushed Emily's skin at the prospect of misrepresenting the truth to Lord Thornburn again and at what he may read into her reactions to him.

"Needs must," her aunt said, patting her cheek. "What we do now, we do for George, regardless of the cost to our own sense of composure."

Emily let out a deep breath and nodded. Whilst shutting herself away at home would protect her from Lord Thornburn, she had to accept that in order to keep George safe and enable them to visit him; they needed the charade of a London Season. And if that meant putting aside her own misgivings and going shopping and to social events, then so be it. But it didn't mean she wouldn't hate every moment.

The coach pulled up outside a small apothecary shop. As they stepped inside, an assortment of aromas assailed them and a dry chalky taste filled the air.

The proprietor, Mr Lewis, a large rotund man with an apron covered in an array of different coloured powder stains, greeted them as they entered. He came around the counter and led her aunt to a chair.

"It is good to see you looking so well." Mr Lewis patted his stomach and a rainbow of powder dispersed into the air to form a kaleidoscope of patterns before drifting to the floor.

"Ah, but if I were well, I would have no need of your services," Aunt Amelia replied.

"On the contrary, it is my medicines that are keeping you well."

"Indeed. I cannot argue with that, and on that note, I would like to request more of your cough remedy. The blue powder one seems to work best."

"Of course. I can make it up now if you care to wait." He returned to his counter and began measuring out various ingredients.

"We can wait. Mrs Shaw has also requested more medicine for her nephew. She asks if you would be kind enough to send it round."

"By all means."

"Wonderful." Aunt Amelia reached into her purse and pulled out some coins. "I have her payment here."

Emily watched as Mr Lewis took the coins and pocketed them. It was an exorbitant amount, and she suspected it was to pay for more than just medicine. She gave her aunt a look, but she blithely ignored her.

Feeling restless, Emily began strolling along the rows upon rows of shelves, each one crammed full of green and blue bottles, big and small. She could tell by how faded the labels were, which were commonly used and which rarely opened.

She recognised the Gum Arabic and Oil of Almonds as they were used in her aunt's remedies. Many others were unfamiliar to her, as the shop had a larger selection than her village apothecary. She strolled along and read the names on the labels; Aconite Root, Cusparia Bark, Basilic Powder, White

Bismuth, and Linimentum Camphor Compositum.

In the far corner, she came to a large jar with a dark metallic liquid inside. She lifted it up, surprised at how heavy it was. She read the label: Mercury.

"What's this one used for?" she asked.

Mr Lewis looked up from where he was mixing his powders. "That's for my less selective gentlemen clients who prefer even less selective company."

"Oh." Emily decided not to pursue the matter further. She put the jar down and began making her way back to her aunt. She came to an abrupt halt when the door swung open and Mr Pykett entered. His nose looking more crooked than usual.

He gave a quick bow to the ladies. "Miss Ellerton, what a surprise to find you here. Your aunt is not ill again?"

"No indeed. We are just here to purchase a renewal of her medicine," Emily said.

Her aunt drew his attention. "I hope it is not ill health that brings you to Mr Lewis's establishment?" Her expression was one of innocent concern, but Emily knew her aunt was playing with him.

"No, I am..." he started and a panicked expression flitted across his face, as though he realised he was supposed to be using subterfuge. "I mean yes, but it is only a mild affliction. Nothing to cause any alarm."

"I'm glad to hear it," her aunt said.

Mr Lewis came around the counter with the package of medicines. "All done, Lady Drayford."

"Splendid. In that case, we shall be off. Good day to you, Mr Pykett." Aunt Amelia rose and headed to the door.

As they were leaving, they heard Mr Lewis asking if he could be of assistance to Mr Pykett and, aware that he needed to continue his charade, he replied that he was suffering from something that he was certain was a common complaint.

"Ah," Mr Lewis replied, "I believe I have just the thing over in the far corner."

His reference to the mercury was unmistakable, and Emily had to clap her hand over her mouth to stop herself from laughing.

Her aunt, though, kept her decorum and, turning to Emily, chastised her for her unladylike behaviour. But Emily didn't miss the twinkle in her eye.

"Where to now?" Emily asked.

"The perfumers," she said, as they were assisted into the carriage for the short drive.

As they entered the shop, the early morning sunlight glinted on the ornately decorated perfume bottles. Behind a locked cabinet sat a collection of bottles with intricate silver covers. Emily smiled at the beautiful designs, wishing there was some gentleman in her life who would buy her such pretty gifts.

The proprietor, Mrs Allenby, entered. "Ah, Lady Drayford. I was informed you wished to choose a new fragrance. Please, come this way." She led them into the back room, where a counter was laid out with a selection of vials for Lady Drayford to sample. Emily lifted one up and sniffed it. She coughed, grimacing at the repugnant cloying aroma, and instantly replaced the lid.

The bell on the door clanged, announcing another customer. Mrs Allenby bustled out to welcome them into her shop. She returned a moment later, followed by Peter Renwick.

Emily glared at him, her blood boiling as he made his bow. She had expected them to be hiding in the shadows, watching, not accosting them at each establishment.

"Has Lord Thornburn sent you to purchase a more appealing cologne?" Her voice rasped against her tight throat.

"No, alas not, although I must admit his is not to my preference either."

"Well, at least one of you has good taste."

He raised his eyebrows as he gave her a quick perusal, "I believe it is only his taste in cologne that is at fault, as I find his other preferences usually match my own."

The hairs on the back of her neck prickled in indignation at his deliberately offensive remark. She handed the vial she had sampled earlier to him, watching him suffer as he took a sniff and tried in vain to maintain a dignified expression.

"Quite a fulsome aroma," he choked out.

"Yes, it comes across as repellent and distasteful. I would not like to be subjected to such a situation again." She replaced the stopper and put the bottle on the glass counter with a sharp clink.

He gave her a quick bow. "Indeed. I would not wish such an occurrence on you again." But a smile tugged at his lips, showing he was completely unabashed.

"Good. See that you do not."

Her aunt paid for a small bottle of perfume and indicated for them to leave.

They bade Peter goodbye and left him standing in the shop.

Leaving the coach, they strolled the short distance to the milliners. The warm sun shone on the square window panes, creating a welcoming interior. On the far wall hung a large mirror, surrounded by several racks of bonnets in a myriad of different colours and styles. Emily removed her own bonnet as the owner, Mrs Haddon, handed her a peach silk organza poke bonnet.

"I think this one will suit you."

Trying on the bonnet, she examined herself in the mirror and laughed at the unflattering effect. "No, not me." She handed the bonnet back.

"How about this one?" Mrs Haddon gave her a gold and blue braid bonnet with a large ostrich feather curling over the top.

Emily lifted it up, looking in the mirror as she did so, and almost dropped it when she spotted Lord Thornburn's reflection as he entered the shop. His gaze caught hers and a lightning bolt shot through her. Her breath locked in her chest and her hands shook. She broke eye contact and concentrated on placing the bonnet on her head. It was slightly askew, like her emotions.

Lord Thornburn shuddered his distaste. She pursed her lips and turned to face him, lifting her chin up in an attempt at condescension. "What's wrong with it?"

"Nothing, it is a perfectly acceptable bonnet for an insipid Miss."

Emily huffed. "Are you calling me an insipid Miss?"

"No, quite the opposite," he said in a husky tone.

"Oh." Emily handed the bonnet back, her chest fluttering at his compliment. "Perhaps not."

Mrs Haddon turned to Lord Thornburn. "Would the gentleman like to make a suggestion?"

Emily's stomach flipped over as his lips quirked suggestively at her question and she remembered the way his fingers had evoked divine pleasure from her last night with the merest stroke. She dropped her gaze from his as heat spread across her skin.

"This one," he said, picking up a crown bonnet in pleated green silk. "It will bring out your eyes."

"It'll bring out everyone's eyes. It's hideous." But she had admired the hat on entering the shop - though she would never admit it.

"Try it."

She sighed. "Very well, if only to prove you wrong." She tried it on and looked at the effect in the mirror.

The owner clapped her hands in delight. "Perfect."

Emily stared at her reflection. The vibrant green of the bonnet emphasised her eyes and complimented her titian hair, but she would not back down.

"No, not for me," she said, removing the bonnet.

"How about a high stove pipe bonnet?" Lord Thornburn indicated the rack to the left and waited for the owner and Lady Drayford to take a look.

Emily turned to examine them and gasped when his fingers skimmed her neck as he tucked a loose tendril of her hair behind her ear. Excitement rippling through her at his gentle touch. But he casually spun away and picked up a high stove pipe bonnet in burgundy and trimmed with black lace.

"Hardly," Emily said before he could hand it to her. "It is more suited to the ladies you normally frequent. It most assuredly is not suitable for a debutante like myself. I must ask you to remember who you are dealing with." She gave him a pleading look, begging him not to embarrass her in front of her aunt. She'd endured enough questions about last night as it was.

"Well, I offered a perfectly suitable suggestion, but you were utterly against it, therefore I assumed your tastes ran to the more daring." His silver gaze lifted to hers and the double meaning of his words struck her with potent force.

"Most definitely not. You completely misconstrue me."

"Do I?" His husky tone sent a dizzying current through her.

"I will take the green silk after all." She cringed at how breathy her voice sounded. Why did he have such an effect on her?

"Very good," Mrs Haddon said, as she placed the hat in a hatbox.

"Send the bill to the house," her aunt said. "We shall call again after we have visited the modiste and have samples for matching items."

"Excellent. I shall look forward to seeing you again."

"Here, let me." Lord Thornburn held the door open for them.

"Thank you," Aunt Amelia said, as she left the shop.

Emily followed her, but as she passed Lord Thornburn, he leaned close and whispered, "I knew you would succumb to my suggestion."

"You flatter yourself overmuch. I had already decided on it before you entered," she replied as she swept past. "Good day to you."

Chapter Ten

"My lord," Jenkins, Nathan's valet, said on entering his bedchamber, "one of Mr Pykett's urchins has called with a message for you. I therefore took the liberty of preparing your green jacket and grey britches, as I suspect you will wish to go riding."

Nathan rolled onto his back and muttered an expletive, which his valet pretended not to hear, before climbing out of bed. In no mood to stand still, he left his valet to chase after him. He, Peter, and Simon had spent the previous evening searching the shops the ladies had attended and found nothing untoward. If it was a ruse, it had worked. He wasn't sure if the ruse had been for him or Emily, assuming she had spoken the truth about not knowing George's whereabouts, and her aunt and uncle were trying to keep her in the dark.

He shrugged into his jacket and strode to his study, where he found a young boy around ten years old eyeing the expensive ornaments in the room. Nathan nudged the tray with scroll edges containing his silver inkpot out of the lad's reach. The inkpot was the perfect size to disappear into the boy's pocket.

"What message do you have for me from Mr Pykett?" he

asked, bringing the boy's attention to him.

The boy removed his cap and clasped it in his hands. "Milord, he says that the ladies have taken the carriage and gone shopping down Oxford Street and that his lordship has gone to his club in St. James's."

"Did he say who he was following?"

"Yes, sir. He said he'd keep an eye on the ladies."

"Of course he did." Nathan reached into his desk and took out a small purse. He pulled out a half crown and gave it to the boy. "Off you go."

The boy took the money and scampered out of the room. Nathan followed him out and, finding the butler, he enquired as to Peter's whereabouts.

"He said to tell you he has gone to see if he can assist the ladies with their shopping," the butler said, with a disdainful lift of his nose.

"Can you have my horse saddled?"

"It is being attended to as we speak, my lord."

* * *

Nathan rode along Oxford Street at a brisk pace. His pursuit of Lord Tysling had been a fool's errand designed to waste his time, and now he was in no mood to be trifled with. His patience was wearing thin and any sympathy for Emily and her family had eroded during his vexatious sitting, waiting and watching her uncle, who'd spent his time at his club first taking a very slow perusal of the newspaper followed by discussing politics with a group of elderly gentlemen who were so set in their ways and views that they could not put together a cohesive sentiment that would have any relevance in the current political climate.

Then, just before noon, Lord Tysling had gone to the betting book and written down a bet. Nathan, wanting to ensure he did not lose his prey, but equally curious to find out what he had put in the book, waited until he was certain Lord Tysling had left but he could still catch up to him and then walked over to the betting book. He thumped the book when he read the entry; 'I bet 10 shillings, Lord Thornburn will, without verbal enticement, read this book before the clock strikes noon on this day.' He strode from the club as the clock chimed to find Lord Tysling climbing into his carriage. On seeing Nathan, he'd had the audacity to wave him a salute, knowing full well he had just won the bet.

Nathan followed him home and waited outside for another hour. Convinced he was not going anywhere else, he decided to find out where Miss Ellerton and her aunt were, as they'd not yet returned home.

Unlike this morning, he was rather hoping he would run into Miss Ellerton as he was determined to release his black mood on someone before this day was out, and right now, she seemed an enticing option.

Finding Peter and Simon, he joined them as they stood talking to each other, whilst watching a modiste shop on the opposite side of the street that Emily and her aunt had entered some time ago.

"Where have they been to this morning?" Nathan asked.

"I followed them into a haberdashery store," Simon Pykett said in a disgruntled tone. "Cotton and lace everywhere and there's me trying to pretend I went in there on purpose."

"I'm sure you made them believe you were a connoisseur of sewing." His response was an angry scowl from Simon. "Where did they go afterwards?"

"To the glover's," Peter said, giving his brother a questioning look. "Miss Ellerton wanted to order a pair of green gloves to match a bonnet she said you chose for her."

"Hmm, it appears she knows how to tell a white lie and is not above causing trouble for me." Nathan's annoyance at Miss Ellerton's hypocrisy gave a sharp edge to his words.

"You're on the defensive today," Peter said, his curiosity echoing in his voice.

Nathan rubbed his face. He didn't need this from Peter. Things were bad enough as it was. They had been in London for over a week and they were no closer to catching George, and now Robert was due to leave. They couldn't afford to lose any more time.

He pulled out his pocket watch. Half an hour had passed and Nathan's bad mood had only increased in the interim. Well, Robert had ordered him to keep the pressure on Miss Ellerton and she'd been in the shop long enough.

Damn it. Miss Ellerton had taken him for a fool. The modiste was the one place George could hide where his sister could visit him and not be followed. Well, he was not about to shy away from his duty.

He shoved his watch back into his pocket and crossed the road, peering into the small windows of the shop to find it empty. A bell greeted him as he entered. It was rather loud for such a small shop, but before he could take any further steps, the proprietor hurried in.

Her look of surprise was fleeting, and recovering, she said, "Good day to you, Sir. I am Mrs Shaw, the owner. How may I help you?" She gave a polite but firm smile.

Nathan scanned the cabinets that stretched floor to ceiling. Each containing examples of the modiste's work. On a counter lay an array of fashion plates. The cramped room was too small for anyone to be hiding.

Ignoring the owner, he strode past her and through the door she'd entered by.

"Excuse me, Sir, but you cannot go in there."

He found himself in another small room with two doors leading off. The nearest door revealed a storage room packed high with bolts of material, rolls of ribbons, and boxes of beads. He shut the door and carried on. A row of long tables dominated the next room. Cotton and silk were rolled across each table with patterns pinned to them. Scraps of material were everywhere, but the room was devoid of people.

Mrs Shaw arrived hurriedly behind him. "Please Sir, I must ask you to leave."

"Where are Lady Drayford and Miss Ellerton?"

"Please Sir, if you wait outside, I will bring them to you."

"Not likely." He strode to the far door and pushed it open. Miss Ellerton was standing with her back to him on a raised block surrounded by seamstresses, pins in their mouths and rolls of gold lace in their hands that they were attaching to the half-finished dress she was wearing.

The ivory silk dress with gold overlay hung open at the back as no buttons had been added yet, revealing soft creamy skin gliding over the notches of her spine as they carried on down the curve of her back.

Right now, if George had been in that room, Nathan would never have noticed as blood pounded through his body and his groin tightened.

A seamstress looked up and screamed, dropping pins everywhere.

Miss Ellerton glanced over her shoulder, and her malachite eyes widened in shock. Her attempts to gather the dress around her just caused the back to gape more, displaying the blush that consumed her, but her mortification soon manifested into anger.

Swivelling, she clutched the silk dress to her breast. "If you were looking for George, you couldn't be more wrong, as it would hardly be appropriate for a man to be in here," she said, giving him a withering glare that could have pulverised rock. "I think you will agree, my lord, that this trespass has crossed the line."

All Nathan could think was that she was magnificent and his heart swelled in admiration of her, but he did not have time to respond before Lady Drayford, who had been seated behind the door, stood up and marched towards him, her walking stick clicking a sharp tempo.

"This is an outrageous affront," she said, backing him out of the room. "Wait until my brother, Lord Tysling, hears about this."

Nathan pulled his eyes from Miss Ellerton as her aunt relentlessly herded him through the adjoining rooms.

On reaching the shop proper, he was joined by Peter, who, looking past Lady Drayford, saw Miss Ellerton peeking from behind the far door, still clutching the half-finished dress to herself.

Peter burst out laughing and slapped his brother on the shoulder, "I told you, you always get the best assignments."

Lady Drayford was not amused and, lifting her walking stick, poked both men in their stomachs as she and Mrs Shaw ushered them from the shop.

On the pavement outside, Peter still guffawed.

"This is no laughing matter," Nathan said. "You have no idea of the apology I'm going to have to make to her now." But his mind would not rid itself of the image of Miss Ellerton stood before him in a dress with no back.

"I shall be certain to be present for that."

"No. This is something I have to do alone," he said, as the need to touch her silky smooth skin consumed him.

"Well, that is most unfortunate, as I'm not giving you the opportunity to do so. Right now, she's got you at a distinct disadvantage and I will not allow her to gain any more ground. Anyway, putting the delicious half-clad lady aside, did you see any evidence of George?"

Nathan brought his mind back to the purpose of his intrusion. "No, he definitely wasn't there and there was nowhere else for him to be hidden."

"Well, that's one more crossed off the list," Peter said, but Nathan was not listening.

* * *

Back inside the shop, Emily shook with a mixture of impotent rage and subsiding shock. Her aunt led her to a seat and Mrs Shaw brought her a drink of tea, with extra sugar, which they made her consume straight away.

After a few minutes her equilibrium returned, but she couldn't quell the strange flutter that skittered through the pit of her stomach when she thought of Lord Thornburn and that primal look he'd given her.

"Well, that could not have gone better," Aunt Amelia said, smiling with unhidden glee.

A mortified Emily turned to her and gasped. "How can you say such a thing?"

"You'll see, Emily. When the time is right, you'll see."

But Emily suspected she would never be able to see anything but Lord Thornburn and his admiring smile.

Chapter Eleven

Handing his hat and cloak to a footman, Nathan surveyed the room. After yesterday's incident, he'd expected her to be hiding away. Oh, but not little Miss Ellerton. No, she'd gone to a party. Not just any party. The most prestigious event of the Season. A soiree being hosted by the Duke and Duchess of Rutterford.

They were renowned for their hospitality, although the event would be more subdued than a ball, as the purpose was to chat over card tables and enjoy the drinks and company.

The heavy burgundy curtains at all eight windows had been drawn closed, giving the large room an intimate feel. Miss Ellerton would be at one of the tables, placed around the edge of the dance floor, as it would afford somewhere for her aunt to sit. He searched the tables, half expecting to find her wearing that dress. Spotting her, he realised she wasn't. To his annoyance, he was rather disappointed. He needed to get that image of her clasping the half-finished dress to herself as she berated him in that magnificent manner out of his head. He doubted he'd ever manage it, but for now he had to get control of himself and the situation.

Peter came and stood by him, as true to his word he had no intention of leaving him alone with the sorrowful-eyed Miss Ellerton, who was sat at a table with her aunt, Sir Richard Hern, and Miss Marianne Kesterton, playing whist.

Nathan gave a quick nod to his brother, who returned an aggrieved glare before he accepted his order and made his way over to the table. After making his greeting, he turned to Miss Kesterton and asked her to dance. She readily accepted and Nathan smoothly took her place.

"May I join the game?"

"In as much as you never stop playing games, I presume there is no point in refusing you," Miss Ellerton said, her green eyes flashing.

"You should know by now there is never any point in refusing me."

The scowl she threw at him gave Nathan a perverse pleasure. If he was going to suffer, then so should she. Although, it seemed anger was not the only emotion he evoked from her as a blush infused her cheeks. Was that merely embarrassment over their last encounter, or did her reaction evolve from something deeper, more primal? A part of him hoped it was the latter, but his gut twisted as he had no right to wish so. He'd forfeited any right to that long ago. He had to stay true to his purpose, no matter how much the part buried deep inside wanted him to do otherwise.

Lady Drayford picked up the cards and began dealing them; she paused when she came to Nathan. "I am extremely surprised to see you here. Surely you have more important things you should be dealing with?"

Nathan leaned nonchalantly back in his chair. "No. I have nothing more important than this."

Lady Drayford eyed him with unconcealed animosity, but he did not back down. With a sharp flick of her wrist, she threw a card toward him and continued dealing.

He picked up his cards, only giving them a cursory glance as he turned his attention to Miss Ellerton, who was trying to ignore his presence. When he casually brushed his arm against hers, the jolt that leaped between them surprised even him. He was sorely tempted to try it again to see if the same thing happened, but one look at her aunt told him she would launch herself across the table at him if he did.

Bringing his mind back to his surroundings, he gave Miss Ellerton a sidewise glance. "I believe we are waiting for you." He indicated the cards already played by her aunt and Sir Richard.

She looked up with a perplexed expression and hurriedly dropped a card onto the pile.

He raised his eyebrow at her.

"It was the best choice I had," she said, giving him a haughty glare.

"Hmm, I think simple arithmetic would suggest otherwise."

"You cannot know what is in my hand."

"No, but out of the fifty-two cards in the deck the worse card to play on top of those already in play at this point would be the two of spades, and as you had five cards in your hand I can tell by simple deduction that you had a least four better cards to choose from."

"There is virtue in cautiousness," she said, rearranging the remaining cards in her hand.

"But not in folly."

"You'd know all about that."

It was a barbed reminder of his foolish intrusion at the

modiste. "My actions yesterday resulted from necessity, not folly."

"Did you find what you were looking for?"

"You know I didn't."

"Then it was folly."

He ground his teeth but did not reply.

With a tone of superiority, Miss Ellerton leaned towards him, "It does not always serve one's purpose to play one's best card first. Sometimes there is advantage in playing a weaker hand and keeping the better card until a more suitable opportunity presents itself. It's your turn, by the way."

She indicated her aunt and Sir Richard, who were waiting for the game to continue. She did not hide her smile when he carelessly dropped a random card onto the pile. She was pleased to see his mind was not on the game before him, either.

The game continued at a much quicker pace thereafter and a smug Miss Ellerton won the round. She tilted a triumphant smile at him in a self-satisfied manner. He pulled irritably at his sapphire cufflinks. Her smile grew brighter. She knew she had riled him. He needed to keep his reactions under control. He couldn't afford to let her get the better of him.

Her aunt hurriedly picked up the cards and began dealing again, but Sir Richard waved his hand in the negative when she reached him.

"I'm afraid I have to decline. A lady in distress requires my assistance," he said, standing and heading towards the dance floor.

Emily hardly noticed him leave, as her attention was on Lord Thornburn. Goading him was a good balm to her embarrassment — a pleasing thought as she did not want him to have a hold over her after he had caught her half-dressed at the modiste. She fanned herself as heat once again swept over her skin. She remembered how his eyes had devoured her with hungry need. She'd never felt so vulnerable or so powerful as he stood staring at her.

Her thoughts came to an abrupt halt when Peter arrived and took Sir Richard's vacated seat. She had not forgiven him for his rude remarks in the perfumers, nor his enjoyment of her embarrassment at the modiste. "You return most unexpectedly. The dance has not yet finished."

Peter lifted apologetic hands. "Alas, an old injury began to plague me, and Sir Richard kindly took my place in the dance for Miss Kesterton's sake." His voice held a touch of challenge, as though daring her to deny it.

"You seem perfectly fine to me."

"If you don't believe me, you can always ask George to confirm it," he said, capturing and holding her gaze.

All the joy of her previous triumph against Nathan evaporated. Dropping her cards, she rose and headed out of the room. Along the corridor, she found an empty parlour. Inside, a fire burned low in the grate and the flickering light from two tall candles on the mantel provided a peaceful sanctuary. She skirted around a table and headed to the windows, where she rested her heated forehead against the cool pane.

A moment later, Lord Thornburn's elegantly dressed form was reflected in the window, his white Marseilles waistcoat contrasting against the dark blue of his double-breasted coat. The sapphire in his tie-pin winked as the twinkling candlelight caught it as he sauntered inexorably towards her.

Heaving a heavy sigh, she pushed herself away from the window and turned to face him. She threw him a warning look and he stopped a foot away from her. "I assume you told Peter how worried I am about George!"

"I did," he said in a neutral tone.

"And yet he still goads me."

"I'm certain he did not mean to upset you."

Emily huffed at him, crossing her arms over her chest. "And I'm certain you did not wish to cause me embarrassment when you burst in on my dress fitting."

"Most—," but Emily held up her hand to stop his speech.

"I would say that you owe me another apology after yesterday's debacle, but I now know from experience that your apologies mean nothing."

"I have a job to do and I was doing as ordered." He jabbed his gloved finger on the polished rosewood table in emphasis of his words.

"You were ordered to follow me into a modiste?" Emily shook her head in disbelief at his attempt to use his duty as a defence for his behaviour.

"You chose to go there, knowing you were being followed."

"That is a poor excuse, even for you. And I did not choose to go into the modiste, my aunt insisted. She is determined to see me make a good match. That is the purpose of the Season, after all."

Nathan clenched his jaw. The thought of Lady Drayford marrying Miss Ellerton off to some other gentleman pierced him. "Well, your aunt should have known better. We made no secret of the fact we were following you."

"How dare you blame my aunt for this? She feels bad enough that her illness has delayed my preparation for the Season and she does not need you accusing her of being at fault for your unforgiveable actions."

"My actions were a necessity of our current situation. And

whilst I concede from your aunt's point of view, so were yours, but—." He held up his hand when she opened her mouth to respond, "But in the grand scheme of things, my situation is of greater import."

"To you, maybe."

"To everyone in this country, if not the continent."

"Are you going to play the national importance card in every argument?"

"Do you have a card that can trump it?"

They stared at each other in the sudden suffocating silence.

After a charged moment, Emily broke the spell. "It still does not change the fact that you should not have followed me into the modiste. I'm amazed it is not mentioned in salacious detail in every society page of every paper."

"That is because Lord Brakenhale ensured the story was forgotten by every editor."

"Just trying to protect his interests," she said through the scathing anger scratching her throat.

"This was not a political incident. It would have no bearing on Lord Brakenhale's career. But he used his political power to save your reputation." The admiration for Robert and his anger that his valuable time should be spent away from his political cause showing in his voice. "He delayed his departure back to the continent where he had urgent matters of national import and instead visited every editor in person and used his most persuasive arguments to protect your reputation."

"Oh," Emily said, getting her anger and humiliation under control. But she still was not ready to concede any point to Lord Thornburn. "Well, that was the least he could have done. After all, it was his order that caused the incident."

"Do you not understand what he gave up to protect you?"

"Do *you* not understand that my reputation would have been ruined beyond redemption if he hadn't? National situations can be repaired, a woman's reputation cannot." She twisted away from him. "Did you even stop to consider that when you entered that shop?" Her voice caught in her throat.

He paused before responding. "Yes, I considered it."

The full import of his words slashed through her and she closed her eyes against the pain of his admission. "So you decided that George's apprehension was worth the risk to my reputation."

Moving around the table, he grasped her shoulders and a shiver of unwanted anticipation shuddered along her full length, leaving a tingle in its wake. She tried to pull free, but he held her fast.

"Please believe me, Miss Ellerton. I would not have done anything to cause you harm if I had thought there was another way. I had to make certain George was not there. I did not make the decision lightly." He pulled her around to face him and held her until she lifted her gaze to his.

A primitive glow shone in the smoky grey depths of his eyes and instinct told her he wanted to kiss her. She let out a shuddering breath. Instead he pulled her against him and wrapped her in his strong arms.

Nathan breathed in her delicate scent. He wanted to kiss her, to taste her lips, to lose himself in her, but that was something he could never have. This was the only atonement he could offer her; anything else was out of the question. He had to ignore the effect she had on him. The connection between them, that weaved around and through them, joining them in ways beyond his own understanding.

Emily stood quietly in his arms. She should not be there. Yet she revelled in the security and strength he provided her. He'd wanted to kiss her. She'd wanted it too, and she respected him for not using their mutual attraction to his benefit and taking advantage of her. Well, her mind did, but her heart resented the fact that he had fought the desire, for if he hadn't engulfed her in his arms, she would have succumbed to the yearning that was pulsating along every fibre of her being.

He tilted his head down and his granite features creased with concern, his arms tightening like steel bands around her.

"You must believe me, Miss Ellerton. I would do anything to protect you from the current situation."

"I know," she whispered back, rubbing her cheek against his chest as she nodded in confirmation of her words.

Nathan sucked in a deep breath, fighting the surging desire her simple action ignited in him. She was in his arms, warm, compliant with a hint of lavender and her full lips only inches from his and that part of him, the part he'd buried so long ago, thrust through him and demanded release. Instinct took over, and he dipped his head.

"There you are Nathan. I've been looking everywhere for you." Peter's voice broke the spell that surrounded them.

Nathan bit back a curse.

Emily jumped free of his embrace and whirled to the window, checking her appearance in the reflection.

"Seems I found you in time to avoid the necessity of another apology," Peter said, giving his brother a pointed look.

"The only apologies required are those from you," Emily snapped, as she spun on her heel to face him. "But I'd rather listen to a snake hiss an apology than be subjected to the poison that infuses your words." She stalked to the door, glaring at Peter over her shoulder as she flounced from the room.

Chuckling at her fiery reprimand, Peter turned to Nathan. "Now I see why you admire her so."

"Enough," Nathan snapped.

"Ah, so I did arrive in time. You'd only be that annoyed if you'd been interrupted before you achieved your goal."

"I am perfectly capable of controlling myself."

"Is that so?" Peter said, with a raise of his brows.

"Yes."

"Well, just remember she's not going to plant her flag with you, so just don't go planting your flag with her."

"I don't plan on planting anything with her."

Peter gave him a level look. "See that you don't."

"It is you who forgets yourself," Nathan said. "I outrank you in every conceivable way, and don't you forget it."

"Doesn't give you leave to be a fool."

"No, I leave that to you."

"Acting a fool and being a fool are two different things."

"Then let neither of us be accused of either. Come, we've done enough for one night," Nathan said, striding from the room.

Chapter Twelve

Sitting in the window seat with her feet tucked under her, Emily curled a strand of hair around her finger. Beneath her, the gardeners tended to the flower beds, where bright yellow daffodils swayed in the breeze.

She'd asked her aunt if she could visit George and she had steadfastly refused, stating it was too dangerous. Her aunt was right, but she wanted George beside her, where she could keep her eye on him. After her aunt and uncle, he was all the family she had left and she couldn't bear to lose him the way she had lost her parents. She needed to see for herself if he was recovering. Needed to reassure him she'd be there for him. She missed him.

As for Lord Thornburn, his mere presence sent a thrum of excitement skittering through her. Why did he make her feel that way? No good could come of it. The less she saw of him, the better.

At the slow click of her aunt's walking stick, Emily uncurled her feet, slid them into her slippers and hurried to assist her. Her aunt waved her help away.

"I can manage. Does me good to do things for myself."

"Well, I have no intention of standing in your way." Emily smiled at her aunt's defiant words. She certainly let nothing stand in the way of getting what she wanted.

Her aunt sat down on the settee, placing her walking stick across the seat next to her. "I wished to speak with you," she said, indicating for Emily to sit on the chair opposite, which she duly obeyed.

"What about?"

"Whether you have any intention of marrying Lord Thornburn?" Her aunt gave her an assessing stare.

Emily leapt off the chair. "No! Most definitely not."

"I did not mean to distress you."

Realising her reaction was distressing her aunt, Emily hurried to sit back down again. "You haven't. I was just not expecting such a question."

"Is it because he wishes to arrest George? You know that will be sorted out in time."

"No, it's not that."

"Then what is it?"

Emily plucked at her lace cuff. The prospect of marrying Lord Thornburn had not even entered her head. As far as she was concerned, with the way things were, it was not even a possibility. But as her reaction had shown, it had deeper reasons than his current need to arrest George. He lived a life she despised. A life spent in constant peril and travels abroad. A life her parents had led, and one that had left her behind, wondering each day when they would return. Until finally, news arrived to say they had been killed.

She rubbed her hands against her skirt.

She still didn't even know where her parents had died; it seemed the reports surrounding the incident were unclear, but that there was no mistake.

It was George and her aunt who had got her through the following days and weeks. She couldn't have coped without them.

She couldn't live such a life again. It was hard enough with George continuing her parents' work without her marrying into such a life. No, there was no way she could ever marry Lord Thornburn. She looked at her aunt. "I would never contemplate marriage to him. I could not go back to spending my life waiting for news."

Her aunt nodded. "I understand. Now this brings me to the root of my discussion."

"How so?" But Emily guessed where this conversation was going.

"I will not be here forever, and you need someone to look after you when I am gone. With that in mind, I want you to put aside everything that is happening with George and Lord Thornburn and concentrate on finding a husband." Her voice was firm.

Emily shook her head. "I cannot. Not with everything the way it is."

"You must. That was the original purpose of our coming to London."

"I know but—"

"I will brook no argument. Tonight, we begin your search for a husband. Is that understood?"

How could she even contemplate trying to find a husband at the moment? She shook her head. "I'm sorry, but I can't."

Her aunt lifted Emily's chin between her fingers and studied her. "Either you actively involve yourself in finding a husband whom you feel acceptable, or I will arrange one for you."

Emily eyed her aunt's determined raised brow. She would not win against her. She had learned that the hard way whilst she was growing up under her watchful eye. It hadn't been easy for her aunt to take on the care and responsibility of two orphaned children. But she'd always been there for them. She had raised her and George as though they were her own children, and Emily loved her dearly. But she could be a formidable woman when she chose. Whether or not her heart was in it, she would have to at least attempt to follow her aunt's edict. "You leave me very little choice."

"It is because I want to ensure you have a choice that I am doing this," her aunt said. "I cannot risk leaving you behind unprotected."

Emily understood her aunt's intentions were her way of looking after her when she was gone. Her heart constricted at the mere possibility and she blinked back the hot tears that pricked the back of her eyes. Family was the most precious thing to her. She loved her aunt and uncle and George. She'd do anything to protect them - as her aunt was doing now to ensure her future after she was gone. How could she prevent her from doing that? It was because her aunt cared that she was doing this. She dropped her shoulders in resignation. "As you wish, aunt, I will endeavour to concentrate on finding a husband."

"Good. Then we start tonight at Lord Attenborough's ball."

Emily let out a shattered laugh. Her aunt didn't waste any time. "Very well."

"And you will wear that new dress."

The mere thought sent ripples of trepidation through her. "Are you sure that is wise?"

"Most assuredly," her aunt said. "After all, one thought

about what happened when you were being fitted for that dress and your complexion will gain a rosy tint, just like it is doing now."

Emily clapped her hands over her heated cheeks. "Aunt, you are the most incorrigible – well, the word has yet to be invented - but when it has, it will describe you to perfection."

"I do not doubt that for a minute," her aunt responded without the slightest hint of compunction.

* * *

With deft fingers, Nathan added the final tweak to his cravat. He scrutinised the finished effect in the cheval mirror. Satisfied, he nodded to his valet who held his black evening jacket up as he slid his arms into the sleeves.

He turned when he heard his butler enter. "Where are they off to tonight?" he asked.

"Lord Attenborough's ball."

"Lord Attenborough's? Rather lively for Lady Drayford, given her health, don't you think?" Nathan said.

"If you say so, my lord."

He shook his head. When Robert had told him that Lady Drayford was not one to miss a party, he had not really believed him. But Robert was correct as always, and with that timely reminder, he resigned himself to the difficult prospect of ensuring Miss Ellerton was kept under pressure. If only Robert appreciated how difficult this was for him. Yet he suspected Robert already knew and this was another attempt by him to try to make him break his self-imposed oath. Well, Robert was going to be sorely disappointed, for this was one oath he could not in all good conscience break.

After the short journey to Lord Attenborough's town house, Nathan handed his hat and coat to a footman and made his greeting to his host and hostess. The ball was an awful crush and again he marvelled at Lady Drayford's desire to attend such events.

The twinkling light from the six chandeliers sparkled in the two mirrors hung on the far wall. The highly polished parquet floor shone as dancers twirled in time to the orchestra playing above in the minstrel's gallery.

Nathan made his way around the edge of the ballroom. Lady Drayford would be stationed where she would have a good view of the activities. He found her in the far corner, the long purple plume in her headdress moving from side to side as she chatted to a group of matrons. Catching her eye, Nathan indicated that he wished to speak with her, and she dismissed her friends with swift efficiency.

He bowed over her hand. "Lady Drayford, you are looking lovely as always." The cane she leaned on only added to her sense of indomitability.

"Spare me your false flattery; I am not some foreign dignitary's wife whom you need to impress." She opened her fan with a sharp flick of her wrist.

"I suspect nothing but stark honesty would impress you."

"Now that is a compliment I will accept."

He nodded his head as he surveyed the room. "Where is Miss Ellerton?"

"Dancing with Sir William." She pointed to the dance floor with her fan.

Nathan searched the dance floor and his stomach somersaulted. Emily was making her way down the centre of the dancers and she was wearing that dress. The gold overlay sparkled in the candlelight as she moved gracefully in time to the music. He gulped in a deep breath as his chest and loins tightened, his mind taking him back to the modiste, with Emily being fitted for the dress. Again her back was to him, but this time her hair was caught up in an elegant arrangement with a soft fiery tendril left to fall loose onto her shoulder; it drew his eye to the soft skin revealed above the dress's back and to the notches of her spine as they descended below the edge of her dress. He remembered how they had continued, notch after notch, after notch. He ran his tongue along the inside of his lower lip.

He looked back at Lady Drayford in time to catch her knowing smile.

"Sir William will make a good husband for her, do you not think?" She dipped her head to catch his reaction.

She was goading him and he had no intention of responding, though blood was pumping through his veins.

Lady Drayford shrugged her left shoulder. "She has to find a husband soon. After I am gone, all she will have left is George."

A heavy ball twisted in his gut. Instinctively he suppressed the sensation. It was not his fault George had betrayed his country, or that Emily would be left defenceless in the world after he was hanged for treason. Not his fault at all. Yet that damned pesky pang of guilt prodded him again. "Sir William is a lecherous old man," Nathan said, more tersely than he'd intended.

"He is a paragon of propriety, as well you know, and I do believe two years younger than yourself."

"Well, appearances can be deceiving."

"And yet at other times they can be most enlightening." She gave him an appraising look.

"If you say so." Nathan bit back a grimace.

Lady Drayford turned away from the dance floor and indicated for Nathan to follow her as she headed to an empty corner behind a large plant pot on a pedestal. She waited for him to join her. "My lord, may I be totally blunt with you?"

"Indeed, it would make a pleasant change."

She returned his level stare before inclining her head in a regal acceptance of his gibe. "Fair point, but now back to my point."

"Go on."

"Even before your pursuit of George, it was my earnest intention of coming to London for the Season with the express purpose of finding a husband to take care of Emily when I am gone. As you are aware, I am not a well woman and I wish to ensure that my niece is well settled before I am gone."

"I'm not the marrying kind, if that is what you are getting at," Nathan said, keeping a tight check on his annoyance. He couldn't marry; his self-imposed oath prevented him.

"Just as well, as you are not on my list of suitors."

His stomach knotted. He should be relieved that he would not have to avoid Lady Drayford's matchmaking. Instead, a picture of Emily in the arms of another man flittered through his mind and anger throbbed in his veins, before being doused by an overwhelming sense of lost opportunity. His eyelids slid shut for the briefest moment. He could not dwell on what could not be. He didn't have the right to dwell on it after what his poor judgement had cost others. After that fateful night, he had pledged his life to the service of his country and made an oath never to marry and experience the joys of a family of his own. He didn't deserve them after what he had done and the pain he had caused.

He reached up and rubbed a large leaf roughly between his fingers before turning his attention back to Lady Drayford. "Then what, may I ask, is the meaning of this conversation?"

"I wish you to leave Emily alone."

Nathan let go of the plant. "I have orders to the contrary."

To Lady Drayford's credit she gave him a look that clearly said his pursuit of Emily had deeper roots. Her attempt to stare him out of countenance was not a battle she would win, but she kept her glare on him for longer than he'd expected before she capitulated.

"I'm not interested in your orders," she said in a brusque tone. "I understand the importance of locating George, but to destroy Emily's chances of making a good match seems rather excessive."

He studied her for a moment. She had the same determined stance as Emily but instead of the stubborn tilt of her chin; hers was raised in calculation. "I see your dilemma, so I will cut you a deal," he said, as he rested his shoulder against the wall. "Tell me where George is and I'll leave her alone."

She kept her features deceptively composed. "Alas, I am unable to oblige."

"That is most unfortunate for Miss Ellerton." Nathan pushed himself away from the wall, ignoring her grasp at his sleeve as he strode past her to the dance floor, as the final few strains of the dance ended.

Seeing Sir William leading Miss Ellerton off the dance floor and away from where Lady Drayford waited, he prowled after them, cutting them off as they reached a side table with a selection of drinks laid out.

"Evening, Sir William," Nathan drawled. "Lady Drayford has bid me to collect Miss Ellerton and return her to her side." He ignored Emily's incredulous look.

"By all means, I will be happy to return her myself," Sir William said, unperturbed by Nathan's menacing presence.

"I don't believe the request was negotiable," Nathan replied.

"And *I* don't believe the request to be true. Miss Ellerton is currently in my care, and I will ensure she is returned," Sir William said, as he placed her hand on his arm in preparation to leave.

Miss Ellerton turned to Sir William and slipped her hand free. "That is most gallant of you, Sir, but I feel on this occasion I would be happy to accompany Lord Thornburn alone." This last said with such forced politeness, Nathan had to bite back a huff of disgust.

Sir William gave a stiff smile and nodded his acquiesce as he lifted her gloved fingers to his lips. "I hope to enjoy the pleasure of your company on many further occasions."

She gave him such a sweet, beguiling smile that Nathan rolled his eyes.

"As do I," she said provocatively as he turned and strolled away.

Nathan waited until he was out of earshot. "That was a sickening display."

Emily snatched up a champagne glass. How dare he reprimand her after his behaviour? "I could say the same about you."

"I hardly think my actions qualify, especially considering your choice of dress tonight." His hungry gaze dipped to rove over her as though she was only half clad as she had been in the modiste.

A spiral of something delicious slid into the pit of her stomach and heat spread out across her skin. She sucked in a deep breath that lodged in her throat when his gaze dropped to her breasts that were displayed to advantage by the low scalloped front of her dress. She lifted her fan to cover her discomfiture and to give her some protection from his smouldering gaze.

"This dress was commissioned for this ball, and if it had not been for you and the distress you caused my aunt, it would have been finished over a week ago. Now, do you think you could find a different topic to discuss in our current surroundings?" She took a hurried sip of her champagne to quieten the butterflies in her stomach.

"I can think of a lot of topics," he said, as he picked up a glass and drained the contents while his gaze stayed fixed on her.

She raised her eyebrows at him in a questioning manner. "You are the last person my aunt would have sent to collect me, so pray tell me, what do you want?"

"To speak with you."

"Do you have news?" Her thoughts instantly turned to George, and she unconsciously lowered her glass.

"About George? No," he said, placing his empty glass down.

"Then we have nothing further to discuss, so perhaps you can do as you promised and return me to my aunt."

"Are you going to marry Sir William?"

Her jaw dropped at his question. "I have not yet decided."

"Of course you have, and you know full well he is not a contender."

"As it does not make any difference to you, I feel that this is not a suitable topic for discussion." She took another quick sip of her champagne, using it as an excuse to look away.

"Your aunt is determined to see you married."

She dropped her head and refused to look back at him.

"Miss Ellerton, is something the matter?" Nathan asked in a gentle tone as he took in her disconsolate posture.

She lifted her face to him. Unspoken pain glowed in her jade eyes. "How can it not be?"

Seeing nowhere appropriate for her to sit, he took her hand, placed it in the crook of his arm and led her out of the French doors onto a small patio. The candlelight from the windows bathed the stone slabs in patterned light. No other guests had ventured out, and they were alone.

"Please Lord Thornburn, I would rather return inside."

"Come." He pointed to a row of steps that led to a secluded arbour with a stone bench set off to one side. Half hidden in shadow, they would not be easily seen. "Sit with me for a while." He was pleased when she allowed him to guide her to the bench.

She sat, taking a moment to arrange her skirts. Nathan sat beside her, turned slightly to face her. Beyond the noise of the music and voices from the house, the dark night held an inviting quietness.

He placed his arm along the back of the bench. "Please tell me what the matter is."

A self-depreciating laugh preceded her words. "Do you really need to ask?"

"Maybe not. But I would like to hear it from you all the same."

She rolled the stem of her glass between her fingers, causing the liquid to swirl and eddy. "You already know of my worries for George and now my aunt insists I must concentrate on finding a husband. But how can I do that?" She stood up and leaned her head against the trunk of a sycamore tree.

Nathan stood and took the glass from her, placing it on the arm of the bench before grasping her shoulders in a firm grip and turning her to face him. "Your aunt is worried about you and your future." He slid his hands down the silky fabric of her gloves, coming to rest at her wrists.

"I know, but how can I find a husband whilst I am so consumed with worry? I am unable to converse in any sensible manner. So how can I assess if we would suit when I cannot even be who I am?"

"If they have any sense, they will see how wonderful you are and if they cannot, then they don't deserve you."

"Eloquent words from a well-schooled diplomat." She lifted her face to him as a soft smile trembled on her lips.

Nathan's heart caught in his throat. When she was not sniping at him, she had a beautiful smile. He smiled in response. "I'm not a diplomat, merely a diplomat's aide."

"And what good is a diplomat's aide who cannot lie?"

"I am no help to Lord Brakenhale if I cannot tell him, of all people, the truth."

"It pleases me to know there is someone to whom you are truthful."

He lifted her hands up so they rested on his chest between them. "I have always preferred the truth over, shall we say misrepresentation, as lies in my line of work tend to end in tragedy." He could not prevent the bitterness and pain that edged his voice.

She twisted away from him. Her one hand rested on the tree trunk and her other placed tight against her midriff, her head bent in a portrait of grief.

"Miss Ellerton, have I said something to upset you?"

She shook her head but would not turn to face him. Leaning forwards, he placed his fingertips under her chin and lifted her face up to him. Her eyes were clenched shut, her face distorted in misery. Unable to bear her pain, he wrapped his arms around her, cradling her head against his chest. What had he said to upset her so?

He stroked her back. There were no sobs. She stood quietly in his arms while the spring leaves in the tree above whispered in the gentle breeze. He did not know how to deal with this. After a few moments, he leaned her away from him and dipped his head so he could see her face. "Miss Ellerton, if I have said something to upset you, I am truly sorry."

"Thank you," she whispered back, but her eyes stayed downcast.

"May I ask what has upset you so?"

She released a shattered breath and nodded.

Sliding his arm around her waist, he led her back to the bench. Sitting, he cupped her cheek in his hand and brought her face up to look at him. She lifted her heartbroken gaze to his, and it pierced him with pain. "Oh God, Emily, what has hurt you so?"

"The loss of my parents." Her voice was devoid of emotion, the emptiness of it clanged through him.

He found her gloved hand and threaded his fingers through hers. "Go on," he said, with gentle entreaty.

Her gaze dipped for an agonizing moment before lifting back to his. The green of her eyes splintered like shattered glass.

"My parents worked for the diplomatic service. They'd be gone for months, then they'd sweep back into my life like a summer's day. They'd talk of wondrous adventures and daring escapades. George loved their stories and the idea of serving his country; it's why he joined the diplomatic service."

Nathan thought this last was a sharp reprimand at him for accusing George of treason, but when he took in her dejected form, he realised she was far beyond using her misery to get at him.

She stopped and took a deep swallow before continuing. "Then a letter arrived to say they were returning home, and that this would be their last assignment. I was so joyful. I remember dancing around the garden with George, whilst my aunt clapped in time to a beat. But our excitement was premature. We waited and waited, but they never came. Then, late one night, there was a knock at the door. I crept out of bed and crouched behind the banister. I wanted to leap out and surprise my parents."

She gave a small smile at the absurdity of such a childish prank, but Nathan saw the young girl she had been, so eager to greet the parents she loved, she hadn't wanted to wait and had hidden in order to surprise them.

She sucked in a deep breath. "Instead, I discovered they had died. I fled to my room and hid under my covers and spent the night crying alone."

Oh Lord, no. She'd been by herself that night with no one to comfort her. Pain seared his chest at her words and he gathered her into his arms, rubbing her back as though trying to comfort that lonely, heartbroken young girl. "I'm so sorry, Emily. Why did you not go to your aunt?"

"I thought I would be in trouble for leaving my room and eavesdropping."

The air left his lungs. She'd been heartbroken but too scared to go to her aunt and instead she had cried alone. He crushed her against him, wanting to wrap himself around her and protect her. His chest ached with the need to take her pain away.

"From what little I could glean from George and my aunt, my parents were betrayed and killed."

Nathan bowed his head and sucked in a deep breath, whistling it out between his teeth. He'd experienced first-hand the cost of betrayal. No wonder his words that lies ended in tragedy had affected her so. He rubbed his thumb across her cheek, noting she was devoid of tears. Her pain may be deep, but it was long enough ago that she'd cried all her tears. He wondered how many tears she had cried. He slid his hand along her sleeve to rest on the curve of her slender shoulder. "You must always remember your parent's bravery."

She sucked in her lower lip at his words, and that was his undoing. He bent his head and caught her lips between his own, moulding them to him. His arms wrapped around her and he gathered her against him. He needed this. Had wanted to do this since the night he'd first seen her at Oakleaf Manor.

His heart soared when she leaned into him, parting her lips in response to his gentle coaxing. With tentative strokes, his tongue explored the fullness of her lips before dipping into her mouth.

He traced the contours of her back with his fingers. She was so small and delicate. He wanted to protect her from harm. Her hands glided up his chest and he released a deep groan. He wanted to do more than just protect her. But when his hand slid upwards along her side, she squirmed and pushed her hands against his chest to free herself.

"This is wrong," she said, as she pulled her lips away from his.

Yet it had felt so right. Nathan fought to get his breathing under control. Damn it. This should never have happened. It was a desire he could not indulge. He'd made an oath and he could not break it. He released his hold on her. "I believe, for once, we are in accord." But she'd been equally affected, judging by the creamy swell of her breast rising and falling rapidly as she struggled to regain control.

She pushed herself to a standing position and wrapped her arms around her waist. "What do you want from me?" She looked so confused.

Now that question provoked a great many images in Nathan's mind. All things he could not have. "To make you feel better," he said with simple honesty as he stood.

"By kissing me?"

The tension left his shoulders and he chuckled. "That is the usual effect."

"Well, maybe you need more practice." She raised her hand against his chest. "That was not an invitation."

"Perhaps, under the circumstances, it was not the best idea." He reached up and tucked a loose strand of her hair behind her ear. He was relieved when she did not pull away. The last thing he wanted was to scare her. He couldn't bear it if she feared him.

"I think the majority of your ideas of late have not been good."

He couldn't argue with her in that regard. "Then let me make it up to you some other way."

"How?"

"Dance with me."

She gave him a stunned look. "You want to dance?"

"Yes. Unbelievable though it may be."

She smiled at him, a sweet, gentle smile, which made his heart swell. Strange that such a small thing could have such a big effect on him.

A warm glow flowed through Emily at the idea of dancing with him. "I would be honoured." It was the least she could do after the comfort he had given her, the kiss notwithstanding. She'd never told anyone before how she had learned about her parents' deaths and to finally do so had lifted a heavy burden from her. And the way he held her as though she were precious made her feel so safe and protected. Adversaries they may be, but perhaps when George had proven his innocence, they could be friends. Her heart squeezed. Friends were the most they could ever be. She decided that for tonight it would be enough, and she placed her hand on his arm, struggling to ignore the ripple of anticipation that skittered through her.

They re-entered the ballroom as the orchestra was striking up the next dance. She let him steer her into the line of ladies participating as he took his place opposite her. In time to the music, they stepped towards each other and something fluttered inside Emily like a butterfly landing on her heart. She should not feel this way about him. It would do her no good.

She was thankful the movement of the dance called for them to turn away and weave between the other dancers. But such feelings could not be suppressed and as they re-joined and crossed hands to spin together, she had to fight the tremble of excitement his nearness caused her.

Releasing his hands, she took a deep breath and inhaled the scent of his spicy cologne as he weaved behind her, all her senses vibrantly aware of him. After this dance, she would have to stay away from him. She couldn't protect George when she was trying to fight her feelings for Nathan. Thankfully, the dance now required for her to partner the man on her left. She dragged her wandering mind back to the dance and found her hands clasped by Peter.

"Evening, Miss Ellerton. I see my brother is taking good care of you."

"I'm surprised you are able to recognise such felicity," she said, as the dance brought them closer together.

"Oh, I recognised a great many things." His eyes flicked from her to Nathan.

A blush crept up her cheeks, but she was spared the need to reply as they separated, following the pattern of the dance to return to face one another.

"How is your injury faring?" Emily asked, to sway the conversation away from her and his brother.

"It comes and goes."

"That must be most convenient."

"It has its uses," he said, catching and holding her gaze.

Emily gave a petulant lift of her chin as she turned away to be re-joined by Lord Thornburn. She did not miss the warning looks the brothers exchanged.

"I hope Peter has not distressed you," he said, as he passed close behind her.

"No, I am sure this was a demonstration of his best behaviour."

He gave a bark of laughter. "You are wise beyond your years." His lips dipped to her ear as the dance called for them to move closer.

She could only draw breath in response.

At last the dance drew to an end and Emily returned Lord Thornburn's bow with a quick curtsey. She allowed him to place her hand on his arm and escort her back to her aunt. She eyed them with a quizzical stare as they approached.

With a sharp flick of her wrist, Emily opened her fan and waved it hurriedly in front of her face in order to divert her aunt's curiosity. "One always underestimates the exertion of a good dance," she said. But her aunt was no fool and she'd know this was a diversionary tactic.

"Indeed," her aunt said. "One would do well to remember that in future and limit the number of partners one agrees to dance with." Her voice held a hint of warning.

"Wise words," Lord Thornburn said. "There are plenty of undesirables, even in attendance at such an event as this."

"Well, you'd know all about that," Aunt Amelia said, turning to him with a pointed look.

Emily bit her lip to hide her smile at his look of pure boyish innocence. She could not believe that a grown man could possess such an expression. She gave him a side-wise glance and her heart skipped at the mischievous twinkle in his eye and that was before he lifted the corner of his lips up in a devastating smile.

Aware her aunt was watching her, Emily smoothed her features into a bland expression and turned to her. "Did you hear that there is going to be a lecture on Lord Elgin's marbles?"

"Do not change the subject. I wish to know what happened to Sir William?"

"He, ah, had to leave, but was desirous of dancing with me again."

"Well, ensure that he does," her aunt said, thumping her walking stick on the hardwood floor.

Emily glanced away and spied Peter Renwick heading towards them. She grimaced in displeasure but was satisfied to see that Lord Thornburn was not pleased by his appearance either.

He made his bow and turned to his brother. "It has been a long day. Perhaps we should call it a night?"

"Why? What have you been up to?" Emily asked.

"Speaking with Lord Brakenhale," Peter Renwick said in a stern tone. "He is returning to the continent tomorrow."

Emily's head whipped around to face Lord Thornburn. "Are you not going with him?"

"No. Not on this occasion. Our services are required in England for the time being."

Emily's lungs expelled her tightly held breath, bringing with it a twinge of guilt; she should be distressed by his not having left instead of relieved. This was a poignant reminder of what she stood to lose if she did not distance herself from him. "What business do you have in England?"

Lord Thornburn's face turned severe, but his brother answered for him.

"The locating of traitors."

Her stomach plummeted at the stark reminder that Lord Thornburn was with her for one purpose only; to use her to find and arrest her brother.

"I think you've done enough for one evening," Lord Thornburn said to his brother before turning his attention back to her. "Ladies, if you will excuse us, we will bid you adieu."

"With pleasure," Emily said, relieved to see the back of him and his brother.

The evening ruined, Emily and her aunt left the ball shortly after. Claiming acute tiredness and an approaching headache, she avoided a conversation with her aunt in the coach. On reaching home, she went straight to her room. She tried to get to sleep, but her mind kept taking her back to the moonlit garden and Lord Thornburn holding her in his arms and kissing her.

She touched her lips, remembering how tentative and almost sad in its gentleness the kiss had been. How tender and caring he'd been with her.

She threw herself onto her front, punching her pillow. She could not have such thoughts about Lord Thornburn. His was a way of life she could never accept, and his need to capture George could not be tolerated.

Chapter Thirteen

Nathan and Peter took the steps two at a time and strode along the corridor into Lord Brakenhale's office.

"Robert, what on earth are you still doing here?" Nathan pulled off his gloves and flung them onto the desk in front of him as he and Peter took a seat. "You should be on your way to Vienna by now."

Lord Brakenhale rubbed his temples. "I would like nothing more. However, the Duc De Orney has sent word to the Hanoverian Ambassador here in London who has, in turn, reported to the King about our mishap with the mission. And now I am to await an audience with His Majesty in order to explain myself. So until that meeting has taken place and King George and the Foreign Office see fit to give me leave, I am stranded here."

"Do they not understand how important our negotiations are?" Nathan said.

"They do, and until I can give a satisfactory explanation, they are withholding the promised 6,000 men we had agreed to send to Malta to support the new coalition." His shoulders slumped in weary resignation.

"But that's political suicide," Peter said.

"There are those in the cabinet who would advocate peace and our situation has played straight into their hands." Robert stood up and walked over to the sideboard. "Drink?"

Nathan waved his hand in the negative. He was too wound up to accept any distraction. Peter followed Nathan's decision and declined as well.

"Never thought I'd see the day when you two turned down a drink."

Ignoring his comment, Nathan took in his friend's dejected stance. "You did not summon us here just to inform us of your delay in returning to the continent. So pray, tell me what information have you received?"

Robert finished pouring himself a drink and then swilled it around his glass as he returned to his desk. He picked up a letter from the large pile stacked in front of him. "I've received a despatch from our Swiss contact that Dubeck has been seen travelling through France to Le Mans."

"He's alive. Thank goodness." Nathan let out a relieved breath. "He may well have the information that can clear your name."

"Let me go after him," Peter said, standing and placing his hands on Robert's desk.

"No. Locating George Ellerton is our first priority," Robert replied.

"But we're no closer to locating him than we were two weeks ago," Peter said, glancing at his brother. "Every avenue we have tried has come to a dead end."

Nathan ignored Peter's look and avoided catching Robert's eye.

Robert wisely decided not to enquire. "Be that as it may. But right now I need something I can present to the King and a confession from George Ellerton could be this mission's salvation."

"No. Peter is right," Nathan said, rubbing his chin. "George's trail has gone cold and I cannot sit around doing nothing when I know we have a lead on Dubeck."

"I'd rather keep you both here in case George makes an appearance."

"But if Dubeck does have information that could clear this mess up, it would explain his disappearance and may be sufficient to prove your worth. It may even flush George out of his hiding place."

Robert drummed his fingers on his desk. "Very well. But I cannot spare you for more than a couple of weeks. If you have not located him by then, your orders are to return to London posthaste."

"Agreed." Nathan stood up and pulled on his gloves.

* * *

'I have news. Meet me in Hyde Park.'

Emily gripped Lord Thornburn's missive. It had been delivered this morning by a messenger who left without awaiting a response. It was addressed to Emily, in a neat handwriting and with Lord Thornburn's seal on the reverse. What did this mean?

"Do not fret," her aunt said, over the sound of the horse's hooves as they drove along Park Lane. "He cannot have found

George. We would have heard."

"How can I not fret? I haven't seen George since we smuggled him out. I need to see him again, to ensure that he is safe and well."

"Of course, but first we still have many things to sort out. Not least finishing choosing your dresses after our rude interruption the other day."

Why must her aunt keep on about clothes? Could she not understand that it was the last thing on her mind? "Can it not wait until a more suitable time?"

"We must keep up appearances, and if all goes well, I will arrange a meeting with George for you."

Emily's gaze shot to her aunt's. "Truly?"

Her aunt gave a regal nod of her head, which made Emily's heart soar as her silent response was as solemn as her word.

They turned into Hyde Park, under the shade of trees lining Rotten Row. A breeze ruffled the silk fringe of her parasol as she searched the sea of people for Lord Thornburn. She spotted him riding towards them on a magnificent black stallion with his brother, Peter, riding by his side. There was no mistaking the familial resemblance as they rode shoulder to shoulder. Their erect carriage a duplicate of each other. Their strong facial features so similar. The matching way that stray lock of hair flopped above their left eye. But Emily's eyes drew her to Lord Thornburn and the sight of him sitting aloft the enormous beast added to his persona of arrogant self-assurance. A powerful man who expected to be obeyed. Yet her body quivered with the gratifying knowledge that she could evoke his gentleness and his desire. A jolt went through her at the sight of his silver eyes, remembering how those eyes had roamed over her near bare flesh in Mrs Shaw's modiste and had dipped to her lips at last night's party before he had kissed her.

A kiss so tentative and gentle. A kiss meant to comfort, to elicit pleasure, but not to overwhelm. She'd been so vulnerable last night, but instead of taking advantage, he'd listened to her worries and offered her comfort in return. If only he didn't work for the diplomatic service. If only he didn't want to arrest George. Her chest constricted. She had to conquer her feelings for him.

As they approached, she fidgeted with her parasol, terrified the news would bring more complications for George.

He drew his horse alongside her carriage. She quelled the shiver that tingled along her spine as she waited for him to make his greeting. When he addressed her, she tilted her head in response, then glanced meaningfully at the footpath that meandered along the side of the Row. She was pleased that he was quick to pick up on her hint.

"It is a pleasant day for a walk. Would you give me the honour of your presence, Miss Ellerton?"

Taking a deep breath and regaining control of her voice, she replied, "I would enjoy the exertion, thank you."

Her aunt gave Lord Thornburn a beady-eyed look. "Don't be long. We have an appointment at Mrs Shaw's modiste to finish our ordering and I will not countenance any more disruptions."

Emily bit back a smile as Lord Thornburn nodded his head in acceptance of Lady Drayford's set down.

"I promise to return her shortly and can assure you of my having no intention of disrupting your activities," he said.

Lady Drayford held his eyes for a long moment before she nodded her acquiescence.

"I'll stay and keep Lady Drayford company," Peter said.

Emily indicated to the driver to pull the carriage over so she could alight and join Lord Thornburn, who had dismounted and was wrapping the reins of his horse around a branch.

He returned to her and took her gloved hand in his firm grasp as he assisted her down. They strolled along in silence until clear of the other members of the ton who were milling about.

Under the shade of a sturdy oak tree, Emily came to a stop and turned to face him. "Please tell me what news you have? Is it about George?"

"In a manner of speaking."

Her heart slammed into her ribs, her aunt's reassuring words lost in fear and dread. "You've arrested him." It was a statement, not a question born out of total conviction, that her worst nightmare had come true.

Nathan grasped her hand as it went limp on his arm. She truly believed he'd found George. Her reaction was not feigned. If he'd needed proof that she did not know where George was, this was it. All the times she'd asserted her innocence, he'd always had that little doubt, that little voice telling him that she must be lying, and now he had to accept that his assumptions were incorrect. Unfortunately, he had been banking on her knowing George's location; his entire purpose in meeting her today was to give her enough information to pass on to flush George out of his hiding place. Looking off into the distance, he began recalculating his strategy.

Beside him, Miss Ellerton sank onto a small tree stump as she struggled for breath. She must have taken his silence as confirmation. All thoughts of stratagems dissolved. He knelt beside her and took her hands in his, rubbing them reassuringly. "We've not arrested George, or found any trace of him." He watched for her reaction.

"You haven't?" Her voice echoed her confusion. He could tell his words had not fully penetrated her fear fogged mind.

"No."

"Then what news do you have?" A tentative hope shone in her moss green eyes and Nathan felt like a total cad for using her love for her brother in this way.

Nathan released her hands and placed them gently on her lap as he said in a carefully modulated tone, "We've received a lead."

"You mean you no longer suspect George?" Her tone echoed her suspicion that this may be a trick.

"Well, there are reasonable grounds to believe our colleague, Dubeck, may have information that could exonerate both George and Lord Brakenhale." It was a partial lie, but he didn't want her to worry more about her brother, at least not until the inevitable happened. After that, there was nothing he could do to protect her.

"Exonerate Lord Brakenhale! Why? What has happened?"

"He's been summoned to attend an interview with the King to explain himself and the mishap with the mission." Bitterness reverberated through his sharp words. "And the only way to help him is to find Dubeck before he leaves France."

"France! But isn't that dangerous?" The trees around them rustled as a sudden gust of wind buffeted them.

"We have no choice. Lord Brakenhale needs us to discover the identity of the traitor and the extent of his actions."

"But..." Emily cut herself off before she said that George must be able to help. Even now, she could not allow her excitement over the fact that the evidence to save George may soon be at hand, make her give him away. She tried to pool her thoughts together. "Will you be gone long?"

"A few weeks. Our information states Dubeck was headed towards Le Mans. We hope to intercept him before he can disappear again."

"Is there anything I can do to help?"

"If George should contact you, tell him Lord Brakenhale is in desperate need of his help. If we do not make it back in time, George may be the only person who can save Lord Brakenhale's reputation."

"Oh." The full import of his words hitting home. "I shall certainly endeavour to assist if I can, my lord."

"Nathan." He tilted his head to one side when she was about to argue. "Please, it would mean a lot to me to know that when all things are considered, we could call each other friends."

Emily considered his words. He'd always acted with respect towards her – well, most of the time – and it seemed fitting to use his given name. She nodded, "Very well, Nathan."

He rewarded her with a smile of genuine pleasure.

"Come," he said, "it is time I returned you to your aunt before she has me flayed alive."

"Indeed, she is not one to be gainsaid." Emily grasped his proffered hand, allowing him to pull her up. They stood facing one another, neither willing to move.

The moment felt portentous, as though things would never be the same again. She gazed up at him, her eyes tracing the arch of his brow, the slope of his chiselled cheekbones, down to his firm lips, trying to commit his face to memory. Her gaze caught his as they closed the gap between them, his head dipping towards her.

Loud voices interrupted them and they leapt apart. The

moment was lost and a tight band encircled Emily's chest.

"We should not have let that happen." He placed her hand on his arm and led her back to her aunt and the awaiting carriage.

He joined his brother, remounted, and in unison they doffed their hats and bade their goodbyes.

An involuntary shiver skittered down Emily's spine as she watched them ride away towards the gathering storm clouds.

* * *

Emily dragged her feet as they entered Mrs Shaw's modiste, ignoring the spots of rain that had begun to fall. How could she think about clothes when her mind was preoccupied with Lord Thornburn's news and her need to see George?

"Ah, Lady Drayford," Mrs Shaw said, "I see you've come to make the final decisions for your niece's wardrobe."

"Indeed," Aunt Amelia said, as she and Emily followed the dressmaker through to the back.

Once there, Mrs Shaw dropped her carefully modulated voice and whispered in a broad Somerset accent, "Everything is as you arranged. From the cellar you need to take the third door on your left."

She handed Aunt Amelia a key before entering the small storage room and moving several boxes aside to reveal a rug and underneath a trap door. She lifted it up to show a staircase.

"After you," Aunt Amelia said, as Mrs Shaw handed Emily a small lantern.

Emily took the first few steps and then turned back to assist her aunt down the narrow staircase. Suspecting where they were headed, she refrained from speaking and on reaching the dank cellar, she quickly searched for the door.

It was half hidden behind crates and large barrels. She wrinkled her nose at the musty aroma. There was a chill to the air. But she could feel no draughts, which meant the room was enclosed. She tried to ignore the high-pitched squeaking and scrabbling coming from the dark shadows. The cellar was larger than the shop above, running under at least three of the shops along the street above. She noticed another staircase descending from one of the other establishments and she worried that someone may discover them.

Her aunt, however, seemed unconcerned and, lifting her skirts above the dust and grime, headed straight for the door instructed by the dressmaker. She slotted the key into the keyhole and with a screeching scrape; the key turned and the door opened.

This led into another cellar, smaller than the last, and a warren of tunnels.

"Where now?" Emily whispered as her aunt locked the door behind them.

"This way," she said, turning right and walking straight on to find another wooden staircase, which she ascended up two storeys, closely followed by Emily.

They were met at the top by a long corridor with several rooms leading off. Her aunt knocked on the second door.

"Who is it?" called a woman's voice from beyond the door.

"Lady Drayford,"

The door was opened a moment later by a matronly woman who resembled the dressmaker and Emily assumed must be her sister.

"Welcome, my lady," she said, opening the door wide and

letting them in.

"How is our patient, Mrs Hewitt?"

"He's faring well."

They found George struggling to sit up in the bed. His arm was in a sling, but his face had colour and he was freshly shaven.

Emily raced to him and touched his forehead. Her shoulders relaxing when he showed no signs of fever.

"That's a nice way to greet me," he said.

Emily beamed a bright smile at him and gave him a kiss on the cheek. "Just checking you are fully recovered from your fever."

"Never better."

"How's your shoulder?"

"Stiff, a bit painful, but I'm getting some movement back into it."

"Good." Emily settled back onto one of the chairs Mrs Hewitt had put out for her and her aunt.

"So what brings you to visit me, other than my wonderful company?"

Emily gave her aunt a look, awaiting permission from her before she broached Lord Thornburn's news. Her aunt nodded her permission.

"Well, what is it?" George asked after watching the exchange.

"We've heard from Lord Thornburn that they may have found a lead and are on their way to intercept him."

"Did they say who they were searching for?"

"Yes, someone called Duboun or Duback," Emily said, struggling to remember the name Nathan had given when she had still been reeling from the fear that George had been captured.

"You mean Dubeck?"

"Yes, that's it."

"Oh Christ, no."

Emily grasped the bed sheet between her fingers. "What's wrong?"

"Dubeck's the one I gave the letters to."

"You mean the one you've been staying hidden in order to protect?"

"Yes, exactly." George pushed himself forwards.

"But then you have to tell Lord Thornburn and save him a wasted journey, especially now, with Lord Brakenhale's audience with the King."

"What audience?"

"The audience to explain what has gone wrong with the mission." Emily released the sheets as she waved her hands in emphasis of her words.

"Damn it, when did this happen?"

"Recently, I assume. Lord Thornburn told me today."

"Today? How often have you met with him?" He gave her a piercing stare.

Emily paused, unsure how truthful she should be. "Not very often, a few occasions at most."

"You must stay away from him." George's voice was sharp.

"If you say so." Emily was taken aback by the ferventness of his request.

He patted her hand. "Good girl. Now did he mention where they were headed?"

"Le Mans in France," she said without thinking as the sky darkened and rain began to lash against the window.

"Good God, no. That means they will be going via Jersey."

He shook his head. "The French know the locations of our safe houses there."

"We must warn Lord Thornburn before he leaves."

"No Emily, they mustn't know you have been harbouring me. They'll arrest you."

"Maybe it is time for you to report to Lord Brakenhale." She placed her hand on his uninjured arm and felt his muscles tense at her words.

"I can't, but there may be another way."

"What way?"

"Best you do not know," George said, as the wind whistled down the chimney, making the fire splutter.

Chapter Fourteen

Emily spent the next four wet and windy days badgering her aunt into letting her visit George again before her aunt finally admitted that he was no longer in Mrs Hewitt's care.

"I knew it." She sank onto the pale blue settee in her aunt's withdrawing room. The heavy rain forming into rivulets as it cascaded down the windows. "He's gone after them."

"We don't know that for certain." But her aunt's gaze slid away from her.

"What other option did he have after I told him Lord Thornburn's news?" Emily dropped her head into her hands; whatever happened now would be her fault.

"Do not distress yourself. He has contacts he can utilise."

"If that is so, why did he not utilise them before now?" She should have convinced him to visit Lord Brakenhale. At least then she would know where he was.

"Because he would be putting them in danger. But now the stakes have changed."

"So now he's putting himself in danger instead."

"He's always being in danger, doing what he does."

"I'm well aware of that," Emily burst out. She gave her aunt a contrite look when she realised her words had hurt her. "I'm sorry, aunt. I did not mean to snap at you."

"It's quite all right. I understand how difficult it is for you after what happened to your parents."

Emily nodded. The pain of her loss was her constant companion. "I'm not sure I can cope with the waiting anymore."

"It is just something we have to bear."

"I loved my parents so much." She glanced up at her aunt.

Her aunt rose on stiff legs and came to sit next to her. "I know you did."

"But," she said, shaking her head, "I know it is wrong of me, and I do not want to feel this way, but I cannot help hating them for going away and dying."

"Shh, you should not talk like that."

"Why not? It was they who left me and didn't come back."

"Oh, my dear child. You must remember they loved you very much."

"Not enough for them to come home to me." Emily pushed herself up and strode to the rain soaked windows. First her parents, then George, and now Nathan. "Everyone always leaves me to go gallivanting off in some foreign country."

"Everyone?" her aunt said.

Emily's mouth opened in dismay that she may have given way more than she intended. She waved her arms in the air as if to dismiss her words. "I meant my parents and George, of course. And now George is injured. What if he never comes home?" What if she never found out what happened to him? She could not bear it. She spun to face her aunt. "It will be my fault for telling him Lord Thornburn's news."

"George knows how to take care of himself."

"I hope you are right," she said in a shattered breath. "But I know one thing for certain."

"And what is that?"

"I do not want to spend my life waiting for news."

* * *

Emily spent the next week in a state of perpetual anxiety. Every time she heard a carriage pull up she rushed to the window, only to be disappointed. She asked the butler so frequently if there had been any letters or messages that he'd begun answering her before she'd even asked. She half wished that he would not, for in that brief moment she had a fleeting sense of hope even if it was dashed a second later.

Finally, her aunt insisted that they go for a ride in Hyde Park, as the sun had put in an appearance, albeit an intermittent one. It was past the fashionable hour, so there would be fewer people about and they both needed the air to help ease their unrest.

As Emily was walking out of the door, the housekeeper called her aunt away to discuss an urgent household issue, so she left them to it and continued on outside.

The sun had made a valiant attempt to escape the clouds and Emily busied herself opening her parasol and so did not see the gentleman who hurried up to her.

"Miss Ellerton, I presume," the gentleman said, causing Emily to gasp in surprise. "Do not alarm yourself, I am Mr Edward Clarrington. I must ask you to excuse the mode of my introduction, but matters of extreme import prevent me from waiting until a more appropriate time."

"Oh." Emily lifted her opened parasol, taking in the tall, smartly dressed man in front of her. She guessed him to be a few years older than her brother - more Lord Thornburn's age. Gathering her scattered thoughts, she asked, "What important matters?"

"Those of national import." His voice was deep and serious.

"Oh!" Emily's heart skidded to a stop. Did he have news of her brother or Lord Thornburn?

"My purpose in intercepting you today was to enquire after your brother, George. Have you heard from him lately?"

"No, not at all," she said, slipping easily into the lie she'd been attesting to since the night Lord Thornburn had arrived at Oakleaf Manor.

"When was the last time you heard from him?"

Emily hastily calculated the last letter from him before he had returned. "About four months ago."

"Oh dear, that is not good." Edward looked swiftly over both his shoulders. "Your brother entrusted me with ensuring your welfare when I returned from the continent as I was due to do some weeks ago, but I was most unfortunately delayed. He should have returned before me by now."

Emily was at a loss as to how to answer him. She didn't know if it was safe for her to tell him George had made it back. And she certainly didn't know if she should tell this stranger that George was now in pursuit of Lord Thornburn who had returned to the continent.

Edward's next words made the decision irrelevant. "Miss Ellerton, I feel it imperative that I warn you that you may be in danger. There are those who would wish ill on your brother and they would not stop short of harming you in order to get to him."

"I'll take care," she said, taken aback by his words.

"Ensure you do, and if George should get in touch, please let him know I have returned and he can contact me in the usual way. In the meantime, I must request you do not mention my presence here today."

"Of course. I will not betray you. But what if I need your help?"

"I'll know."

"You mean you will be watching?"

He gave her a look that clearly said he was doing it for her own benefit before casting a swift glance at the house. "I must take my leave. Adieu, then, my fair lady, and I apologise for not being able to meet you under better circumstances." He bowed swiftly before he turned on his heel and disappeared across the road.

Her aunt joined her at the foot of the steps. "What was all that about?"

"I'm not certain that I know," she said, deciding against lying to her aunt who'd obviously observed the meeting.

"Maybe you can elaborate on our drive."

Emily gave her a distracted glance before shaking her head to clear it. "No aunt, I don't think we should venture out today."

"Did that gentleman threaten you?"

"No, he said George had sent him to keep an eye on me some weeks ago, but he got delayed. He seemed distressed when I told him I'd not heard from George." She closed her parasol and headed back inside. "Do you know him?"

Her aunt followed her. "No, I don't believe so."

"He said he would be watching."

"Not another one."

"I'm afraid so."

"Seems we may need to stay indoors for a while."

"So it would seem." Emily glanced back down the street the way Edward Clarrington had gone, but she could see no sign of him.

Chapter Fifteen

Whilst getting dressed that morning, Emily's maid had laid out her pale aqua morning dress. She'd first worn it when George had last been home, over a year ago now. He'd taken her to the local fair. They had sampled the tasty treats on offer and watched the acrobats and stilt walkers. She'd tried to enjoy herself and not dwell on the fact that he would soon be gone again. Seeing a stall selling ribbons, George had purchased one to match her dress. It was such a frivolous gift, but she loved it. She asked her maid to fetch it and she threaded it through her hair. The wearing of it made her feel closer to him.

By unspoken agreement, Emily and her aunt now spent the hours each day in her aunt's withdrawing room whilst they awaited news. This way, if her aunt desired to retire, she did not have far to go, and Emily could stay nearby.

She gave the fire an agitated poke, earning a few more flames. "Are you certain you're warm enough? I could ask for more wood to be put on."

"That will be sufficient for now. Please come and sit down."

She put the poker back on its stand and came over to her

aunt. She pulled her aunt's shawl tighter around her shoulders and then plumped up the cushions she lay on. She needed to keep busy, to take her mind off her worries. She knew her aunt worried about George, but she desperately tried not to show it. But Emily had seen her fidgeting with her shawl when she thought no one was looking.

They'd both endured sleepless nights, wondering if he was safe, followed by all the hours of each day to fill. Her aunt had even stopped her insistence that Emily pursue finding a husband. They'd gone to one ball after she had seen George, but they'd not stayed long. The absence of Lord Thornburn was a stark reminder that he had gone to the Continent in pursuit of the man George had been trying to protect. A man George may be at this very moment risking his life to protect.

It had been a strain for both of them and worse still, she suspected her aunt knew that she was not just worried about George, but about Nathan as well. She couldn't bear the thought that something might happen to him and remembering her parents' loss and George's fevered dream did nothing to quell her uneasiness.

The gilt bronze clock on the mantel struck eleven.

"How about I ring for tea?" Emily stood up almost the moment she had sat down and walked over to the bell-pull. "A nice hot cup of tea would do you good."

"A nice hot cup of tea would do us both good," her aunt replied.

As soon as the maid laid the tea on the table, Emily poured her aunt a cup with an extra spoon of sugar to help keep her spirits up.

She was pouring herself a cup when the butler entered and announced that Lord Thornburn had called. Emily's heart stuttered to a momentary stop as relief flooded through her, then began a triple beat in apprehension for the reason for his call; her hands shook as she finished pouring.

"Tell him to wait in the white salon." She looked at her aunt for permission to attend his call alone in there, rather than inviting him into the withdrawing room they were occupying at present. She wanted to protect her aunt if it was bad news, so she could break it to her gently. Her aunt nodded her assent and Emily took one quick fortifying sip of her tea before she placed the rattling cup and saucer down and headed to the salon.

She entered to find Nathan staring into the empty fire grate, his body taut, his hands balled into tight fists on the mantel. She had taken several steps into the room before he looked up and what she saw in his splintered grey gaze stopped her in her tracks. "What's happened?" She wrapped her arms around her body, numb with trepidation.

He straightened into a dignified stance, his movements stiff; rigid, as though he was trying valiantly to hold himself together. It took him a moment before he regained control over his throat.

Unable to do anything else, Emily waited.

The muscle in his jaw convulsed as he began to speak. "There was an incident in Jersey," he said, pausing again, his voice raw and cracked.

Emily stood, her breathing suspended, her heart racing. George had admitted the French knew about their safe houses in Jersey. It seemed he had been right to worry. She swallowed, but it lodged in her throat as fear for George consumed her.

"Peter's dead. Shot." His gaze dropped from hers and he turned back to face the mantel.

"Peter?" It took a moment for her to absorb the fact that it was Nathan's brother who was dead. She'd been worrying all this time about George and Nathan and hadn't even considered Peter's safety. Not really, not if she was honest with herself. "No, it can't be true." She stepped forwards, coming to a halt beside Nathan, the boyish curl falling across his brow, the same boyish curl his brother Peter had shared. It was unimaginable to believe he was gone.

He twisted his head, his metallic silver eyes boring into hers. "It's true, and we both know who is to blame."

No, her heart screamed. George could not be the culprit. "It can't have been George."

"Then tell me you know for a fact George was here in England instead."

But she could not. She twisted away from him. "You know I do not know where he is." She'd given this lie so many times in the past to protect George and now she spoke it in truth it could mean his death knell. The sickening irony was not lost on her. Desperate to defend George, she enthused her following with defiant certainty, "But my lack of knowledge does not condemn him."

"It doesn't exonerate him either."

The truth of his words nibbled away at her convictions, but her loyalty rose to the surface. She would not allow Nathan to make her doubt George's innocence.

"What about Dubeck?" she asked, turning back to face him, her hands in supplication that something good must have come out of this.

Nathan's gaze fell away from hers, bitterness etched across his taut features. "Our information was false; we could find no trace of him."

Emily was struck by the full force of Nathan's agony that Peter had died a pointless death. After all he had done for his country, to die in such a futile, unsuccessful mission was an insult and an indignity past bearing. But it was a pain Nathan would have to carry all his life. And in that moment, Emily tasted every bitter drop of his torment with the added vile twist that her own brother may have been the cause of Peter's death and Nathan's anguish.

She pressed her fist against her lips, trying to suppress her shuddering horror that Peter was truly gone. She remembered the last time she had seen him in Hyde Park, bidding farewell as he and Nathan rode away. A young man full of vitality and vigour, now lost because of a futile mission. Her eyelids slid shut as a sluice of tears overwhelmed her.

"He can't be gone, he's too young, too..." she said, her words trailing off as she was unable to express the senselessness of Peter's death. She reached out and laid her hand on his sleeve, squeezing his arm in shared sorrow.

Nathan looked down at her pale hand squeezing his arm, her compassion for him and her anguish at Peter's loss reflected in her wide, shimmering jade eyes. The urge to protect her, to take away the pain for her, ripped through him. He placed his hands on the sides of her cheeks, wiping away the tears that marred her perfect alabaster skin with his thumbs, but still it wasn't enough; he needed more.

Leaning forwards, he kissed her tears away, before his lips sought hers, in need of solace, of comfort, of a haven in his world of pain and misery.

Emily let his kiss consume her, comfort her, and torment her with images of the youthful Peter lost forever and the fear that her own brother may have been the cause of his death.

She stood in Nathan's embrace, crying tears for the loss of his brother. Comforting the brother of the man whom her own brother may be guilty of killing, the brother she had sent after Nathan and Peter. A gut-wrenching realisation slashed through her. If what Nathan said was true, then that made her just as culpable. She gripped the sleeves of his jacket, pulling him closer to her as she poured out her grief and sorrow and guilt into a kiss that was the result of events pulling them together while tearing them apart.

This would be the only kiss they would ever share again, could ever share, as after today there could never be anything between them and the poignancy of it made her want to give him her all, body and soul. Her tongue traced the contours of his lips, tasting him, memorising him.

Nathan accepted her invitation, his hands sliding into her hair, holding her head as his lips moved over hers. He twisted them round so her back was pressed against the wall and leaned into her, his hands sliding from her tangled hair to trace the smooth curves of her body, cupping her breast.

She arched her back, thrusting her chest more firmly into his grasp and he moaned with desire, with need, with a shuddering groan of regret.

They were lost in a world where the only thing that mattered was being in each other's arms, but the spectre of Peter and George's involvement swirled around them bringing them back to the world where betrayal, loss and pain were their daily companions and love just a fleeting dream beyond their grasp.

Nathan pulled free of her lips, but he was unable to release her fully. He wrapped his arms around her waist and rested his head on top of her dishevelled coiffure. This was a taste of heaven in his hellish world, and he was reluctant to relinquish it.

The removal of his lips sent a soul-screaming wrench through Emily. She was not ready to end the kiss yet, but one look at the struggle playing out across Nathan's tormented features held her still. She stood in his embrace, a feeling of comfort and impending loss consuming her.

He lifted his head and her heart squeezed at the pain and regret etched across the planes of his handsome face. As the silence lengthened, the hairs on her arms and nape vibrated with tension and foreboding.

She watched as his steely resolve regained control. He was back to being the resolute Nathan, whose sole aim was the arrest of her brother. She stiffened as he spoke.

"Emily, I feel it is only right to forewarn you that after everything that has happened." He swallowed the lump in his throat. Then looked away for the merest of moments, his grip on her tightening. His gaze returned to hers and his granite eyes held a lethal calmness. "You'd better pray I do not find George, for if I do, he won't live long enough to be questioned by Robert."

Emily bit her lip. She understood his loss and need for retribution, but loyalty forbade her from absolving his intentions completely.

"George is innocent," she whispered. She may have her doubts about his involvement in recent events, but her doubts did not prove George's guilt.

He shook his head, "I wish more than anything that he were, but too many things point to his complicity."

"No."

"Shush, Emily." He stroked her back as though comforting

a child. "You must not punish yourself for George's actions."

Emily twisted free of his grasp, fearful he may suspect her own misgivings about George. The last thing she wanted was to give him more reason to believe George guilty. For if Nathan thought, for even a moment, that George's own sister and loyalist campaigner could think him guilty, he'd have total conviction in his beliefs and nothing would stop him from punishing George for the losses he'd suffered. She placed a placating hand against his chest. "Please promise me one thing."

Heat burned Nathan where her hand touched his chest. He took one look at her youthful, innocent, heart-shaped face and shook his head. "I know what you wish to ask, but I cannot."

"Please," she said, searching for something to give him. She pulled the aqua ribbon George had given her from her mussed hair. "Promise me one thing, in memory of what we have shared here today," she said, as she tied the ribbon solemnly around his wrist. "Please do not harm my brother."

Nathan heaved a deep sigh. His sense of righteousness and chivalry warring against his driving need to avenge his brother's death. His fingers brushed the silken ribbon. "I can only promise to try not to hurt him."

A tear rolled down her cheek and landed on his hand.

"Thank you, Nathan. As the good and righteous man I know you to be, that shall be enough." She leaned closer and placed a heartfelt kiss on his rugged cheek. Then she whispered in his ear. "You know George; you know he could never do anything like this. Look into your heart and you'll know the truth. Just look."

He shook his head. "I have, but there's too much evidence against him."

"Then you haven't looked deep enough." She smoothed down her pale aqua silk morning dress and ruffled hair, giving his hand one last squeeze before she turned and left.

Nathan looked at the ends of the ribbon swaying in the breeze of her departure. He couldn't believe the unshakable faith she had in both him and George. But how was one to keep such a promise against seeking justice for the death of a loved one?

He feared that this time her unshakable faith may truly have been misplaced.

Chapter Sixteen

Pausing, Emily took a deep breath before nodding to the footman, who opened the door to the morning room for her. Sweeping past him, she re-joined her aunt on the settee.

She'd spent the last twenty minutes in her room trying to regain her composure; having bathed her tear-swollen face in the cold water from her washstand and rearranged her hair into some resemblance of respectability. Her mind was numb, unable to think of anything beyond the practical, and now she sat next to her aunt, knowing she must tell her of the tragic death of Peter Renwick.

Her aunt reacted with shock and sorrow. She grasped Emily's hands as they sat in shared misery. After a few minutes, her aunt asked, "Did Lord Thornburn meet with George while he was away?"

"Not from what I could gather," Emily said, as the servant's door swung open.

"Should my ears be burning?" George said, stepping into the room.

Emily leapt up from her seat and hurled herself into his arms.

He grimaced as pain shot along his injured shoulder with the force of her embrace, but it didn't stop him from returning her hug in equal measure.

"Oh my, your shoulder. Did I hurt it?" Emily straightened and searched her brother's face for any sign of pain.

"No more than normal. It still hurts when I try to move it, but it's bearable."

"Thank goodness you are well." She paused, and choosing her words carefully, said, "Are you aware of what has happened to Peter Renwick?"

"I am." He set Emily aside and walked over to his aunt and gave her a kiss on her cheek.

"It is good to have you back," her aunt said, giving George's cheek a pat in return.

He was about to sit down when he turned and gave Emily a curious look. "How do you know about Peter Renwick?"

Her cheeks reddened with guilt as the kiss she'd just shared with Nathan came vividly to mind. The kiss itself being born of shared sorrow, but the current underneath had thrummed with something more, something that had been building between her and Nathan for some time and she could feel the truth displayed for all to see across her face. She glanced quickly away, her mind searching for the answer to his question. "Nathan, I mean Lord Thornburn," she hastily corrected, "called this morning and informed us of his loss."

"Why did he call on you?" George said, taking a step towards Emily, his face stern as his blue gaze swept over her.

"He, erm, he wanted to know if we had heard from you."

"What did you tell him?"

"Nothing. I had nothing to tell, except that I didn't know where you were." Emily fought the urge to back away from her own brother as he reached out and grasped her chin, turning her face towards him.

"What else happened?" His voice held an angry edge.

Emily's eyes widened. "Nothing, nothing happened." She pulled free of his grasp.

"You don't normally wear your hair in that fashion," he said.

Emily's hand instantly went to her hair. Too late, she could do nothing to hide her impulse.

His perceptive gaze looked her all over before returning to her hair. "Where is the blue ribbon I bought you to match that dress?"

Words failed her. She couldn't tell him she'd given it to Nathan in the hopes he'd spare his life, or why he'd accept such a trifling token in exchange for a life unless there was more to it than that, when there wasn't. But there was her heart cried. She pushed the thought away. She could never explain it, and George would never accept any explanation anyway.

"How long have you had feelings for him?" George demanded.

"I..."

"He will never marry you."

"I don't want him to."

"Then what do you want?"

"I want him to stop trying to arrest you." Her voice was a cracked whisper. "It's all I've ever wanted. To have you back and know you're safe from arrest." She caught his hand and rubbed it against her cheek.

He pulled her into his arms, being careful of his injured shoulder. "It's all I want too, and hopefully soon it will be as we both want."

"Truly?" She leaned back so she could see into his face.

He nodded. "It seems my colleague made it safely out of France. I just need to locate him."

"Then this will all be over?"

"Yes, but in the meantime, I forbid you from seeing Lord Thornburn."

Considering everything, Emily doubted she would ever see him again. "As you wish," she said, ignoring the sudden sharp tug of forfeiture.

George patted her arm. "That's my girl. Now I believe I may have stayed longer than was wise, so I'll take my leave."

"So soon?" She wanted to grab his hand and not let go. He'd come home to her and now he was leaving again. She hated that she would be left wondering if he was safe.

"I'm afraid so."

"Where will you go?"

"I'll stay at Mrs Hewitt's hideout for now. But if I should need to leave, I will send word."

"I'll miss you." She curled her fingers around the heart-shaped pendant her parents had given her.

"All being well, it should not be for long." He kissed both Emily and Aunt Amelia goodbye and disappeared the way he had come.

Chapter Seventeen

Heavy cloud dulled the late afternoon sun, leaving Nathan's study in gloom. No candles had been lit and the smouldering fire was the only light.

Lord Brakenhale pulled off his gloves as he entered. He found Nathan slumped in his chair behind his empty desk. "I heard about Peter. What happened?" His voice was gentle and concern creased his brow.

Nathan lifted his head from his hands. "He was shot. We found no trace of Dubeck, but you will be pleased to know that we found out the traitor has stated that the arrival of the 6,000 British men in Malta will be proof of the validity of his information. So the threat to withhold the men may well be our saving grace after all."

"Damn it man, your brother's dead. The mission can wait."

"Wait! He died getting you that information." Nathan strode over to the fire and attacked it with a poker, causing sparks to cascade over the grate. "And you think it can wait?"

"You know that is not what I meant. Right now there are more important things for you to be concentrating on rather than the piffling matters of national intrigues."

"But aren't those national intrigues your sole raison d'être?"

Robert shook his head. "Not today. Today, the only thing that matters is you and ensuring Peter's memory is preserved in a manner befitting his contribution to his country and, more importantly, his family.

"But I will need to talk to you and soon, but not now," Robert continued. "Come to my office tomorrow evening after eight."

When Nathan made no reply, Robert picked up his gloves and headed for the door. "My office at eight," he reiterated as he left.

* * *

Nathan pulled his collar up higher as he strode along the wet street. After Robert had left, he'd spent the night in his study. He'd opened the decanter of Peter's favourite blend of brandy and toasted his brother with it. God, it was horrible stuff. But he'd drunk every last drop. It didn't help to numb the pain, but it did help him sink into blissful oblivion, at least until a few hours ago when he'd woken with the painful moment of Peter's shooting searing across his memory.

Now he was late for a meeting with Robert, but his hung-over head couldn't bear the noise and jolting of a carriage, so he had decided to walk, hoping the cool crisp evening air would clear his mind. It wasn't working so far.

Taking a shortcut down a narrow alley, his well-honed senses snapped into focus; he wasn't alone.

He reached for his gun and squinted into the fog-shrouded

shadows. "Show yourself, George, or are you a coward as well as a traitor?"

"You know full well I am neither." George stepped into a pool of light that shivered in a reflection on the wet cobbles. "But if you truly believe me to be the spy that betrayed your brother, then you had better shoot me now. I'll not stand before you if you doubt me for even a moment."

Nathan lifted his gun and pointed it at George's heart. "My brother is dead because of you."

"Then why am I still alive?"

"Even I couldn't kill you in cold blood. Unlike you, I still have a modicum of morals."

"Morals be damned, your brother is dead. If you believe I am to blame, then shoot me." George took another step forwards.

Nathan gripped the gun tighter and Emily's blue ribbon fluttered against his wrist; he hadn't taken it off last night, and until this moment he had forgotten he still wore it. Promises; he'd promised Emily he'd not harm George, but he'd promised Peter he would gain justice for him. And himself. Oh, he'd promised himself he'd seek revenge against the traitor who had led his brother to his death. And he could fulfil two of those promises now with a squeeze of a trigger, but that would be at the detriment of his promise to Emily and her faith in him. He took a long, slow swallow.

"After everything I've witnessed in the last few days and the proof I've collected, I'm tempted to do just that." Nathan's voice bounced off the wet brick walls of the alley.

"Proof! So tell me, Nathan, how quickly did you collate the evidence to condemn me? Too quickly, by my reckoning. Let's face it; I was not the only one in contact with the French conspirators."

Nathan took a step forwards. "Are you trying to accuse myself or my brother? I suggest for your own sake you do not attempt anything so foolish." He swiped the cold rain from his face. The constant drip, splash, drip, a loud concerto to the sudden silence of words.

George took a step back. "I didn't come here to antagonise you."

"Then why did you come?"

"To tell you to stay away from Emily. She doesn't need you turning her head in an attempt to get to me."

"You flatter yourself," Nathan said. But until that moment, he'd believed that their association was at an end and he'd accepted it as the inevitable conclusion that he'd known all along it would be. But now he wanted more than anything to see her again, needed more than anything to see her, and the words of her traitorous brother would not stop him.

George's eyes formed into slits. "And you, my lord, overstep yourself. She's an innocent in all this. I will not have her harmed."

"It's rather late in the day to be playing the protective brother, when she's the one who's being protecting you all this time."

"The loyalty of a caring sibling is nothing to be ashamed of."

Nathan released a bitter laugh. "So you admit she has been protecting you?"

"I'll admit nothing of the sort. But I'll warn you again, stay away from her."

Well, that was one promise he was not going to keep, as first thing tomorrow he was going to have a long chat with Emily and the first question was going to be how long she had been in contact with George. But he suspected he already knew. He lowered his gun as George's footsteps echoed away down the alley.

And if his suspicions about George's involvement in his brother's death turned out to be true, then that meant Emily was as culpable of Peter's death as George.

The sickening sensation of a hot boulder sliding through his stomach overcame him. It was he who had given the information to Emily that had caused George to be in Jersey and, therefore, he was ultimately the one to blame.

He retched in the middle of the alley.

Chapter Eighteen

The next morning Nathan strode away from Lord Tysling's town house, slapping his gloves against his thigh. He'd been refused entry to see Emily and had demanded the butler tell him on whose authority the order had been given. Miss Ellerton's was the reply. Well, she'd certainly played him for a fool.

How could he have let himself be taken in by her? The lying to protect her brother he could understand, even admire. But her duplicity in the portrayal of her feelings for him had been beyond the bounds of integrity and dignity.

Oh, he was honest enough with himself to accept that he'd invoked the feelings of women in the pursuit of his country's goals in the past. But he'd never misled them into believing their feelings were reciprocated with the total conviction Miss Ellerton had displayed to him.

She'd fooled him on every possible level imaginable. Peter had been right '*she's the sister of a traitor and she doesn't deserve any special consideration.*' Peter's words brought him to an abrupt stop while his mind struggled to readjust to the reality that his brother was dead and not coming back. Dragging in a ragged breath, he fought against the pain and headed to his club. He wasn't in the mood for company, but he couldn't bear returning to the house echoing with the emptiness of Peter's absence, and he needed a drink. One drink. That's all he would allow himself. After all, he had responsibilities and details pertaining to Peter's death to deal with. Some very important responsibilities.

* * *

Emily rested her head against the window's cool glass as her gaze clung to Nathan striding away down the road. She was about to turn away when he paused. Was he going to return? A skittering of hope fluttered through her. If he came back, she would disobey George's command and agree to see him. She waited, but without a backward look, he strode on and disappeared from view.

Pushing away from the window, she went to the morning room to join her aunt. She spent the next few hours absentmindedly adding random stitches to her sampler as they sat in muted silence until the butler entered with a letter he presented to her aunt on a tray.

Seeing her aunt's reaction, Emily jumped up and peered at the writing. It was addressed to George.

"Who is it from?" Emily asked.

"Never you mind," her aunt said as concern creased her brow.

"No, you are not keeping something like this from me."

Her aunt gave her a considering look. "Very well, it's from

Lord Brakenhale."

"Are you certain?"

Taking the envelope to the window, her aunt scrutinised the seal. "It looks authentic."

"Maybe this is the news George has been waiting for."

Her aunt did not reply.

"We must take it to him."

Tapping the letter against her fingertips, her aunt chewed her lip. "I feel it would be remiss of us not too, although I do wish it were not so."

"What do you mean?"

"I feel this letter may be portentous." Her aunt sighed. "One way or another, it will bring events to a head and I wish that I was not the one for whom the task of delivering it must fall."

"Then let me take it."

"No, I would not allow you to be burdened with the consequences."

"I will not be prevented from knowing what that letter contains. Like it or not, I intend to see George receives it." She stood with her hands on her hips in a resolute stance.

Her aunt nodded. "Of course, after everything you have done for George's cause, it is only right and proper you should know the contents of this letter and the implications. But for the sake of preserving George's location, I suggest we perform some more subterfuge."

Emily eyed her aunt suspiciously, not sure if part of this subterfuge involved hoodwinking her into the bargain. "Very well," she said, taking the letter from her aunt. "But I will keep hold of this."

* * *

Ensconced inside the carriage, with her lady's maid, Emily rode around Hyde Park. After the recent rainfall, the grass was lush and the leaves on the oak and chestnut trees were a bright green. Birds chirped and swooped around them. The air held the excitement of spring, but Emily could not bring herself to share in the joy. Her mind was too preoccupied with worry and uncertainty. She exchanged mundane pleasantries with the matrons of the ton, assuring them that she and her aunt were well and would look forward to joining them for this soiree or that Venetian breakfast when they would attend none. No, once everything was resolved with George, she would head back to the country and never return to London, as it would always be a place of guilt and pain for her.

Clutching her reticule to her with George's letter tucked inside, she informed the driver to take her to Mrs Shaw's modiste. She'd given her aunt enough time for her to have gone on a round of misleading visits. Now it was time to re-join her and deliver the letter to George. She prayed it held good news.

They found George flexing his shoulder, his shirt unbuttoned and his jacket and cravat flung over the back of a chair. He hurried to dress as he greeted them. "What brings you here?"

"We've received a letter for you." Emily held the letter out to him. "From Lord Brakenhale."

He hesitated before taking it, then scrutinised the seal and handwriting. He glanced at Emily and Aunt Amelia. "Thank you for bringing this. Mrs Hewitt will see you out." His brow was creased in a perplexed expression.

"Are you not going to open it?" Emily asked, hurt by his curt dismissal.

"Yes." He walked to the door. "After you have gone."

"No, I can't allow it." Emily stood resolute before him. "Whatever it contains, we need to know. We can't have you disappear and have no idea where or why you have gone. Please, for our own peace of mind, we need to know what that letter contains."

"The information in here may be too dangerous for you to know. I do not want to put your safety at risk."

"And I can't let you put our safety before your own, not after all the days and hours we have spent worrying about you over the last few weeks. Please, I could not bear it again."

George heaved a heavy sigh. "Very well, but I do not do this lightly, and I am certain it goes without saying that the contents of this letter must not be divulged to anyone else, no matter what." His stern blue gaze swept over both her and her aunt.

Emily nodded her head while her Aunt Amelia regally inclined hers.

Satisfied, George broke the seal and pursued the short missive. "Lord Brakenhale states he has received information that could prove my innocence and requests we meet. He has suggested an abandoned woodcutter's cottage located outside the small village of Tilde Green at seven o'clock tonight."

"But that's wonderful news," Emily said.

George didn't look so certain.

"What is it?" Aunt Amelia said.

"He makes no mention of where this information has come from."

"Maybe he is just being cautious," Aunt Amelia reasoned. "He has no way of being certain that this letter would reach you or that it would not be intercepted in the process."

"True. Well, the only way to find out is to attend the rendezvous."

"Alone? Is that wise?" Emily asked.

"You're not coming with me, under any circumstances. But don't worry, I have someone I can trust to come along."

"Who?"

"Now, that's one question I will not answer." George took a quick glance out of the window. "It's time you two were getting back. I promise to contact you as soon as I return. Who knows, I might even arrive via the front door."

Emily leaned forwards and placed a kiss on his cheek. "Just make sure you come home safely."

"I will," he said, as he gave Aunt Amelia a kiss. "Take care of each other and don't worry. I forbid it."

Chapter Nineteen

Dismounting, Nathan flung the reins at the groom and strode to the door of Lord Tysling's town house. He pulled off his gloves and slapped them against his thigh while he tried to get his temper under control. He should be sorting out his brother's funeral arrangements. Instead, he'd received a visit from Simon Pykett's street urchin with the information that a letter had been delivered addressed to George from Lord Brakenhale. Shortly thereafter, Miss Ellerton had been sent on a ride around Hyde Park while Lady Drayford had gone on a large excursion involving visiting many establishments.

Wondering why Pykett was bothering him with the information that Lord Brakenhale had finally taken it upon himself to contact George was beyond his comprehension. He'd dispatched the child back to Pykett with the message that he was not to be disturbed again in any matters regarding George Ellerton or his family.

He'd returned to the list he was drawing up of tasks required. He was only doing that so as to delay the actual process of making a start on the things he needed to do pertaining to Peter's death, as once he did, then that meant he'd accepted Peter was not coming back. In the finish, he'd used the interruption as another excuse to delay doing what was necessary and had gone to visit Lord Brakenhale.

That had been a mistake.

Robert was adamant that he had not sent a letter and insisted that Nathan find out the contents.

Now, he was in the one place he did not wish to be, about to face the one person he did not wish to see, but orders were orders, and duty was duty. He rapped heavily on the door knocker and waited.

As soon as the door opened, he barged into the house. "I'm here on official business for His Majesty. Please kindly direct me to Lady Drayford."

"This way, my lord," the butler intoned with a bow and led him to the salon.

He entered to find, to his annoyance, only Emily present. He cast his scathing glance over her as she stood up. She looked at him in muted silence, whilst they both tried to gauge each other's mood and intent.

"Where is Lady Drayford?"

She remained standing, ignoring the dictates of etiquette, and waved her hand vaguely, "She's gone out."

"Again!"

Her eyes blasted him as the full importance of that remark proved her family's every move was still being watched. "As you should no doubt already know," she spat contemptuously.

He ignored her remark and stepped further into the room. Not towards her. No, he couldn't bear to be any nearer to her. Instead, he paced the outskirts of the room as she turned to watch his progress.

Coming to a stop by the windows, he faced her and folded his arms across his chest as his gaze took in the defiant young lady before him, her chin tilted in its familiar position when confronted by him. Her chest rising and falling in long, even breaths while her eyes searched his. He watched the myriad of thoughts displaying across her expressive face. His heart ached with what they had lost. His past mistake meant he did not deserve to feel the way he did about her, but she had got under his defences. She'd shown faith and belief in him and made him feel as though he wasn't the worthless wretch he knew himself to be. Then he'd discovered that she'd been lying to him the whole time. Protecting the man who had killed his brother. His fingers tightened on his arms. He wondered for a moment if she was ignorant of the letter, but her apprehensive stance spoke for her and in no mood for games, he got straight to the point. "I've come regarding the supposed letter to George from Lord Brakenhale."

Her spine stiffened. "I do not know to what letter you are referring."

"Yes, you do. And the reason for my call is to inform you that the letter is a forgery."

Emily let out a sharp laugh at the audacity of his tactic. Obviously, her aunt's run around earlier had fooled them sufficiently for them to be unable to locate George and this was merely a ruse to trick them into panicking and giving his location away. She stared at him. This morning, when he'd called, she'd adhered to George's edict to turn him away, but she'd instantly regretted it. From the first moment they had met, she'd been drawn to him. His admiration of her when she was standing in his way made her appreciate his integrity and rectitude. The way he'd comforted her as she told him about her parents had opened her heart to him. How, even devastated by his brother's death, he had accepted her ribbon and given his pledge not to harm George. It was then she knew she loved him. She blinked away the hot tears that burned the backs of her eyes. She was a fool. He didn't care about her. Today there was nothing of the gentle, compassionate man she'd fallen for. The only thing he cared about was the arrest of her brother. And she couldn't let that happen.

"You presume too much if you insinuate such a letter exists." Emily folded her arms across her chest in imitation of him.

"Very well, let us assume for the moment that the letter is real. As it came from Lord Brakenhale, he knows what he wrote and therefore I would not need to call here, at this house and associate with this particular family. I do have other more pressing things I should be dealing with right now, as I am sure you can appreciate."

A sharp stab of sympathy pricked Emily. She understood all too well the distressing things he should be doing instead. "Then I will detain you no further." Her voice caught in her throat. This interview may be the final time they saw each other; it seemed such an unfitting end.

"Unfortunately, that is no longer an option. Lord Brakenhale did not send that letter and for George's sake, we need to know what the letter said."

His attempt to suggest George's safety was at risk to get to her washed away her feelings of regret for what they may have lost. Her ire rose and, in no mood to be toyed with, she turned fully to face him. Looking into his familiar face was nearly her undoing. But she had to put George first. She was the only one who could protect him. "If Lord Brakenhale had sent a letter, it would have his seal on as proof it was from him." She raised her brows, daring him to deny it.

"His seal was faked."

"No, my aunt confirmed its validity," she said with conviction. She realised the error of her words the moment she spoke them. All this time, she had been so careful. And now she had let everyone down. Her stomach writhed in mortification. How could she have been so foolish? She expected to see satisfaction from Nathan at her slip, but instead he shook his head.

"There is a secret office that trains men from the diplomatic service to forge seals so well they are indistinguishable from the real thing. How do you think we gain our intelligence and ensure our enemies do not suspect?"

A chill slithered through Emily. If what he said was true, then George was truly in danger. She lifted her gaze to him, searching his face for any clue that he was lying, but there was none. "How can I believe you?"

"Think. What do we gain by sending George a letter and then denying it is real?"

Emily racked her brain for an answer. Something that would make sense. Something that would mean George wasn't about to set off for a rendezvous with an unknown assailant. Suddenly, the risk was too great to ignore. She couldn't let George ride straight into a trap. She had to warn him. But would that not lead Lord Brakenhale and Nathan straight to him?

Seeing her trying to assimilate the possibility that the letter was false, Nathan took three swift steps and grabbed her wrists. "We need to know what the letter said."

"I, I cannot say."

"Please Emily. If we had sent that letter, we would not need to ask. The only way to save George now is to tell me."

Emily lifted her gaze to his. The silvery depths shimmered like a beacon in the night and in that moment she knew she could trust him. "It was to arrange a meeting with him and Lord Brakenhale."

"Where?"

She had no intention of waiting around this time. "I'll take you."

"No, it's too dangerous."

"If you truly do not know the contents of that letter, then the only way to find the meeting place is to follow me, but first I need to change. I cannot go riding in this."

Nathan let her go with the sickening realisation that he had no other choice than to race to the rescue of the man who may have killed his brother. It was like spitting on his brother's memory.

Chapter Twenty

As time was of the essence, Nathan arranged for Emily's horse to be saddled and brought out front to join his mount. Unable to stand around waiting, he went outside and began soothing his horse. It was pawing the ground with the same intense restlessness that thrummed through him. He flicked open his pocket watch. It was half past four.

Hurried footsteps announced Emily's arrival as she strode towards him wearing the cornflower blue riding habit she'd worn the first night they had met at Oakleaf Manor. Her hair was caught up under a matching dainty hat, leaving her glorious slim neck bare and drawing his eye to the heart-shaped flesh displayed tantalisingly above the tightly buttoned bodice of her jacket. He swallowed as his heart thumped into his ribcage; sending blood surging through his system, and that was before she stopped next to her mount and waited for him to assist her into the saddle.

Taking a moment to regain control of his rioting ardour, he patted his horse's flank before turning towards her. Cupping his hands in front of him, he braced himself as she placed her foot inside his hands and, grabbing the pommel, heaved herself up with his assistance. He closed his eyes as her long curvaceous body slid against his highly charged form, the rough wool of her riding habit only heightening his senses. He waited while she adjusted her skirts.

"Ready?" he said in a hoarse voice.

"Yes," she replied, but she glanced away as though she had been equally affected.

Relieved to have something that gave him some distance from her, he twisted around and, in one swift motion mounted his horse. "Lead the way," he said, this time in more normal tones.

They rode for over two hours before Emily pointed to a small deserted lodge half hidden behind a grove of trees about a half mile away. Slowing their mounts, they crossed a wide bridge over a quickly flowing river and headed to the east side of the building. The dilapidated, two-storey lodge had been deserted for some time. The windows were devoid of glass and it looked on the verge of collapsing. With dark clouds obscuring the sun, the building was cast in shadow, giving it an eerie appearance.

Nathan surveyed the area; no horses were present. If anyone was here, they had purposely hidden their mounts a distance from the lodge. No one wanted to tip their hands. Obviously, George was wise enough not to take the letter at face value. That was so typical of him. The thought brought a stab of remorse for the loss of his loyalty and friendship, but the stinging bitterness at his recent actions soon eroded the sensation.

Dismounting, he led the horses to a small copse that hid them from the lodge before assisting Emily down and wrapping the reins around a sturdy branch.

He put his finger to his lips to show they should be quiet. Ducking their heads under the low-hanging branches, they edged their way to the side of the lodge.

Muted voices came from an upper window as they rounded the corner and pushed the dilapidated door open, slipping quietly into the small entrance hall.

The musty smell of damp greeted them. Cobwebs stretched across the rotting timbers and hung down from the ceiling. Mould covered the walls and Emily pulled her skirts away to avoid contaminating her habit. To the left, narrow stairs led upwards and, taking Emily's gloved hand in his, Nathan led the way cautiously up the stairs.

The voices were coming from a room to the rear.

Nathan halted at the top of the stairs and whispered, "Stay here. If anything happens, you are to take your horse and head straight back to London." He reached inside his greatcoat and pulled out his pistol, not at all certain what he would find beyond the door.

He waited until she nodded her compliance, then he took a deep breath and stepped into the room. It was devoid of furniture. A half rotted bird's nest lay on a soot filled fire grate and a cold wind blew in through the empty windows.

Three pairs of eyes flicked to him.

"Is this a private party, or can anyone join in?" Nathan said, taking in George Ellerton, with his gun pointed at Robert Darnell, who was pointing his at George and finally Simon Pykett, who was also pointing his gun at George. With the exception of George, he was surprised by the other occupants of the room.

He gave Robert a questioning look.

The exchange did not go unmissed by George, who glowered

at him. "Depends on what brought you here?"

Nathan returned his gaze to George. "My fortitude."

"Wrong answer," George said, transferring his gunpoint from Robert to Nathan.

Nathan pointed his gun at George in return, but directed his comment at Robert. "I'm surprised to find you here."

"Lady Drayford informed me," Robert said.

George swivelled to face Robert. "I don't believe you; my aunt would never betray me."

Robert gave an indifferent shrug. "She thought you were in danger. She was trying to protect you."

"How did she know she could trust you?" George demanded.

"She used to work for me and my uncle a long time ago; she was the one who recommended you to my service."

Accepting Robert's explanation for the time being, he turned to Simon Pykett. "What about you? How did you know I was here?"

"Robert ordered me to accompany him." He scowled, his crooked nose giving his face a sinister expression.

"Doesn't mean you didn't send the letter first," George said.

"Yeah, I'm well known for my letter writing skills, being slum educated."

"Well, he's right there. He'd hardly be able to forge my scholarly handwriting," Robert said.

"No, but *you* could!" George faced Nathan.

"The handwriting, yes, but not the seal. There are only two people I know who have been trained at the Bureau Noir and that's you and Edward Clarrington."

"It's not him," George said.

"How can you be so certain?" Nathan took a casual step towards him.

"Because he's the one person I know to be on my side."

"And what side is that?" Robert asked.

"The same as yours," George bit back. "Just with a little more faith in me than you have shown."

They stood there, arms outstretched guns pointed at one another. Old friends turned enemies.

"If you believe in Edward so much," Nathan said, "I'm surprised you came here alone."

"I didn't."

Dark dread descended on Nathan. He'd left Emily in danger. He spun to face the door, but he was too late.

Chapter Twenty-one

Emily leaned towards the wall, not willing to press her ear against the mouldy expanse as she tried to discern what was transpiring in the room beyond. On hearing George's voice demanding an explanation from Robert, she had been both relieved and fearful and she strained to hear more.

A masculine hand gripped her shoulder. She gasped and spun on her heel; her scream frozen on her lips as she beheld Edward Clarington stood before her, a gun in his hand.

Fear locking her lungs, she stepped away, but her boot heel caught in the long skirt of her riding habit. Twisting awkwardly, her back collided with the wooden door and, losing her balance, she stumbled through into the room.

"Miss Ellerton, no," Edward shouted.

Struggling to regain her balance, she found herself the centre of everyone's attention.

A furious George lunged at Nathan, but Simon held him back. "I told you to stay away from her." George's voice was a growl.

"I went to her because I thought you were in danger and your damn stubborn sister refused to be left behind."

"That's still no excuse," George shouted.

"Well, I'm sorry, but I didn't realise Edward was covering your back." Nathan reached behind him and pulled Emily away from Edward as he lifted his gun to point at him.

"Well, this is an interesting collection," Robert said. "Perhaps now I can get some answers." His voice held a lethal calmness.

George huffed. "I'd rather not answer questions at the end of a pistol."

"Would you rather answer them at the end of a rope?" Nathan replied.

"No!" Emily yelled, trying to push closer to George.

Nathan took a side-step along with her, his polished boots kicking up dust and leaves that had blown in from the empty window. He put himself protectively in front of her as everyone moved as well so that they could still keep their guns trained on their respective targets.

"I have one question," Nathan said, looking at Edward. "How long have you been back?"

"Long enough to know you've been chasing the wrong man." His jaw tightened as he glared at him.

Nathan gave him a sceptical raise of his eyebrow. "What makes you say that?"

"I met with Dubeck in France. He was on his way to London with vital evidence."

"When?"

"Three weeks ago."

Nathan let out a relieved breath. His good friend was still alive. "Where is he now?"

Edward looked away. "I'm not sure. He had to make a detour."

"Where to?" Nathan asked.

Edward shook his head as he lifted it slowly to Nathan. "Saint Clement's."

Emily saw the spasmodic tightening of the muscles in Nathan's jaw. She didn't understand the significance of Edward's remark, but it had a profound effect on Nathan.

"It's the seven-year anniversary of their passing," Edward said.

"I'm well aware," Nathan bit back. "Now tell me where you were when Peter was shot."

"I was in London looking for George. You can ask Miss Ellerton."

Nathan twisted so he still had Edward in his sights, but could see Emily's profile. "Is this true?"

"Yes, he turned up on my doorstep a week ago."

"Well, that explains your whereabouts." Nathan swung around to face George. "Where were you when Peter died?"

Emily felt the tenseness emanating along Nathan's arm as his fingers clasped tighter around her wrist. She glanced from George to Nathan. She was in the middle of an explosive situation and she didn't dare move or breathe for fear of igniting the atmosphere. Her gaze swivelled back to George as he opened his mouth to reply.

"Searching for Dubeck," he said, as his gaze bored into Nathan's.

"In Jersey?" Nathan demanded. His grip biting into Emily's wrist, but she knew better than to complain.

She saw George's eyes flick to Nathan's white knuckled hand clamped on her arm, and then his lethal gaze lifted to Nathan as he uttered one word. "Yes."

"You'll die for this." Nathan let go of Emily and dived

at George. He collided instead with Robert's solid shoulder, knocking his hat to the ground, but Robert held him back with implacable purpose.

"If Dubeck does have evidence," Robert said, giving Nathan a warning look as he restrained him, "then we may be able to turn this travesty around. But until he arrives, I need George's help."

Nathan raked his disgusted gaze along George's length before returning to look at his superior - a man he admired and revered. Yet still his reluctance to relinquish his desire for retribution for his brother's death fought hard against the need to save the mission, a mission he'd worked towards alongside his brother. He clenched his jaw. He owed it to his brother to allow his revenge to be delayed in deference to saving what his brother had given his life for.

Nodding, he stepped away. "As you wish."

"Thank you," Robert said simply. "I knew you would do what was right as you always do, and I know what this last concession has cost you."

Nathan dropped his gaze from Robert, hiding the unbearable pain his words of approbation brought. This was one man he would do anything for, and it was humbling to hear him acknowledging his sacrifices. It reminded him of why he did what he did for him.

Robert, understanding his need for a moment, turned to George and lowered his gun. "Will you answer me at least one question?"

George eyed the gun still pointed at him by Simon. "Very well, for old time's sake, you may ask one question."

"What made you realise we had been betrayed?" His expression was of gentle entreaty. An expression he had honed during his long years as a diplomat.

George heaved a sigh. "The contact mistook me for the traitor and handed me a letter requesting to know where the 6,000 British troops were going to land. They were also expecting me to hand over the documents I'd brought. I stalled them and drew up a new proposal. Being able to forge your seal comes in useful sometimes," George said, giving Nathan a level stare. "That's why the other diplomats thought you were double dealing. The contact obviously tried to use the information to discredit you. For that I'm sorry."

Robert absorbed the information, stroking his chin as he contemplated the possibilities. "The troops were part of the Austrian deal," he said. "Whoever betrayed us had to have been involved in the negotiations."

Nathan's head lifted at Robert's words. He'd worked on the Austrian diplomatic project, but that had been prior to Pitt the Younger taking power and actively pursuing the formation of a third coalition. But the only two people in this room who knew that were him and Robert. Everyone else knew of his high-profile role in Austria and they would all conclude the same thing — that he was the traitor. And any moment now, Emily would comprehend what Robert's revelation meant by the crackle in the air and all the attention turning to him.

A straight denial would prove useless, and in this volatile situation, positively deadly. He looked at Robert — waited for him to correct their assumptions — but instead he gave him an imperceptible shake of his head and indicated Emily.

Nathan ground his teeth at what Robert was asking him to do and to give up. His jaw hardened as he looked at George, who had all but admitted to having a part in Peter's death. Robert wanted to remove him from the temptation of exacting retribution and instead use the distraction to allow him to get Emily out of danger. So much for Robert's fine words, they had not only been praise for his past sacrifices but a pre-emptive strike towards his goal of ensuring Miss Ellerton's safety.

Giving Robert one last mutinous look, he stepped behind Emily, grabbed her around the waist and dragged her backwards through the empty window.

Chapter Twenty-two

George ran to the window fully intending to jump out after them but Robert pulled him back. "I've not finished with you. You should have come to me straight away. You know how important this mission is. So you'll have to do a lot to convince me you are as innocent as you've been making out."

"Damn it, Robert. He's taken my sister."

"Don't worry George, I'll get the blackguard," Simon Pykett said from the window as he took aim.

George dived at him and knocked the gun in the air as he shot. "When it's your sister, you can take potshots."

"Aww, come on, you know I wouldn't have hit the little miss."

George punched him in the face. "Don't you ever raise your gun against my sister again!"

"Thunder an' turf," Simon cried, as he wiped away the blood pouring from his already crooked nose.

George swung back to Robert. "You have to let me go after her."

"I can't. I need you to come with me."

"Then at least send someone after them. Please," George pleaded.

Robert looked from Edward Clarrington who also had a lot of questions to answer to Simon who was currently coughing up blood and looking more in the mood for revenge against Miss Ellerton than saving her. But he had to send someone.

* * *

Nathan scrambled up from the bushes they'd fallen into and hauled Emily to her feet. He tried to drag her towards the horses, but she dug her heels into the ground. In no mood for her stubbornness and with the urgency of the moment pulsating through his body — punctuated by the gunshot from the window — he lifted her bodily over his shoulder and strode to the copse of trees where they'd hidden their horses. He ignored Emily's struggles and screams as the branches scratched her back and snagged her bonnet, pulling it unmercifully off her head and releasing her hair in a tangled web over her face.

On reaching the copse, Nathan flung a writhing Emily onto his horse, wrapping the long skirt of her riding habit around her, binding her limbs fast against her. He swung up and clamped her between his arms and thighs. His horse sidled in displeasure at the extra weight and the uncomfortable position of Emily. He grabbed the reins of her horse and on command both horses bunched their muscles. With the thud of hooves on the dry earth, they raced away from the cottage.

Chapter Twenty-Three

Pinned between the hot sweating body of the horse and Nathan's muscular thighs, Emily fought for breath as each bounce jolted the air from her lungs. She tried to quell the fear that coiled inside her. She had to be ready to get away, to get away from Nathan. Tears of disbelief burned her eyes. Nathan a traitor? How could this be happening? She'd believed in him.

Reaching the bridge they'd ridden over earlier, she heard Nathan sending her horse clattering away along the dirt road before he pulled their horse to a stop. Through the tangle of her fallen hair, she watched as he dismounted. Listening hard against the gurgling of the river beside them, she took a deep breath and held it ready.

He grasped her waist, and she stiffened at his touch as he hefted her off the horse. As soon as her feet touched the ground, she tried to pull away, but he clamped his strong hand over her mouth. The fine lines that criss-crossed his fingers only an inch from her eyes. She tried to suck air into her lungs but instead breathed in the deep earthy scent of him.

"Keep quiet," he growled into her ear, his words vibrating through her. "I'll not harm you, but I need you to keep quiet.

Do you understand?"

Scared to do anything else, she nodded as much as his tight hold would allow.

"Good girl. Right, I'm going to release you now. Don't try anything foolish," he said, as he loosened his grip and, turning, sent his own horse galloping off after hers.

Emily did not miss a beat; she lifted her heavy skirts and raced into the maze of trees.

"God's teeth," he said, as he charged after her. She hadn't made it ten paces before he caught up to her and wrestled her against a sturdy tree trunk.

"You damn stubborn woman." He held her hands pinned between his hands and the rough bark, his infuriated face mere inches from hers, his chest rising in rapid gasps that matched her own. His impatient grey eyes caught and imprisoned hers. "Now listen to me. You were in danger in there, and I had to get you out as expediently as possible."

"You mean you needed to get yourself out of there and I was just a handy hostage." She lifted her chin in mutinous disdain.

"I wasn't the one in danger and believe me, the last thing I wanted was to be anywhere near you," he said, his voice echoing his disgust.

"Is that so?" Tears pricked her eyes in humiliation at his frank admission of his not wanting to be around her, but her wounded pride erupted in angry indignation. "Well, it seems to me George's revelations put your recent diplomatic conduct under suspicion," she said as she struggled to free her hands from the tree bark biting into her soft flesh.

"No, his revelations merely highlighted a possible lead." Her writhing was doing nothing to dislodge his firm hold on her.

"That pointed to you. You were involved in the Austrian deal; that was obvious from everyone's reaction, especially yours."

"My involvement was prior to Pitt's authorisation of British troops. Robert knows I was not privy to that particular proposal."

"Then why didn't he say anything?"

Nathan gave her a contemptuous look. "Because he needed to ensure I got you safely out of there."

"You would say that."

"Think about it; if he'd revealed the traitor's true identity, they'd have threatened you." His eyes traced her features as though trying to reassure himself she was unharmed.

"Just like you did."

"Exactly like I did, yes. But Robert had to be certain that whoever took you wouldn't hurt you, as they were innocent. That's why he didn't disabuse the other's misapprehension that pointed to me."

"My brother would not have harmed me."

"Your brother is still under suspicion."

"Then we have to go back and save him." Emily struggled more fiercely against him now George's safety was at risk.

"Damn it, Emily. Do you not understand the severity of what went on in there? Robert has given up his best chance to find out the truth in order to protect you," he said, loosening his grip on her. His eyelids slid shut momentarily before he lifted his lids to reveal storm cloud eyes glittering with pain. "Don't let another sacrifice be in vain."

The rawness of his voice reverberated along Emily's taut nerve endings and she felt contrite; he was referring to his brother's pointless death. She couldn't argue against that. Her shoulders drooped in resignation and Nathan released her.

"We need to get away from here," he said, holding out his hand to her.

Emily eyed it hesitantly. He'd never done anything to harm her in the past. If anything, he'd always tried to protect her. She bit her lip in contemplation. Did she trust him? Her heart did a triple beat. She'd never trusted anyone more than she trusted Nathan. Even George.

She placed her hand in his and felt the tension leave his shoulders. She allowed him to lead her to a moored boat where he assisted her onto the wooden plank that served as a seat.

They fell into silence as Nathan cast off, took the oars and began rowing them swiftly away down river.

Chapter Twenty-Four

They sat in silence. Only the sound of the rippling water interrupted the taut hush that had descended between them. Nathan steered the boat towards a small jetty as the sun sank below the tree line. He assisted Emily out and placed the oars inside the boat as he gave it a hard shove and sent it back into the strong current of the river.

The jetty led to a narrow road bordered by a hedgerow with fields beyond.

"Come, we need to find somewhere safe to stay for the night."

Again they walked in silence, Nathan alert to the sounds of pursuit. Several times he raised his head to listen and then motioned for them to hurry and take cover, waiting while a lone horseman or cart passed by. Nathan heaving a sigh of relief when it wasn't someone in pursuit of them.

Emily sensed this was a frequent occurrence for him and she suspected for George and, before him, her parents also. Had George endured this during the hours before he'd arrived at Oakleaf Manor with a bullet wound? He must have suffered unbearable fear knowing Nathan was on his tail.

The last rays of light made the sky to the west glow and shimmer. An owl swooped low over them and headed towards a silhouetted barn in the distance.

"That looks promising." Nathan stopped by a dry stone wall that surrounded the edge of the field the barn overlooked. "Stay out of sight while I check it out."

Emily pressed herself against the rough wall. She couldn't believe it had come to this; George arrested and she on the run with Nathan. All she had been trying to do was protect those she loved. Instead, she had put everyone in danger.

When Nathan returned and took her hand, she made no complaint as he led her to the rear of the barn. He had pried a few loose boards aside, providing a gap big enough to squeeze through. Once inside, he replaced the boards behind them.

A wooden ladder climbed to the upper hay loft and Emily clambered up, followed by Nathan. Across the barn nestled in the oak struts sat the owl on a nest, scowling at them with big, intense eyes that even in the gloom shone ominously.

"I don't think she likes us," Emily said.

"She's just protecting her brood."

Well, she could certainly empathise with that. She took in Nathan's taunt features. After the sickening wrench of his brother's loss, it was a sentiment he had experienced firsthand.

He removed his greatcoat and laid it down on the hay for her to sit on. She sank onto it gratefully as Nathan dropped down next to her, resting his arm on top of his bent knee, the sleeve of his grey superfine jacket pulled back, revealing the cuff of his shirt.

Emily's breath caught in her lungs; the ends of her blue ribbon peeked out from the edge of his cuff. Lifting her gaze to his, her mind reeled back to the cottage and George's words to Nathan when she'd fallen through the doorway. "*I told you to stay away from her.*" It could only mean one thing. "You encountered George after our previous meeting." The ramifications pulsated through her.

Nathan looked into her upturned face, her hair in riotous abandon, forming a fiery halo around her. Her brows pressed together in suspended belief, waiting for him to confirm her conclusion. The look of veneration in her eyes for his forbearance in keeping his promise to her, whilst disgust and loathing for not taking his opportunity then and in the cottage against the man who'd all but admitted to his brother's murder burned his soul. But he couldn't let Emily know that. He turned away as he uttered one word. "Yes."

"What transpired?" She laid a hand against his arm and urged him to face her.

He let out a long sigh. He had tried so hard to blot out the knowledge that he had let his brother down, but the images of his failure haunted him. "He followed me into a deserted alleyway and tried to persuade me the evidence I'd collected was false."

"And what did he say about Peter?"

"He didn't claim his innocence, if that's what you think." He almost wished he had. Then at least he would not feel like the ogre he was; letting her believe he was honourable when in truth he was a failure. He'd not only let his brother get killed, but he had let his murderer get away.

"Did he tell you he was guilty?" she said, her hand tightening on his arm.

"Not in so many words."

"Not in any, I suspect."

Nathan allowed her that. "True, but my brother's death was not what concerned him."

"But it's what concerned you and it's your actions on that occasion that concern me now. So please tell me, did you threaten or try to harm him?"

Nathan grasped her chin between his thumb and forefinger and tilted it so he could see her unguarded features in the beam of moonlight glinting through a small gap in the roof. Needing to see her face, to see something to wash away the pain of his lost chance of retribution. To know that there had been an element of good in what he had given up. To know that someone would feel the magnitude of his forfeit and value him for it and give him the absolution he could not give himself. His thumb stroked her bottom lip before he let his hand drop. "No, I did not threaten or attempt to harm him. I let him walk away after he warned me to stay away from you."

A hot tear rolled down Emily's cheek; she had wrapped her ribbon around his wrist, knowing what she was asking him was beyond difficult. But she had not fully realised the magnitude of her request, nor the depth of gratitude she would feel knowing he had honoured her plea. She lifted her hand and curled it through his hair, pulling him towards her, touching her lips to his in the merest of a kiss. "Thank you," she whispered against his stubble roughened cheek. "I understand the depth of restraint it took for you to do that, and I'm humbled by the knowledge you did it solely for me."

Intense gratitude touched his strong face. His gaze caught and held hers imprisoned by the swirling need glowing in his eyes, their breathing joined in a unison of quick short bursts. Her eyes slid shut as he grasped a loose tendril of her hair laying against her over-warm cheek. A tingle skittering through her as his fingers glided along the strands to her neck, curving around her nape and placing enough pressure to guide her head towards him, towards his waiting lips.

A jolt reverberated through her as their lips met. The corner of his lip lifted up at the contact. He wanted this as much as she did. The knowledge caused raw need to pulsate through her. Due to the events of the last few weeks culminating in the altercation at the lodge, they would never be together again after tonight. Could never be together. What they felt for each other could never be reconciled against the actions of her brother and the loss of Nathan's brother and her own culpability in sending George after Nathan and Peter.

The outcome of that action lay on her conscience, pained her to the centre of her heart, and she needed to atone for it. To seek forgiveness from the very man whose soul she'd inadvertently destroyed and who at this moment needed her as much as she needed him. But a kiss wasn't enough. She wanted, needed all of him, to release her soul to him and share her body. To set them free of their grief of past crimes and a future that was lost to them. To give them the solace they both so desperately needed, knowing as she did so that this was goodbye.

They still had now, tonight, to share themselves. One night to carry with them through the rest of their days. It may be short-lived, but it would be fully lived.

Kissing her cheeks, Nathan tasted the salt from her tears; tears she'd shed in gratitude of his restraint against her brother. He pulled the few remaining pins holding her dishevelled coiffure free, crushing his fingers through her unbound hair as he leaned over her, pressing her down onto his greatcoat. His lips commanding hers to open, and when they did, his tongue plunged in and tangled with hers as he drew her tongue into his mouth where it entwined with his.

Emily let out a groan as wonderous sensations raced through her. In response, his hand roamed down over her jacket and found the swell of her breasts, moulding them firmly under his strong fingers.

"Emily." His hot breath caressed her sensitive ear, sending ripples of excitement through her body. "I need to be inside you, but only if you want this too."

Knowing what he had done for her, she could not withhold herself from him now. She twisted her head and found his lips again, kissing him with ardour and unbridled desire. It was answer enough.

His fingers sought the buttons of her jacket, undoing them in quick succession to reveal her silk shirt, her nipples taut beneath the thin fabric.

He kissed the long column of her neck, trailing kisses to her ear. "I have longed to remove this riding habit from you since that first night at Oakleaf Manor." His voice hoarse with desire, admiration and a tinge of regret.

His admittance of his attraction to her since the very beginning of their acquaintance sent a wave of pleasure through her. She reached up and entwined her hands around his neck, her fingers digging into the dark curls of his hair as she pulled him firmly against her.

He eased his fingers between them and began unbuttoning her shirt, caressing her breasts through the thin material of her chemise, her nipples hardening in his grasp.

She moaned in delight, instinctively arching her body towards him, but she needed more.

He straightened up and Emily cried her dismay at the loss,

only to see him tugging his cravat loose and tossing it aside. He began to shrug out of his jacket and she sat up and assisted him, pulling his arms free of his sleeves. He reached for his waistcoat buttons, but she stopped him and began undoing them herself.

Nathan stilled as a dishevelled Emily sat in front of him and slid her hands along his waistcoat, undoing him one button at a time. It was exquisite agony. He reached out and removed her open jacket, shirt and stays, sliding her chemise off her shoulders to reveal her creamy breasts in the silvery shaft of moonlight.

Urgency raced through them as Nathan helped Emily out of her skirts and chemise while he shed the rest of his clothes and they stood facing each other; Emily naked except for her silk stockings and Nathan wearing nothing but a blue ribbon tied around his wrist.

The poignancy ripped through Emily. She grasped his wrist and kissed the swaying ribbon, her lips trailing a path along the warm inside of his muscled arm, along his shoulder, to his rough-hewn chin to find his lips again. She traced the contour of his mouth, pressing herself fully along his aroused body. Breathing in the scent of him; his spicy cologne, and the deep earthy scent hidden beneath, mingled with the sweet smell of the hay surrounding them.

He scooped her up, his one arm around her back and the other under the crook of her knees. His lips on hers, he lowered her onto his greatcoat as he followed her down, covering her with his body. His hands moulding her curves before skimming along to her breast.

The touch of his hand was almost unbearable to Emily in its tenderness and when the ribbon grazed her sensitive nipple she cried out in exaltation.

His lips left hers as he kissed the pulsing hollow at the base of her throat before he dipped his head and invoked divine pleasure from her breasts, his lips and tongue circling and then suckling on her tight buds.

Excitement pierced through her in sharp bursts and she dug her fingers into his hair, holding his head upon her breast. His hand slid lower, gliding over her abdomen and sinking between her legs. Caught in the rapture of the moment, she writhed at the intimate touch and welcomed his questing fingers. Gasping at the pleasure he evoked from her as he caressed her most intimate place, expertly evoking excitement and fiery desire from within her.

Shifting position, he placed his manhood at her entrance and whispered, "I never wanted to cause you pain, but there is no other way, and it will only last for a moment."

She raised her gaze to see him poised above her, his body taut with restraint. "I trust you."

Her words erupted through Nathan, sending pride surging through him, and his restraint broke. He eased himself into her part-way, feeling the barrier that prevented further entry. "Look at me," he commanded.

Emily opened her eyes. Remorse was etched across his face for what he was about to do, his apology haunting his silver eyes. She reached up and brushed the unruly lock of hair that fell across his brow. His jaw tightened as he pulled back and thrust into her.

She cried out, and he soothed her discomfort with his lips, kissing apologies along her mouth. When her pain subsided, he moved back and forth within her, the pain replaced by an increasing rhythmic pleasure. She relaxed into the motion, lifting her hips instinctively as he took her hands, encouraging her to explore his body. She glided her hands over the crisp hairs on his chest, brushing his nipples and causing them to rise under her fingers. His teeth grazed the taut tendons along her neck, causing rivulets of desire to build and join the excitement that was intensifying in the pit of her stomach.

She pressed her head back as his strokes increased. Something beckoned to her, calling her on to an inevitable peak, and her body answered.

"Go with it," Nathan said, his arms holding him braced above her, waiting for her to reach her crescendo.

She gave a guttural cry as her body bucked and Nathan, unable to hold back any longer allowed himself release.

They crested and peaked, and in that moment attained solace. A moment of togetherness to carry them through a lifetime of separation. It would never be enough, but it was all they would ever have.

Nathan withdrew, then rolled onto his side, taking Emily with him. He held his arm protectively around her, gently stroking her back. Her heart beat against him, getting slower with each stroke, her head nestled against his shoulder.

Emily lay cocooned in his strong arms, each stroke of his hand a sweet torment. His warmth permeating through her whole body. This was the last night they would spend together. The silence of the unspoken truth enveloped them.

Unable to speak the words they desperately needed to say, they lay instead in each other's embrace while the night ebbed away.

Nathan held her as the silver light of the moon moved along her slender body as the night drew on. This was the last time he would hold her, the last time he would have her in his arms, and he wanted to lie next to her and watch her sleep. He wished he could stop the earth from turning, for he did not want this night to end. He leaned closer and placed a kiss on her forehead, breathing in the delicate floral scent of her hair, the soft contours of her body pressed against him, all the while knowing, come the morning, he would have to let her go.

Chapter Twenty-Five

Dawn made its way across England's green fields, over London town, and crept towards a small barn stood on the edge of a farm.

Inside, Emily stirred. Her bare arms and legs entwined with Nathan's limbs. Her body sated with last night's lovemaking. Overwhelmed at the knowledge Nathan had kept his promise to her. His actions proved how deeply he cared for her. Her chest filled with joy and pain. What they had shared had been the perfect expression of the love they felt for each other and it hurt so much knowing there could never be a future for them. Their love could never be reconciled against the actions of her brother and Peter's loss, along with recent events and her own culpability. She could never atone for her involvement in Peter's death. Last night had not only been a demonstration of her love for Nathan, but an attempt to atone for the unforgiveable.

She looked up as Nathan placed a gentle kiss atop her head, but he glance away before she could catch his eye.

"It's too dangerous to stay any longer."

They were not the words of love she had been expecting. But what could she say to express the emptiness and crushed hope that consumed her? What could either of them say?

Across the barn, the owl gave an irritated hoot and flapped her wings at them.

Nathan untangled himself from Emily's slender limbs and stood. He brushed the loose hay from his hastily discarded clothes as he dressed, pulling his shirt cuff over the blue ribbon still tied around his wrist. He should never have made that promise to her. His eyes slid shut as he remembered her look of adulation for not harming her brother. He had needed the absolution she had granted him. But he didn't deserve it. For even now, he would give anything to gain revenge against his brother's murderer. He opened his eyes. Emily's brow crumpled with uncertainty. Well, maybe not anything, but that was the problem. Too much lay between them.

He reached out, and taking Emily's slim hand, he assisted her into her clothes. His greatcoat was soiled with their lovemaking and the evidence of Emily's lost virginity. He could not bear to touch it and left it where it lay.

His heart was heavy as they prepared to leave. A sense of deep loss and profound admiration for Emily consumed him. He so wanted to tell her he loved her. To shout it to the world. But even love could not undo all that had happened. After today, they would go their separate ways. What good would those words be to her then? No, they were words he would have to keep to himself. To speak them would only cause more pain. And he had inflicted enough already.

With nothing left to keep them in the hayloft, they had to leave behind all that they had shared. He climbed down the ladder and assisted Emily as she descended to join him.

Outside, cold air greeted them. Above, a golden dawn stretched across the sky. Birds sang amongst the treetops, the sun warming all that it touched. It was a dawn that spoke of hope and new beginnings, but for them, it heralded an ending.

A shiver prickled along Emily's body as she stood in the shade of the barn. Today they would part. She opened her mouth to speak, but no words formed. Her throat tightened at the hopelessness of their situation. He was a man of integrity and honour. He'd kept his promise to her against insurmountable odds. Yet, all they'd done, all that they'd shared and felt for one another could not overcome the difficulties that lay between them. Today was the day when they would have to say goodbye. Today was the day her heart would break.

She blinked back the hot tears that threatened to fall. The last thing she wanted was to cause him further pain with her tears.

He walked over to her and wrapped an arm around her. "Are you cold?"

She gave a weak smile. "Not anymore."

He looked away from her, glancing across the fields. "It's dangerous to hang around any longer. We need to be on our way."

She nodded. "I understand."

His arm dropped from around her and she sucked in a shattered breath as they parted. Soon, they would be parted for ever.

As Emily was too tender to ride, Nathan arranged for a farmer to drive them in his cart to a coaching inn, where he hired a coach for them.

They sat in the confines of the coach in muted silence until they reached a crossroads, but instead of heading back to London the coach turned the other way.

Emily straightened. "The coachman is going the wrong way."

Nathan shook his head. "I have some things to attend to that I cannot postpone any longer. It won't take long." At least he hoped it would not.

"But we have to get back for George."

"Robert will not do anything until my return. He'll be safe until then."

"How can you be so sure?" she demanded.

"I know Robert." It was a tone that stated there was no point in arguing. But in truth, Robert could do nothing until he returned as it was his testimony that would convict George. He hated to cause more heartache for Emily, but he could not let his brother's murderer walk free. Justice had to be done.

Emily sank back against the squabs, unable to do anything but accept the delay.

* * *

Two hours later, the coach drew up to an ornate gatehouse of red brick with cream stone overlay. Greek style carvings adorned the arched entrance that loomed over them. The coachman informed the gatehouse keeper that Lord Thornburn requested entry. The gate was duly opened and as they swept past, the keeper bowed and intoned, "Welcome home, my lord."

"Thank you, Davies. Please invoke protocol safe as houses."

"Right you are, my lord."

"What was that about?" Emily asked, peering out of the

coach window at a large pale stoned mansion with a colon-naded entrance and large mullioned windows.

"A safety procedure to ensure an advanced warning is given of any visitors."

"You still think we're in danger?"

"I don't intend to take any chances, especially not with my family in residence."

Emily bolted upright. She was arriving at his family home in a state of utter dishevelment. She ran her fingers through her hair, but it did nothing to ease her tangled tresses, and the discovery of a piece of hay only increased her dismay.

"Do not alarm yourself. I shall explain your appearance." His voice was firm, as though no one would question his word.

Was he mad? His family would take one look at her and know exactly what had gone on between them and she'd be escorted out of the house forthwith. She sucked in a deep breath. She did not have long to discover her fate as the coach drew up in front of the house and a footman lowered the steps.

Nathan descended and turned to assist Emily out. She took his hand, the first contact between them since last night. Ignoring the tight squeeze of her heart, she lifted her head, trying to convey an air of dignity she was aware her appearance undermined.

She studiously avoided the eye of his servants as they strode into the house. The butler, however, was well-trained enough that, as soon as he'd registered her unkempt form, had the grace to glance away and act as though his master had arrived home with an utterly respectful young lady in tow.

"Your mother and sister are in the morning room. We have no other guests at home at present."

Mortification consumed Emily, aware that was in reference

to her, to let Nathan know her appearance would not be noted by anyone other than family. She didn't know whether to be relieved by the news or offended by the butler's assumption that it was important his master be made aware.

"Is there somewhere I can go to freshen up?" Emily asked.

"Yes, of course—"

"Nathaniel, darling, welcome home. Oh, I see we have a guest." Her voice was well modulated, but her tone lowered when she spotted Emily.

The look Nathan gave Emily was inscrutable, and he hesitated before turning to his mother. The pause was long enough for Emily to feel his embarrassment at his mother seeing her. She feigned absorption in a Chinese vase resting on a rosewood hall table, trying to pretend she was not hurt by his behaviour. She looked up when he mentioned her name.

"Yes, mama. Please let me introduce Miss Emily Ellerton. Miss Ellerton, my mother, the Dowager Countess of Thornburn. Please excuse our appearance, but we were involved in an unfortunate incident."

"Oh my, I hope you were not harmed."

"No, just suffered some inconvenience with regard to accommodation and travel," he said.

"Miss Ellerton, is it?" Only the slight lift of her right eyebrow gave away her surprise at her son arriving unexpectedly at her home with an unkempt young lady by his side.

"Yes, Lady Thornburn."

"Well, we must get you sorted out. Reeves, please arrange for a bath to be brought up to the guest rooms and ask Dorothy's maid to sort out some suitable clothing for our guest. They should be about the same size." She turned to Emily and threaded her arm through hers. "Come, take tea and sandwiches with me while the preparations are made."

"I couldn't impose on you while I am so un-presentable."

"Oh, balderdash. It is no imposition, any friend of my son is a friend of mine. Plus, you seem in need of a good cup of tea and some sustenance, and I intend to ensure you receive it."

With no other choice Emily allowed Nathan's mother to guide her into a sunny morning room, decorated in gilt and white, with delicate French chairs and a Greek mythical scene painted upon the ceiling that was echoed in the carpet's design spread out below.

A young lady about a year younger than Emily stood as they entered. Nathan introduced her as his sister, Lady Dorothy Renwick. She had Nathan's striking dark hair and silver eyes, but her mouth and cheeks were delicate and feminine. She welcomed Emily with easy manners and although her expressive eyes showed her shock at Emily's state, she made no comment and invited her to take a seat next to her, which Emily duly complied with.

She possessed the grace of a well-trained hostess, pouring Emily a cup of tea and offering her a sandwich from the plate laid before them.

Feeling drained, Emily readily accepted both.

"May I ask what brings you here this time of year?" Lady Thornburn asked her son.

Emily glanced at Nathan as he took a fortifying sip of his tea, before placing the cup on the saucer with deliberate care and cleared his throat.

The hairs along Emily's nape prickled with foreboding, his demeanour reminiscent of his visit to her after his returned from Jersey. It was then that she realised what she'd sensed was amiss within the house. It should have been a house of mourning, but the servants were not wearing black armbands and Nathan's mother and sister were not wearing mourning clothes. They'd not been informed of their loss; she closed her eyes in sympathetic pain for the unsavoury task Nathan must now undertake and the grief that would be inflicted on his mother and sister. She placed her hand on his sleeve and gave him a comforting squeeze. He glanced at her with a subdued glance, then turned his attention back to his family.

"I came to inform you about Peter." His eyes dropped from his mother as he took a shuddering breath. "There was an incident in Jersey. A shot was fired and Peter was hit. He stumbled backwards over the cliff edge and into the sea. I tried to find him. We launched a boat and searched for three hours before we lost the daylight."

Emily listened to his heart-rending recounting of his beloved brother's loss. His pain vibrating through the raw strain of his voice. She wondered if her own brother had truly fired that shot. Could he really be responsible for causing such pain? She held her breath as Nathan struggled to finish informing his family.

"I stayed for another two days." He swallowed before continuing. "Waiting for his body to be washed up, but the sea had taken him. There is no body to place in the family vault."

A wail split the air. Dorothy sat rooted to her seat, too shocked to react as her mother fainted.

Emily leapt up and took Lady Thornburn's hands in hers and began chaffing them, trying to restore her. "Nathan, call for help. Does your mother use smelling salts?"

"Yes, she keeps them in her room."

"Then I suggest we remove her to there."

"Yes, of course." He summoned the butler. Lifting his

mother up himself, he carried her up the stairs, while Emily assisted his sister, following in his wake.

He laid his mother on her bed and waved her smelling salts under her nose. She smacked them away from her. Dropping her head, she curled into a ball and began sobbing.

Dorothy sat on the bed beside her and wrapped her arms around her, while Nathan handed her a handkerchief, his hand resting on his sister's shoulder.

Emily stood watching Nathan's grief-stricken family, not knowing if her own brother was the cause of the scene before her. She wanted to help, but what could she do?

The butler tapped quietly on the door and Emily slipped out. "Yes?"

"Your bath is ready, Miss."

"Oh, I see." Emily hesitated as she deliberated about what to do. She was intruding on a private family matter, but she did not think it right to leave so she could bathe.

The door opened behind her, and Nathan stepped out. "I can take it from here. You go and get yourself sorted out." He glanced at her, but would not look her in the eyes. "We'll be able to manage on our own now."

"I understand." She had been dismissed; he had no intention of involving her further in his family's mourning. He had no intention of involving her in his life. She suspected that come tomorrow a carriage would be arranged to transport her home and that would be that.

She'd thought their last moment together would be spent in each other's arms, but instead it was to end with her a witness to the tragic consequences she may have inadvertently been to blame for. She would let this be her penitence for that fateful decision.

* * *

Nathan watched Emily being led away to the guest rooms. He regretted how things had ended, yet maybe it was for the best. His conscience pricked him. No, whatever lay in their past, she did not deserve this, but he could never make it up to her and there would be no point even if he could. Though she could no longer see him, he bowed to her; he owed her that courtesy at least.

Chapter Twenty-Six

The unfamiliar creak of the door woke Emily. She rolled onto her back as the maid who'd assisted her last night entered her room.

"I have your clothing ready, Miss."

Emily eyed the dark brown travelling dress; it was as she expected. Nathan wanted her gone and had arranged for her to be sent home. Well, she would not stay where she was not wanted.

With the assistance of the maid, she dressed and made her way downstairs. As she reached the bottom step, she heard voices coming from the breakfast room.

"Will you be making her an offer of marriage?" came Lady Thornburn's voice.

"You know I cannot."

In the hallway, Emily's heart thudded to a stop. She'd known there was no future for them. But to hear Nathan state it with such finality as though she was too far beneath him for him to even contemplate was beyond humiliating. She was a guest, an unwanted guest, in his family's home, and she was going to have to look his mother in the eye as though Nathan had not said those words. To know what his mother must think of her and all she could do was endure it with as much fortitude as her tattered pride could muster, whilst knowing she could not utter one word in her own defence. She lifted her head up, put her shoulders back and headed towards the room to face the consternation she was certain awaited her. However, the dowager's next words stopped her.

"I take it from your unceremonious arrival and your behaviour to each other that her virtue is no longer intact."

Emily waited as she heard Nathan stride across the room and attack the fire with a poker before the dowager walked over to him in a swish of skirts. "I understand your reasons for refusing to marry, but under the circumstances you need to do right by Miss Ellerton." Her voice was gentle but firm.

"And do wrong by my vow and the memory of those I let down."

"You cannot continue living in the past."

"I have no right to be living in the present, not after what I did."

Emily gasped as his revelation penetrated her shocked mind. He'd taken a vow not to marry, but why? It was wrong to eavesdrop, but glancing around to make certain no servants were about, she took a step closer to the room so she could hear more clearly.

"Your first duty is to your family and now Peter is gone," the dowager cleared the catch in her throat, "it is your duty, a duty that was yours to begin with, to continue the family name and to produce the next heir."

"Even if I was to accept that, marriage to Miss Ellerton is impossible," he said with implacability.

In the hallway, Emily heard the exasperation in his voice.

She understood he could never explain to his mother that he could never marry her, as her brother may have been to blame for Peter's death.

"Well, in that case, the least we can do is escort her back to London in a respectful manner."

"Mother, you cannot go to London. You're in mourning."

"And Miss Ellerton cannot return without a chaperone after two nights alone with you. For the sake of her reputation I need to accompany you both on your return and make it known that you'd met with me on the first day and on hearing the news of Peter's death had come back here with me and you are now escorting myself, your sister and Miss Ellerton to London."

"That will not be possible."

"Considering what has happened between you, the least I expect of you is to do everything in your power to preserve her reputation."

Emily held her breath as she awaited Nathan's response. Not sure what she hoped for; just some sign acknowledging that what they'd shared had meant the same thing to him as it did to her.

"In as much as her family's reputation is about to be publicly ruined beyond redemption, I'm afraid there is very little I can do to protect Miss Ellerton from that."

"The least you can do is try after what she has given up for you."

"I cannot," he said, frustration threading through his voice.

"Why not?"

"Because I'm the one providing the evidence to condemn them."

"Is there something you are not telling me?"

Silence filled the air, sucking the oxygen out of Emily's

lungs. She stood rooted to the marble floor, waiting for Nathan's response, afraid he would reveal George's possible involvement in Peter's death to his mother.

"I will not have this conversation with you," he said in a clipped tone.

"And I will not be left in ignorance. Either you tell me what is going on or I will demand an explanation from Lord Brakenhale."

He did not respond.

"Very well, but know this," the dowager said in a tone of unarguable authority. "I intend to escort Miss Ellerton home and make it known she has my support."

"I must beg of you not to do that, for your own sake."

"Unless you can give me sufficient reason, then I shall have to consult my own feelings on the matter and act accordingly."

"It is your feelings I wish to protect."

"Then tell me why I cannot lend my consequence to a young lady who has gained the love of my eldest son."

"Because her brother killed your youngest son." The words tore from Nathan as though ripped from his heart.

A chair creaked as the dowager sank onto it. Emily contemplated entering the room and ending the discussion, but her bravery had been squeezed out of her by the betrayal of Nathan's words. She dropped her head in shame.

The dowager's voice drifted out to her in a strong and defiant tone. "That does not make the guilt hers."

Emily's head lifted, her jaw dropping in surprise at the dowager's defence of her, but Nathan's next words wiped away her shock.

"You think not!" he burst out. "Who do you think told him where to find us?"

Her eyes slid shut, and she fought against the sharp piercing stab of guilt which cut through her at his words and at the verification he'd known all along that it was she who'd sent George in pursuit of him and his brother and as a result she was as guilty as George for his brother's death.

"She sent him after us," Nathan said, in a tortured whisper, "and look at the result. She is as culpable as if she'd pulled the trigger herself."

His confirmation of her thoughts sent a icy shiver slithering down her spine at the hatred threading his voice. She couldn't believe how much he detested her, not after how tender he'd been with her two nights ago. She shook her head in disbelief that he'd known about her possible involvement in Peter's death, and yet his caresses had been gentle, almost reverent. Had it all been an act? Her heart screamed a denial. He couldn't have feigned those feelings, but informing his family of Peter's death may have been enough for him to realise how devastating her own innocent actions had been. His mother must despise her by now as well.

But she was wrong.

"Dorothy can no more be guilty for your actions as Miss Ellerton can be for her brother's, regardless of what preceded it. You know that as well as I do, or you would never have spent the night with her. Your feelings for her go far beyond any perceived guilt. Now do me the honour of understanding the true worth of that young lady, her brother notwithstanding, and allow me to act in accordance with my own judgement."

"I cannot allow it."

"You cannot stop me. That girl loves you, and as my son, I know you love her. I do not pretend to understand what has gone on between you, but I do know she gave herself to you knowing that you could never accept her and for that, I will protect her to the full extent of my consequence." She stood up and strode from the room.

Caught in the act of eavesdropping, Emily expected to see revulsion in the dowager's eyes after she'd defended her so resiliently. Instead, she laid her hand against Emily's cold cheek and said, "We leave in an hour," before heading up the stairs with a swish of her black mourning dress. Humbled by her actions, Emily stared after her, unable to believe her gallantry, but her admiration was cut short as Nathan walked into the hall. He gave her a scathing glare, then turned on his heel and strode away.

Emily bit her trembling lip, trying to stop the tears from falling. She'd been so gratified by the dowager's belief and fortitude in her and so crushed by Nathan's disgust. She felt like a china cup falling to the floor, waiting for the moment it would shatter.

Chapter Twenty-Seven

Nathan rode ahead of the coach. He refused to ride inside, ensconced next to Emily, with his mother trying to convince him to forsake his oath to repair her reputation. She'd known what she was doing and had accepted the consequences. His mother did not understand that although marriage may save Emily's reputation, it would be the ruin of her. They could not live together with what lay between them. Such a life would destroy them both and he'd destroyed enough lives already.

His horse sidled to the left, causing Nathan to ease his taut grip on the reins. Reaching down, he patted the flanks of his horse in apology for his tenseness. He glanced back at the coach. What his mother asked was impossible. A sense of loss descended on him. Instead of fighting it, he embraced it. This was his punishment for his mistake of old and he should suffer for it, though he greatly regretted that Emily would suffer too. She did not deserve this, but they had needed each other that night in the barn. Now they had to carry on with only the memory of that night to keep them going through the difficult times ahead.

Inside the coach, the atmosphere was subdued, and Emily could not look at the mourning clothes of the dowager and Dorothy without feeling a sense of acute regret and guilt for their loss.

Lady Thornburn leaned forwards and took Emily's hands in hers. "Please, Miss Ellerton, you must convince him to give up his oath and marry you, for more than just your reputation, for Nathan's own salvation." Her eyes were imploring. It was painful to see how desperate this strong, resolute woman had become.

Emily wished she could comply. But she couldn't. It wasn't possible. Unable to bear the desperate, pleading grasp of the dowager, she pulled her hands free. "I am sorry, my lady, but I cannot."

"Because of your brother and Peter?"

As if that wasn't enough, but Nathan's role in the diplomatic service made it an impossibility. She couldn't bear to live the life she had lived before, sitting at home and fearing the worst whilst waiting for news. "That is one reason, yes, but there is more beyond those things that prevent me from doing so."

"You will not even try?"

Guilt pierced her. Lady Thornburn had defended her and under such difficult circumstances and now she denied her the hope that she could persuade Nathan to change his mind and relinquish his oath; that she would not even try. "I am sorry. It would do no good."

Lady Thornburn gave a sad nod and glanced out of the window as a heavy silence descended inside the coach.

Emily was relieved when the entourage pulled up outside her uncle's town house and the dowager bid her a sombre farewell. She sucked in a deep breath as Nathan opened the coach door and, taking her hand, assisted her down. Her fingers were clammy inside her gloves as she walked beside Nathan, the man she loved, the man who wanted nothing to do with her. She struggled to keep her spine stiff, to stop herself from collapsing. So many emotions crashing through her. She stared resolutely at the door before her. All she had to do was make it up the steps and into the house. Then she could put all this behind her. The butler opened the door and Nathan handed her over without ceremony, then turned away. Her eyes clung to his retreating form. He did not look back as he remounted his horse and rode away. Drawing a shattered breath, Emily turned and entered the house.

She hurried to her aunt's drawing room and found her pulling at a loose thread on her shawl where a large hole had now formed. "Aunt Amelia, please do not damage that shawl any further. I am home. I am safe."

"Oh, my child! Where have you been? Lord Brakenhale called and told me he'd ordered Lord Thornburn to take you away from the meeting, but I expected you back the same day." Her eyes were wide with fear and confusion.

"I'm sorry to have worried you. Lord Thornburn had yet to inform his family of Peter's loss, and so we spent the days there." She gave her aunt a hug, grateful her aunt could not see the lie written across her face. "Is George home?"

"No. Lord Brakenhale has detained him, as he was awaiting the return of Lord Thornburn, but now he is back, I am sure he will release him soon."

"Lord Thornburn is going to report to Lord Brakenhale first thing tomorrow. Hopefully, George will be released soon thereafter." She could not tell her aunt that Nathan's return may mean George's demise. Grasping her heart-shaped pendant, she squeezed it between her fingers. George was innocent. Regardless of what Nathan had to say, George would prove his innocence. He had to. His life now depended on it.

"If he is not back home by tomorrow afternoon," her aunt said, "we shall call at Lord Brakenhale's office and find out what the situation is."

Emily nodded, unable to speak. She was desperate to see George. To know she would not have his death on her conscience as well. She squeezed her eyes shut, praying that whatever the outcome, she would not meet Nathan. For how could she look upon the man who had broken her heart and would willingly condemn her brother to death?

Chapter Twenty-Eight

"You're doing what?" Nathan ripped the words out in an incensed growl.

"I'm releasing George," Robert repeated, leaning back in his chair with an unarguable expression on his face as he steepled his fingers in front of him. The late morning sun slanting across his desk.

"Is my word not good enough for you?" Nathan surged up from his seat and walked away from Robert's desk as he ran his hand through his hair.

"I dispute neither yours nor Simon Pykett's substantiation, but I am not prepared to convict George on that basis alone."

Nathan spun on his heel and stalked towards Robert. "It is enough for a court of law to have him hanged for treason."

"True, but it is insufficient for me to use to the King in order to clear myself of any wrongdoing, so I cannot condemn George to death on the same basis."

Nathan pressed his white-knuckled fists against Robert's desk and said in as civilised a voice as he could muster, "Your judgement is flawed."

"Be that as it may, my decision is final."

Nathan shook his head, his voice an empty rasp. "He all but admitted to killing Peter."

"No, Nathan. He merely admitted he was in Jersey at the same time. That's not enough to convict him."

"He was trying to rub my nose in it. Knowing there was nothing I could do about it. If that isn't evidence enough." Nathan shoved away from Robert's desk.

"No, it's not. And on that note, I am releasing him on the morrow."

"You're letting my brother's murderer go free?" Nathan said with a huff of incredulity.

Robert came around his desk and stood in front of Nathan. "George has answered all my questions fully and explained his actions that you witnessed, and I do not believe him guilty of betraying either us or his country. Therefore, he has no motive for murdering your brother."

Nathan rocked his head from side to side, a muscle throbbing in his jaw in disbelief at Robert's gullibility. "I'll not work with him."

"I understand, and I believe it is best that George is released from his duties," Robert said.

"That's the least that should be done."

"At the same time, I must insist that you stay away from him." His stern expression brooked no argument.

Nathan could not believe this was happening. George was being released, and there was nothing he could do. His brother's death would go unavenged. He glanced at Robert; he was awaiting his reply. "As you wish," he said between clenched teeth.

"Oh, there is one more thing I require from you."

"What?"

"Please call on Miss Ellerton and her aunt and inform them of my decision. I know they will be worried."

Nathan glared at Robert. "You cannot be serious?"

"Have you ever known me to be otherwise?" Robert returned Nathan's gaze with one of absolute resolution.

"You know not what you ask."

"Then pray tell me."

Nathan swung away and rubbed the back of his neck, his fingers biting into the taut tendons. How could he explain to Robert about what had happened between him and Emily? He would insist that recompense be made to her and he could not give it. Knowing he had no choice but to accept Robert's instruction, he turned back to him. "Forgive me, I overstated my grievance and I would be pleased to deliver such good news to Miss Ellerton and her aunt."

"I'm pleased to hear it," Robert said, waving his dismissal.

Nathan grabbed up his hat and gloves and, with a curt bow, left the office.

* * *

Unable to sleep, Emily lit her candle and carried it to the window seat, where she sat with her legs pulled up to her chest and rested her head on her knees.

She stared at the candle's flame dancing in the window's reflection. The flickering flame blurred into an image of Nathan, the stray lock of hair falling across his brow. Would the man she loved condemn her beloved brother to death? Did he love her enough to lie to Lord Brakenhale for her sake? He was righteous and resolute. He would do what he thought was right, he was incapable of doing anything else. These were the qualities she admired in him. Yet she feared those same qualities would result in her innocent brother being hanged for treason.

Lifting her head, she traced the reflection of the candle in the window with the tip of her finger. A future between them was impossible because of the situation with George and Peter and her own feelings about the diplomatic service, but she'd not realised he'd pledged an oath never to marry. Even without the situation with George and Peter, he'd not have married her. She had given herself to a man who'd had no intention of ever marrying her.

If she'd known, would she have changed her mind? She pressed her hand against the cool pane. The answer was no, she'd needed to be with him that night and she would never regret giving herself to him.

She let her hand slide down the window and prayed George was innocent of Peter's death; it would not change the situation between her and Nathan, but it would ease her guilt where Nathan was concerned. She did not want to be someone he despised. Even though they could never spend the rest of their lives together, she couldn't bear knowing he was out there somewhere, hating her.

She lifted her eyes to the lightening sky with trepidation, wondering what this new day would bring.

* * *

As the clock chimed ten in the morning, Emily paced across her aunt's drawing room, ignoring her aunt's request that she sit. Surely if George had been acquitted, he'd be here by now?

Her uncle had offered to go to the Foreign Office on their behalf, and her aunt had agreed, disregarding Emily's protestations. So now she waited, like she always waited. She rubbed her arms, praying that this time it would be good news.

Footsteps echoed along the corridor and she turned, expecting to see her uncle. She gasped as Nathan appeared from behind the butler.

"I have news," he said, stepping into the room, his stern features punctuated by clouded eyes.

The tangled knot in Emily's throat made her voice harsh. "You've condemned him to death." She sank onto the settee. "And now you have come here to gloat!"

"Believe you me, the last thing I feel like doing right now is gloating. Lord Brakenhale has decided to release George." His words rasped against his tight throat.

But Emily didn't hear his tone as she clapped her hand over her mouth and gave her aunt a fierce hug.

"Did I not tell you George would prove his innocence?" Aunt Amelia said, once free of the embrace.

"You did indeed," Emily said, as her heart danced. Nathan stood with his body taut, but he gave her a slight smile, showing he was happy for her. She wished things could have ended well for his brother too, but his death would always be a burden of guilt and grief for him.

"Now if you will excuse me," Aunt Amelia said, "I believe Lord Tysling is back and I wish to share the good news with him if he has not already heard."

"Of course." Nathan bowed to her as she left.

Emily sucked in a deep breath to calm her skipping heart. This may be a happy outcome for her and her family, but for Nathan, the search for the traitor and his brother's murder remained unresolved. He'd been so certain that both were George and that his evidence was irrefutable. Her brow furrowed. If that was so, how could George have been released?

"Was this your doing?" she asked, but when he gave her a blank expression, she clarified. "George being released, after you were so adamant that your evidence would convict him. Did you withhold some vital information?"

He glanced down at the floor before lifting his granite gaze to her. "No, I withheld nothing from Lord Brakenhale."

"Oh." Her chest tightened at his blunt admission, but what else had she expected from the principled man before her? "In truth, I did not expect otherwise."

He stepped forwards, hands outstretched in a gesture of conciliation. "It would not have made any difference if I had, as Simon Pykett was a second witness to George's suspicious behaviour. My information was merely confirmation of what Mr Pykett had already told Lord Brakenhale. By the time I arrived, he had already decided to release George."

She nodded. He'd regretted what his information could have caused for George, but he did not apologise for doing what he believed to be right. Even so, his betrayal stung. "Is George still under suspicion of killing Peter?"

He gave a mirthless laugh. "No, according to Lord Brakenhale, as George is innocent of betraying his country, he has no motive for killing Peter."

Emily let out a deep breath.

"I'm glad it gives someone peace," he said in a bitter tone.

She had not meant to be so thoughtless. He had always

done what he could to comfort her and protect her, even when in pursuit of her brother. Her prayer that George would be exonerated had been answered, yet Nathan had been left with nothing. She grasped his arm. "If I could do anything to bring you answers, I would do it, for I cannot bear to see you in such pain."

His gaze dropped to her hand and lifted back to her, and her breath caught in her throat as a myriad of emotions blazed in the depths of his grey orbs.

"I'm used to it," he said.

"You shouldn't have to be."

"Maybe not, but it's my cross to bear. Please do not take any more upon yourself. It would not be fair of me to allow it."

"Let me worry about that," Emily said as a tear slid unbidden down her cheek. She turned to hide it, but he caught her chin between his finger and thumb and lifted it up to him.

"Save your tears for someone who deserves them."

"I have," she said, on a shattered breath.

He released her chin. "I have done as I was ordered; now I must leave."

Her jaw dropped. Done as ordered! He hadn't come here for her benefit, but because Robert had ordered him. Had she meant nothing to him? "You mean you only came here because you were ordered? You were happily going to leave me and my aunt in ignorance of George's acquittal when you knew how important this news was to us?" She wiped away the tear she had shed for him. "You are right. You don't deserve my tears."

He twisted away from her and dropped his arm to his side. "How can you expect me to want to tell you such news when it brings me only bitterness?"

"Because I thought you cared enough about me to want

to bring me some sense of relief after the weeks of worry regarding George."

"At least for your brother you have a happy ending, not so for mine."

"You still hold George responsible?" She shook her head. How could she have revered this man when he held such a deep grudge against George?

"I can see no alternative. I wished that I could."

"You have made your feelings clear," Emily said, crossing her arms over her chest. "Well, you have done as you were ordered. I suggest you take your leave."

His gaze slipped from hers and he paused for an agonising moment, then gave a sharp bow. "Good day to you, Miss Ellerton."

"Goodbye, Lord Thornburn." She turned her back on him as he left.

Chapter Twenty-Nine

Emily sat in the drawing room with her aunt, the tick of the ormolu clock marking the seconds and minutes as they waited for George's return. The clock struck midday as she fiddled with the cuff of her dress, unable to rest until he was back home. Yet her conscience pricked her about her behaviour towards Nathan; she'd not been fair to him. Whilst George's release had been the best news she could have hoped for, it left Nathan bereft of answers for his brother's death. He already suffered deep regret. He should not have to carry the pain of not knowing who'd murdered his brother. A pain she'd suffered with the loss of her own parents, taken from her with no explanation of how or who was to blame.

She had mistreated him. He'd been so compassionate towards her at Lord Attenborough's ball when she'd told him of her loss. And now, instead of returning his compassion, she'd chided him for not being pleased for her about George's release, when he, like herself, had been left without answers. He'd always put aside his anger at her brother and treated her with respect and now she'd failed him; so caught up in her own happiness, she had not considered his pain. She bitterly regretted her lack of forethought. But how could she apologise when their dealings were at an end? She wished she could say she was sorry.

A loud commotion brought her back to the present as George strode into the drawing room. She leapt up and threw her arms around him. "You've proven your innocence."

"Of course, although Nathan is still not prepared to let things drop." His face was drawn and his eyes haunted.

"You mean about Peter's death?" Emily said, wincing as she remembered her behaviour to Nathan.

"Among other things. He wants to see justice done for Peter and if he can't get a conviction for his murder, he is prepared to get me on something else."

"But he has no evidence."

"None."

He sank into an armchair as though he was too weary to stand. The last few weeks had taken their toll on him. Emily's heart constricted at her brother's lost vigour. As a boy, he had never stayed still. He'd grown into a great sportsman and always kept himself busy. Now he looked lost and devoid of spirit. She may no longer need to keep him hidden, but she still felt the need to protect him. "Have they found out who the real traitor is?"

George shook his head. "Lord Brakenhale has dispensed with my services though, as Nathan will not work with me now."

"But you loved your job," Emily said, in his instant defence, but her heart skipped with joy that she would no longer have to suffer the distress of waiting behind while he was away. Yet it was unfair that he was still subjected to distrust, even after clearing his name. Until the real culprit was caught, it would be very difficult for anyone to trust anyone else and that must hurt her loyal brother so much.

"Well, I'm glad to have you home," Aunt Amelia said, "and if you'll both excuse me, I will return to my bed and get some sleep. I've had several restless nights."

"Of course. Let me assist you," George said.

"No, I'll manage. You just enjoy being home."

As soon as she was out of earshot, George turned to Emily. "Now that we are alone, I have some things I need to ask."

"Like what?" Dread seeped through her; did he suspect the truth? She glanced at the doorway as she tried to calculate how quickly she could feign some excuse and get away?

"What happened to you after Nathan removed you from the cottage?" He skewered her with a sharp look.

She had to keep to the truth as much as possible, but she couldn't let him know what had really happened. "We went to visit his mother. She had yet to be told of Peter's death."

"On foot? We found your horses."

"No, we went via boat."

"The river goes the wrong way. You'd have never made it before nightfall."

She hesitated. Just for a second, but it was long enough for George to read the truth in her face.

"That son of a bitch," he said, surging to his feet. His cheeks mottled with anger.

"No, it wasn't like that."

"Wasn't like what?"

She didn't have an answer. Not one she could explain.

"Oh, I know exactly what it was like. And Nathan is going to pay."

"No! Please, you mustn't hurt him."

"This is not your concern," he said, pushing past her.

Emily stamped her foot. "Not my concern! I think it is more my concern than yours."

"Not anymore," George said as he strode out of the room, his boot heels clicking on the tiles.

Emily gnawed on her lip. She loved both George and Nathan. She didn't want harm to come to either of them. Whatever was she to do?

Chapter Thirty

Wearing his shirt open at the collar, Nathan stood with his arms braced against the mantel over the empty fireplace in his study. He regretted his behaviour to Emily. She'd done nothing except put her trust in him and for that he'd treated her with rude contempt when his feelings for her could not be further away.

He dropped his head and stared into the dead embers. He had to forget her, to move on and erase her from his heart. Her brother had been cleared and so their involvement with each other was at an end, as it should be. He should not have slept with her, but he didn't regret doing so; he'd needed her that night and she'd needed him. But it had been wrong, for he could not offer her marriage afterwards. At least she'd got what she wanted where George was concerned; she had her family back.

But for him, it was so different. His brother's killer was out there, somewhere. As Robert had made abundantly clear, George had been cleared of betraying his country, so it also absolved him of murdering Peter, as he now had no motive. But that left Nathan with no-one to blame, no-one to punish.

He hadn't wanted it to be George for Emily's sake as much as his own, but for him it was better than it being some unknown assailant, someone he would walk past in the street and not know that they were his brother's murderer. He'd insisted that Robert dismiss George from the diplomatic service. It wasn't right as he had no proof George had killed his brother, but even so, he could not work alongside him, wondering if it had been him.

He pushed away from the mantel and walked over to his desk. He sat down in the stiff green leather chair and pulled open a drawer, taking out paper, wax, powder, ink and a quill.

His mother had requested he send an announcement to the papers, but he did not know where to begin. What could he say about his brother that would do him justice? With a determined dip of his quill in the ink, he began to write. Then he neatly put a line through the words and began again. And again.

Sometime later, the butler entered.

"My lord, a messenger has come for you."

"Send him away." Nathan didn't look up as he crossed out his last sentence.

"He says Lord Brakenhale has requested your attendance forthwith."

"Can you not see I am busy?" Nathan shouted, throwing his quill down and causing ink to splatter across the page and his shirt.

"Begging your pardon, my lord, he said it was imperative that you attend, and I was not to take no for an answer."

Nathan eyed his butler for a moment. Robert would never request his presence under these circumstances unless it was imperative. Even so, the thought of having to deal with something else on top of everything was overwhelming. But orders were orders and he'd never disobeyed Robert before.

He rubbed his temples in resignation. "Very well."

"I've arranged for the carriage to be put to."

"No, I'd rather walk," Nathan said, straightening from his chair.

"His lordship's messenger did express the urgency."

"Trust me, it will be better if I walk and clear my head first."

"Very good." The butler bowed as he left.

Nathan headed to his room and changed his ink-stained shirt for a clean one and then, with the help of his valet, he tied his cravat into a simple knot and shrugged into a dark blue jacket.

His valet handed him his greatcoat and beaver hat and Nathan strode from the house.

Outside, a stormy grey sky held the threat of rain. Ignoring the biting wind that tugged at his coat, he headed along the London streets at an impatient pace. He turned down the alley where he'd met George a few days ago. He heaved a disbelieving sigh. "I know you're there, George," he said, turning around to face him. "What do you want this time?"

"Your blood," George said, as he punched him.

* * *

Gripping her pendant, Emily ran it back and forth along its chain as she looked out of the window, waiting for George's return. As he came marching along the street, she breathed a sigh of relief and braced herself.

He entered the parlour and strode to the fireplace, where he stood with his foot on the fire grate without uttering a word. She studied him for a moment. His clothes were ruffled, but not badly enough to suggest he'd been in a fight. So that meant it hadn't come to blows. For that, she was grateful. But it led to another possibility. "Did you call him out?" she asked in a fearful voice.

"No, we settled matters between us."

"What exactly did you settle?"

"That he was not to come near you again. But then he'd already decided that before he bedded you."

Her eyes slid shut. They'd both known there was no future for them. That this one time was all they would ever have and accepted that afterwards they could never see each other again. Yet it hurt so much to be reminded of it and in such a disapproving tone. She understood how angry George was with her, but she'd known what she was doing and that they would have to walk away from each other forever.

Now she needed to hear everything that had taken place between George and Nathan, because this was as close as she would ever get to him again. "Please tell me what happened?"

"You let him ruin you," George said, his eyes slicing over her.

The shame she'd brought on her family burned her like a hot coal. But what she'd done had been right for her and Nathan. George would never understand. This would be her punishment for disobeying the dictates of society in order to demonstrate her love for Nathan. But Nathan did not deserve to be vilified for what they'd shared. "The decision was mutual."

George spun around. "Oh, you poor deluded child. Do you

not see he used your naiveté and youth against you?" His voice was harsh and his face showed the pain she had caused him. But he didn't understand.

"That's not true. He loved me."

George bowed his head and heaved a deep sigh. "He made you believe he loved you so he could take advantage."

"No, he'd never do that."

"How many women do you think he has seduced over the years, all in the name of duty?" George said, pointing out of the window as though pointing to all of Nathan's previous conquests.

Emily shook her head, denying George's words. Of course there had been other women in Nathan's life. In his line of work, seduction was a powerful weapon, but this was different. "They were just a means to an end, but I meant something to him."

"He was using you to get to me, using you in every conceivable way."

"No, you mustn't think that." She lifted her hands to him in supplication.

"He admitted it," George said, gripping her shoulders. "He admitted he'd had no intention of marrying you."

She dropped her hands. "I knew he couldn't offer me marriage. It wasn't possible with the way things were."

"Oh, good God." George threw his arms up in disbelief at her gullibility. "He didn't love you, he just wanted the challenge of trying to bed you and to use you, all so he could avenge himself on me."

"No."

"He thought I'd killed his brother. What better revenge could he take than to ruin my only sister?"

His words were daggers piercing her heart, yet she had to defend him. "You're angry, I understand that. But you don't understand what Nathan and I shared."

"No, Emily, I understand what you felt for him was real and pure and innocent. I truly believe that, but as far as he was concerned, you were a traitor's sister, the sister of his brother's murderer. Do you really think he could feel anything more than hatred for you? He didn't want anything to do with you."

Nathan's words to her after he'd dragged her out of the cottage came back to her. *'The last thing I wanted was to be anywhere near you.'* He'd truly not wanted anything to do with her. George's words started to penetrate the barrier of love she'd erected to protect herself. Everything she'd believed about Nathan and his feelings for her shattered. Her eyes slid shut, the truth hammering at her heart.

Unable to bear George's recrimination, she ran from the house, making her way along the gravel paths through the garden to the stables. Intending to groom the horses like she used to when she was young and upset, to use the soothing presence of resting her hands against the warm flank of the horses to calm and restore her.

Striding past the stable hands, she grabbed a comb and entered a stall with a docile mare and through a blur of tears, she began rubbing her down. The action of losing herself in her work usually had the desired effect, but she'd not considered her location. The scent of hay; that sweep crisp aroma had surrounded her and Nathan in the barn. She closed her eyes, and she was back there with Nathan as he stood before her with her blue ribbon tied around his wrist, his hands caressing her with gentle reverence. Those had not been the actions of someone acting in revenge, but someone in love.

Her eyes flew open. She had to see him, to find out what he truly felt for her. Hanging up the comb, she left the stall and headed out of the side entrance that led out onto the street.

Chapter Thirty-One

Nathan limped into Lord Brakenhale's office to find him staring out of the window, a letter clasped in his hands behind his back. It caught him off guard to find Robert not at his desk working, but instead staring lost in thought. Whatever had caused Robert to summon him here it wasn't good, but right now he had more immediate problems.

His presence must have penetrated Robert's contemplation, because he spun to face him. "My God, Nathan, what happened to you?"

Nathan stood before him with a torn coat, cut lip, bloodied nose, missing cravat and blood-stained shirt. "I bumped into George." He held his side where he suspected he had a couple of cracked ribs. He took the proffered glass of brandy Robert hurriedly poured him and brought it to his mouth, wincing at the sharp sting of pain the brandy caused to his cut lip.

"I thought I told you to stay away from him," Robert said.

"He came looking for me."

"What the hell for?"

"To avenge his sister's honour."

Robert lifted his eyes skyward. "I thought you'd have had

more restraint than that."

"Oh, come on, Robert. We both know why you tried to force me into close contact with Miss Ellerton. You wanted me to break my oath."

"Damn it man, I thought she'd be safe with you because of your stupid self-imposed oath."

"It wasn't celibacy I swore to."

"Well, maybe it should have been."

They stared at each other across the expanse of Robert's desk before Nathan lowered himself gingerly into a chair. "What was I supposed to do? You're the one who forced us together. I told you I didn't want that assignment and then you order me to get her out of the cottage. It was late evening by then. I didn't know if we were going to have someone pursuing us. I had to find somewhere safe to hide her."

Robert dropped into his chair and shook his head. "I thought the one person who'd be able to keep his hands off her would be you, especially with her connection to George. What on earth possessed you?"

Nathan lifted his gaze to Robert. The man was so astute when it came to political intrigue, but when it came to romantic matters, he didn't have a clue.

"Oh dear God," Robert said. "You're in love with her."

Very well, he did have a clue when it came to romance. Nathan shifted uncomfortably in his chair. "Not that it matters anyway. We both knew there was no future in it."

"Yet you still took advantage!" His voice was harsh and held a wealth of disappointment.

"It was mutual." Nathan felt like a school child trying to justify himself to his headmaster.

"You're not the one whose reputation was at stake."

"Yes, I get your point," Nathan bit back. Being reprimanded by his superior, who he admired beyond measure was almost as painful as the beating George had given him.

"Well, at least now your oath is immaterial. You're going to have to marry Miss Ellerton and start living the life you have been so diligently protecting."

"No, I'm not." Nathan grimaced as he shifted in his chair, trying to find a more comfortable position.

"But George will insist."

"Actually, he insisted the complete opposite."

Robert stared at him. "You ruined his sister and he demanded that you not marry her?"

"Yes, he'd rather have a tainted sister than taint his family's bloodline. Now if you've quite finished upbraiding me, maybe you will tell me why you summoned me."

* * *

Emily hurried along the streets, feeling conspicuous without an escort or chaperone. She should go back and get her maid, but she could not face George until she found out Nathan's true feelings for her. Instead, she tugged her bonnet more tightly around her face, put her head down, and forged onward.

She weaved between pedestrians, around courting couples taking a leisurely stroll, past hawkers and street sellers, ignoring the unsavoury comments shouted by the tradesmen. Hurrying past them, she appreciated the reason for having a companion to accompany a young lady when she was out and about. It definitely was not wise for her to be wandering the

London streets alone.

As she passed the entrance to a circulating library, a hand shot out, grabbed her around the waist, and pulled her into the shaded doorway.

* * *

Robert picked up a decanter and poured himself a dash of brandy, which he knocked back before he returned his attention to Nathan. "I've received an account of transactions from our man of affairs in France. A sizeable sum of money has been withdrawn. It isn't for anything I have authorised." He eyed Nathan with speculation.

"You think it was me?" Nathan leaned forwards in his chair and gasped in pain.

"No. I know it wasn't."

Puzzled by his remark, Nathan asked, "When were the funds withdrawn?"

"Six days ago."

Nathan drew his brows together. He'd been back in England then, breaking the news of Peter's death to Emily. "Then who withdrew the funds?"

"According to this report," Robert said, lifting the letter up, "Peter did."

"Peter! But he died twelve days ago." Nathan knew this for a fact. The whole incident was imprinted on his mind and he'd been counting the days ever since.

"Not according to this report." He stood up and came around his desk, stopping in front of Nathan. "I'm sorry to have to ask you this, but did you actually see Peter die?" His tone was gentle, but his gaze searched his face.

Nathan pushed himself to a standing position, his anger numbing his pain, as he looked Robert straight in the eye. "Yes. I saw him die."

"Did you see his body?"

"No, he fell into the sea."

"So, you do not know for definite he is dead."

"I know what I saw," Nathan ground out.

"And so does my man of affairs." Robert gave him the letter.

Nathan stood motionless. Could his brother truly be alive? With shaking hands, he opened the letter and read the missive. It contained an account of all transactions and the code name for the withdrawer. And there in black and white was Peter's code name, Pierre Perdrix. "He must have made a mistake." There couldn't be any other explanation.

"He knows Peter, and he's a stickler for accuracy. There's no mistake."

"Peter's alive," Nathan said, rolling the words around his mouth to see how they felt. They felt good.

"So it would seem, but it does raise one more question."

Nathan dragged his gaze from the letter and looked at Robert. "What question?" But suspicion as to what Robert was implying about Peter begun to surface.

"If it was Peter who withdrew that money, then what was he intending to do with it? That amount is much too high just to allow him safe passage back to England."

"You think he had an ulterior intention?"

"That would seem the only logical conclusion."

Nathan stood there, not quite believing that a few minutes ago he'd thought his brother dead. Next, he'd experienced elation at the possibility he may be alive, and now he had to face the possibility that his own brother could be the traitor they'd all been searching for.

He almost wished for the blissful ignorance of a few hours before.

He shook his head in denial. No, there was no conceivable way his brother could be the traitor. Could there?

Nathan balled the letter in his fist. "If he is alive, where the hell is he?"

* * *

Heart in her mouth, Emily prepared to scream when her brain recognised the familiar features of Nathan.

Only it wasn't Nathan, it was Peter. Logic told her it couldn't be. Hope prayed she was wrong. With uncertainty threading her voice, Emily spluttered, "Peter, is it truly you?"

"Aye, Miss Ellerton, it is me, but you look like you've seen a ghost."

"Well, I have, in a way." Joy spread through her. Peter was alive. Her brother wasn't guilty of killing him. Maybe there was hope for her and Nathan after all.

There was a pause as he digested her words. "You thought I was dead?" His face showed his shock.

"Yes."

"But why?"

Emily looked at him. Did he not remember being shot? "Nathan said you were shot and fell into the sea."

"My God, so it's true then."

"What's true?" Emily asked.

A muscle throbbed in his jaw. "I've just spent the better part of a week in a French gaol and, according to Dubeck, it was all courtesy of my dear brother."

"No." The denial burst from her. "Nathan was devastated by your death; you should have seen the state he was in when he told your family."

"He's told my mother and sister that I'm dead!" Peter removed his hat and crushed it in his hands.

Emily took in his horrified face, his stiff shoulders and his fingers that had turned white where they gripped his flattened hat.

"My God," he said, shaking his head in disbelief. "He truly did not want me to survive prison. The coward was just not willing to kill me himself."

"No, you mustn't think that. He was distraught over your death." She had to convince Peter he was mistaken.

"Do I look dead to you?"

"No." Emily shook her head, partly in emphasis of her words, partly to clear it.

"No. Then he could not have seen me die. What he told you and my family was a lie."

Emily's insides sank. How could Nathan have lied to his own mother about the death of her youngest son? The enormity of that deceit was despicable beyond words. Had he done it merely to keep up the facade he'd presented to her or did he really intend for Peter to rot in some prison cell and decided as he wasn't coming back, he may as well tell his family he was dead? It was incomprehensible. But then that meant the rest was an act too – his fortitude in not harming George became easy as he knew George had not killed Peter as he wasn't dead.

Oh God, she'd given herself to him, for keeping his promise to her to not harm her brother, but now it would seem to have been such an easy promise for him. Nausea overwhelmed her. The noises around her became muffled, the world tilted, and the last thing she remembered was Peter catching her.

Chapter Thirty-Two

In Lord Brakenhale's office, the seconds ticked by, heralded by the tick-tock of the walnut clock on the desk.

"You should go home and get your injuries seen to."

"And what am I to say to my mother about Peter?" Nathan stood, his left hand clutching his ribs while his other hand supported his weight against Robert's desk.

"Say nothing till we know for sure."

"Say nothing! I'm supposed to be writing his obituary and arranging his funeral. How can I stop doing that without telling my mother why?" He sank onto the chair and pressed the hand holding the crumpled letter against his forehead.

"I'll arrange for my carriage to take you home. Once there, I suggest you get treated and then rest. Once you've had time to digest everything, you can decide what to tell your family, but first you need to sort yourself out."

Nathan nodded, then wished he hadn't as his head pounded with the combined beating from George and the staggering news about Peter.

Robert was right, he needed to go home.

* * *

Bright candlelight burned the backs of Emily's closed eyelids. Opening them, she blinked against the harsh light to find herself lying on a daybed in a strange apartment.

She sat up, pushing a strand of loose hair from her face. She was alone. In the fireplace, a fire had been recently lit and crackled quietly. The dark panelled room had few paintings or ornaments. This was a very masculine room. She should not be here.

Hearing a door creak open, she twisted around. Peter entered, scrutinising the small bottle he held. "Ah, Miss Ellerton, you're awake. You gave me quite a fright."

"Where am I?" She pushed herself up into a sitting position.

"In a friend's apartment. As he's not here, I've been trying to locate some smelling salts. I'm not sure what this bottle is supposed to hold." He put it on the table. "If only I had that bottle of perfume you made me smell in the perfume shop, then that would have roused you in a heartbeat."

Emily gave a slight smile at his quip. "I would rather stand next to the Thames in high summer."

"Yes, that would definitely be the better choice."

His teasing words restored her composure, but she needed to return home to the sanctuary of her room, where she could gather her thoughts about Nathan. "Well, I'm recovered now, so there's no need. If you would escort me home, I would be very much obliged."

"You're much too pale to go anywhere. Plus, I've sent the maid to make some tea and she will be back soon. Once you've had a fortifying cup, maybe then I will think about taking you home. For now, you've got to put up with my company, I'm afraid."

Emily bit her lip as she considered her situation. She shouldn't stay here, but she didn't want to risk walking back home alone and one cup of tea wouldn't be an imposition, surely? She nodded, and Peter sat next to her.

They sat in silence listening to the snap and crackle of the fire, as questions ran around in her mind, making her unable to put a coherent sentence together.

The entrance of the maid gave a welcome distraction, and she set about pouring the tea. Peter, however, made a point of adding an extra lump of sugar to her cup. "For the shock. I don't want you fainting again."

"Nor I." Emily stirred her tea to ensure the sugar fully dissolved. She eyed Peter with curiosity. "Can I ask what happened that day in Jersey?"

He tapped his fingers on his knees. "There was a dense fog. I remember a gunshot, but I was not hit. Instead, someone pulled me backwards, next there was a blinding pain and I don't remember anything until I woke up in a French gaol." He gazed into the distance as he spoke, a crease deepening his brow.

"Well, there you go." Emily twisted to face Peter. "That matches what Nathan saw or thought he saw. He heard the gunshot and saw you go over the cliff. When he couldn't find you, he assumed you'd fallen into the sea."

"It was low tide; there was no sea for me to fall into."

"You must be mistaken. Nathan would never harm you or anyone."

"You think not."

"I know it," she said.

"Do you want to know what he said about you when Lord Brakenhale ordered him to watch you?"

"I'm not sure that I do." Emily lifted her teacup, using the action as an excuse to look away from him.

"He said the only thing you were good for was a quick toss in the hay."

His words, so close to the truth, caused Emily's jaw to drop. The tea missed her mouth and ended up in her lap. Jumping up, she pulled a handkerchief out of her pocket and began drying her dress.

"I'm so sorry Miss Ellerton, I did not realise." He lifted his hands in apology.

Mortified that her reaction had given away the humiliating truth of what she had given to Nathan after his falsehood, she tried to deny his assumption with a dismissive wave of her hand, but she failed.

"It seems it is not just me who has suffered as a result of Nathan's lies." He indicated for Emily to sit again.

Swallowing her embarrassment, she retook her seat. "I don't understand why you believe Nathan lied." She needed to get her head around Peter's and Nathan's conflicting stories. Peter was not the same driven, determined man she'd known before. He looked deflated and his voice was despondent.

He heaved a deep sigh. "The only reason I am here now, still alive even, is because Dubeck broke me out of prison. At first I was ready to drag him back to England to face trial, but then he showed me the documents George had given him to safeguard."

"You've seen the documents?"

"Yes."

"Where are they now?" Emily asked, putting her cup and

saucer on the table.

"In my possession, but I will not say where."

"But this is wonderful news; I must inform George at once."

"You mean you can get a note to him?"

"Yes," Emily said, smiling.

"So you know where he has been hiding all this time?" Peter gave an admonishing shake of his head.

"He's not in hiding anymore," Emily said with a pointed raise of her brows, but she didn't deny knowing where he'd been.

"He's not? What caused him to come out of hiding?"

"A letter, a false letter to be exact, which requested a rendezvous with Lord Brakenhale. It led everyone to him. Then Robert interviewed him and released him without charge. Well, except for dismissing him from the diplomatic service by request from Nathan."

"Ah, another that has paid the price for Nathan's lies. We have to stop this."

Emily decided that until Nathan was advised of the situation and had a chance to explain himself that it was not worth arguing further with Peter on this point. Instead, she did what she usually did with most men and agreed to go along with them until matters could be sorted out properly. "Very well, how?"

"I think you should ask George to join you here. That way, he can escort you home. It would be best if you were seen leaving here with him rather than me."

"Yes, indeed. Where does your friend keep his writing materials?"

"Let me find out." Peter rose and headed to a small bureau. He brought the items over to her and she wrote a quick note.

"I'll have the maid arrange for someone to take it," he said, pulling the bell pull.

Chapter Thirty-Three

A dejected George climbed the steps of his uncle's town house. His visit to Edward Clarrington had proven fruitless.

They'd gone over everything, but still nothing made sense. It didn't help that George couldn't concentrate after his unsavoury confrontation with Emily. He'd had to make her see Lord Thornburn was not worth her tears, for if she knew the whole truth, it would break her heart. That was the one thing he was trying to protect her from, but he had not wanted to upset her to the extent he had. He needed to make it up to her, but he didn't have a clue as to how.

He walked into the morning room to find it empty. His aunt had returned to her bed, but he'd expected to find a worried Emily waiting for him. It worried him now that she was not here.

He checked her room, but there was no sign of her.

He rang for the butler and was about to interrogate him when the butler handed him a note in Emily's elegant handwriting, saying it had been delivered a few minutes ago. His heart beat stuttered as he took the note, terrified about what he would find.

The note read:-

George, I have startling news. Meet me at the above address.

Emily.

"Oh God, what has she got herself into now?" He swung on his heel and headed back out of the house.

Ten minutes later, he found the address and, barging past the maid, took the stairs two at a time. He burst into the parlour to find Emily and Peter sitting together on the settee.

"Get your damned filthy hands away from my sister."

* * *

Refusing the assistance of the butler, Nathan grunted with pain as he climbed the stairs to his room. Ordering a bath to be drawn, he headed to the mirror.

He had a swollen left eye, a bloody cut across his nose, and a split lip. His teeth felt tender but none were loose, for that he was thankful.

He dipped a cloth into the washbasin and began cleaning his face. Wincing with pain, he stopped, poured himself a liberal slug of whisky, and sipped it through one side of his mouth as he finished wiping his face.

His valet arrived and was assisting him out of his coat when the butler knocked on the door.

"What is it?" Nathan winced as his lips screamed in protest at his sharp words.

"It's the street urchin, my lord."

Nathan shook his head. Now what? "Send him in."

"Cor, Gov'ner, that's a blinder you got there," the lad said, as he sauntered into the room.

"Just tell me why you are here."

"Mr Ellerton give me a letter to take to Lord Brakenhale and I remembers how you said to bring you anything sent from the house first."

That wasn't quite what Nathan had ordered, and he suspected his diligence in bringing the letter here had more to do with receiving an extra coin for his trouble. He held his hand out, and the boy handed him the letter.

"This is open."

"Yes Sir. That is how it was when he give it me. He said as to take it to Lord Brakenhale with all haste."

Nathan looked at the front; it was addressed to George and written in an elegant hand. He turned it over and read the brief message, his heart lodging in his throat. The startling news was obviously Peter's resurrection, which was confirmed by the address — a bachelor apartment belonging to a good friend of Peter's. Any doubts he'd had about his brother's complicity were wiped out completely.

His brother was a traitor. His stomach churned at the horrific realisation. But he couldn't dwell on the implications. Emily and George were in danger. He had to get there.

He shoved the letter back at the urchin. "Take this letter straight to Lord Brakenhale. No detours this time. Take his carriage. It's still outside."

"Yes, my lord," the boy said, as he turned on his tail and raced out of the house.

Nathan turned back to his valet. "My coat," he said, as he

hurried to pull it back on, ignoring the scream of pain through his body. His pain was the last of his worries.

* * *

Peter stood, holding his hands up in a gesture of innocence. "We were only having tea. She fainted when she saw me, so I brought her here to recuperate. There's nothing untoward going on."

"No, indeed, George," Emily said, coming to her feet. "He has the documents you gave to Dubeck."

"Does he have them here?"

"No, he's put them somewhere safe and will take you to them after you have returned me home."

"Well, that's good of him. After all, he wouldn't want you or anyone else to witness him murdering me and the destruction of the documents that convict him, now would he?"

"What are you talking about?" Emily said. "The documents prove your innocence."

"Well, they would do as it was Peter's complicity I discovered, only I didn't realise it at the time."

"No, you must be mistaken." Emily shook her head. None of this made any sense.

George took a step towards Peter. "This is not the first time you've tried to lure me out into the open with a letter, is it?"

"I don't know what you're talking about."

George gave a huff of disbelief at Peter's continued pretence of innocence. "Five days ago I received a letter with Robert's seal on it requesting a rendezvous, only it wasn't from Robert.

Someone had faked his seal, someone who trained at the Bureau Noir, someone like you."

"I've only just got back from France, having been liberated from the gaol you put me in." His angry words reverberated around the room.

"Don't talk daft," George said, shaking his head.

"You were in Jersey when I was knocked unconscious."

"I'll not deny I was there, but I was searching for Dubeck and the letters I'd given him."

"He says different."

"I doubt that." George took another a step closer to Peter.

Peter sidled around the red striped settee, putting more distance between them. Bracing his hands on the back of the settee as he leaned towards George. "Strange that you're not surprised by my being alive, just angry. So, my dear friend, what is it about my appearance that angers you so much?"

"Your damn lies."

"Mind your language, we have a lady present," Peter snapped back.

"You keep her out of this."

"Afraid she'll hear the truth about you."

"You have no idea what truth is," George said, his eyes forming tight slits.

"You think not? How about I tell your sister what Dubeck told me?"

"Oh please do, I could do with a good fairy tale."

Peter's jaw hardened. He turned a face full of pleading to Emily. "Dubeck told me how he intercepted a letter from one of the French diplomats to George." He looked at George, with hatred flaring in his eyes. "How you ran off into hiding when he confronted you with your cowardly tail between your spindly legs."

"No," Emily said, moving around the settee. "You must be mistaken. You said the letters exonerated George."

"There's no mistake. George went to Jersey to dispose of Dubeck before Nathan and I could find him. I was getting too close, so he attacked me and deposited me in gaol," Peter said to Emily before swinging back to George.

"But this doesn't make any sense," Emily said. "George gave the documents to Dubeck to take to Robert. That's why he had to stay in hiding so he could protect Dubeck's identity and he only came out of hiding when he found out you had discovered Dubeck's whereabouts."

"Oh, how convenient. I'm surprised you could keep your face straight while you told her that lie," Peter said.

Emily scrunched her brow. George had been terrified when she'd visited him, but his fear had not been for himself but for the safety of his colleague. That much she knew was true. "He told me the truth," Emily said, staring at Peter.

"Finally catching on," George said.

Peter returned Emily's look, but pointed at George. "If that's true, then ask him why he's not surprised that I'm still alive."

"Oh, that's easy to answer," George said. "Because with you dead, nothing made sense. But now everything has become clear. Only you weren't working alone, were you?"

"What do you mean?" Emily asked as her skin prickled with foreboding.

George let out a self-depreciating laugh. "I don't know why I didn't see it before. They hit on the perfect ruse. Make out that Peter had been killed, most probably by me and whilst everyone is feeling sorry for Nathan, he gets to utilise the situation to his advantage."

"No, you're wrong," Emily cried, her heart screaming the denial along with her voice. Nathan could not have feigned his anguish.

"Oh, you think so?" George said, giving her a look that clearly said she was only fooling herself. "By using Peter's death, he convinced Robert to sack me, so I could no longer investigate what happened and expose him. Using Peter's death, he deflected any doubt about himself. And finally, by using Peter's death, he convinced you to lead him to me, then persuaded you into believing that you both loved each other and that due to the situation of Peter's death and my involvement that there could never be a future for you and that the only thing you could ever have is one night together."

"No, it wasn't like that," Emily said, beseeching George to believe her, regardless of what else he may believe Nathan of right now, she could not let him believe that. Her gaze roved over him, trying to find something that would convince him of the truth about Nathan. Her eyes riveted on his swollen hand.

"Your hand is bruised." She stared at the purple circles forming around his knuckles. A horrifying suspicion pierced her.

"Courtesy of Nathan and his full admission of guilt regarding the night he seduced you," George said, lifting his hands up as though his bruises were evidence of Nathan's guilt.

"But there's not a mark on you." Emily took in his unblemished face, but the bruises on his hand told another story. Oh God, what had he done to Nathan?

"Like I said, he admitted his guilt in full. Although I didn't realise how much he had to confess to."

Her stomach tightened as the truth hit her with fearful clarity. "You mean he didn't raise his hand against you; even to defend himself."

"Because he knew he had no defence. Good grief, Emily. You were just another conquest. He even kept this as a souvenir," George said, reaching inside his coat and pulling out a small scrap of material. He dangled it in front of her.

Emily drew her eyebrows together in confusion at the unfamiliar material. What was it? Her heart slammed into her ribs. He held her ribbon, but it was no longer blue but red.

Blood red.

Nathan's blood.

Emily paled at the sight before the full meaning hit her and she leaned her head back, blinking the prickling of tears away. Nathan had kept his promise to her, even whilst George was beating him, he'd still kept his promise to her to not harm her brother.

A sharp movement from her left caught her attention. Peter, having mistaken George's movement as him reaching for his gun, now stood with his own gun pointing at George.

George didn't miss a beat as instinct took over and in one swift movement, he drew his gun on Peter. The sudden movement causing him to wince as pain streaked along his shoulder.

Peter's eyes formed slits of satisfaction at his display of pain.

"Why didn't I see it before?" George said, shaking his head at his own short-sightedness. "There's only one person who could have shot me as I left Dubeck in France, whilst Nathan and Simon chased after me, so that left you."

Emily swung to face Peter. "You shot George!"

"Not me. But I'm more than happy to rectify that."

"Just try it," George said, holding the bloodstained ribbon clasped tight in his right hand that now pressed against the trigger of his gun.

Emily stared at the ribbon. She remembered the day she'd tied it around Nathan's wrist and the solemn promise he'd kept to her, even with the deepest of suspicion and the greatest of provocation. How even when her brother had thrashed him, he'd kept his promise to her and had not raised a hand against George, even to protect himself.

She looked from George to Peter, stood guns raised against each other and knew after all of Nathan's restraint against her brother she could not let George harm Nathan's brother now. She had to protect him. Seeing George's finger tighten around the trigger; she only had one choice.

* * *

Pushing past the maid, Nathan hauled himself up the stairs, grasping the wooden banister like a lifeline and racing as fast as his battered body would allow him.

Raised voices from the room above echoed down to him.

'Because he knew he had no defence. Good grief Emily. You were just another conquest. He even kept this as a souvenir.' Oh God, that was George trying to convince Emily he didn't love her. Please don't let her believe him.

But he didn't have time to dwell on George's words as his next brought a chill to his heart.

'Why didn't I see it before? There's only one person who could have shot me as I left Dubeck in France, whilst Nathan and Simon chased after me, so that left you.'

'You shot George!' Emily's incredulity echoed his own. Could

his brother truly have tried to kill George? Breathing hard and clutching his ribs, he reached the top of the stairs. Beyond the open doorway, George stood, his gun pointing across the room.

He heard Peter's denial, *'Not me, but I'm more than happy to rectify that,'* and he let out a ragged thankful breath that was short-lived as George replied, *'Just try it.'*

"No," Emily screamed and in that heart-stopping moment Nathan knew what she was about to do and there was only one way he could save her.

Dragging all his reserves of strength together, he lunged at George.

Chapter Thirty-Four

Two loud bangs rang across the room and the whistle of a bullet hissed over Nathan as he and George hit the floor.

But those were not the sounds Nathan would remember for the rest of his days. No, that accolade would go to the high-pitched yelp of pain Emily expelled as the bullet hit her.

Scrambling up from the floor, he raced to her side. Peter was kneeling over her. Nathan grabbed him by his collar and shoved him into the bedroom, where he took the key and locked the door. "I'll deal with you later; I dare not deal with you right now," he growled.

He returned to Emily and cradled her against his chest as he examined her; she'd been hit in her upper arm. He breathed a thankful sigh as the bullet had passed clean through; all she would need were stitches.

She lifted her head, looked at the blood pouring out of her arm, muttered, "Oh my," and fainted dead away.

George drew up by his side. "Get away from her."

"Now is not the time, George. She needs help."

"She's shot. But how?" He knelt beside Nathan, his worry

for his sister washing all other thoughts away.

"She jumped in front of your bullet."

"Why would she do that?"

"She was returning my promise to her."

"What bloody promise?" George demanded.

"That I not harm her brother." Nathan took in George's look of dawning understanding.

"Is that why you did not shoot me in the alley?" George said, his brows drawing together in disbelief.

"Yes, and why I did not lift a finger against you earlier."

"You bloody fool. I mistook your restraint as an admission of guilt."

"Well, that too, in regards to your sister, at least."

"So she jumped in front of Peter to protect him, even though he is the traitor?"

"Yes," Nathan said, gently brushing a lock of Emily's hair from her pale cheek.

"And all because of a promise you made to her?"

"You know how loyal and honourable she is." Nathan smiled at her, pride and admiration swelling his chest at the knowledge he had gained her trust and faith in him.

"Yes, and damn stubborn," George said.

Nathan lifted Emily up, the adrenalin coursing through his body dulling his physical pain as he placed her on the daybed. "Find the maid and see if she has needle and thread and something to clean her wound with."

George called the maid, who produced a bottle of whisky and went off to get a sewing basket. He passed the whisky to Nathan, who held the bottle against Emily's lips and made her take a long swig.

She sat up, coughing and spluttering. Nathan made her take

another sip, ignoring her attempts to shove the bottle away. "You are going to need this, believe me."

"Yes, just like I did when you helped Aunt Amelia stitch up my wound," George said.

Nathan gave George and Emily a peeved look. "I had convinced myself she knew nothing about your whereabouts, at least to begin with." He poured a liberal shot of whisky over Emily's injury, her hiss of pain slicing through him.

George patted him on the shoulder. "Sorry, old boy, but that's my Emily. Loyal and protective, just like you said yourself."

"I was trying to forget her trespasses."

Emily lifted herself up. "But I had to do it," she said, waving her uninjured arm around.

"Never could hold her drink," George said.

"That's probably for the best." Nathan picked up the thread and held it to the eye of the needle.

"To protect those that deserve protecting," Emily proclaimed in a stage whisper.

"He didn't deserve it," Nathan said, indicating the room he'd locked Peter in.

"But he's your brother. I had to protect him," Emily rasped. "For you."

Nathan forgot the needle and thread and looked straight at Emily. Deep in the pale jade centre of her eyes, the truth shone. She'd protected Peter not just because of the promise he'd made to her, but because she wanted to protect him from hurt. His heart constricted at the depth of her feelings and compassion for him. He did not merit her good opinion, or anyone's good opinion, not after his deadly mistakes of the past. Feeling humbled and unworthy, he glanced away. "Hush now. We need you to be still."

George took up the needle and thread dropped by Nathan and, with trembling hands, tried to pierce Emily's skin. "Ow."

"What's wrong?" Nathan asked.

"I cannot push the needle through."

"Does your hand hurt too much from punching me?"

"Yes," George spat back. "And you deserved every punch."

"I couldn't agree more, but right now, we need to stitch Emily's arm. Here, give me the needle."

George clenched his jaw as he debated his choice. He thrust the needle at Nathan. "Try not to hurt her."

"That's all I've ever tried to do."

George was quiet for a moment before he half glanced away. "Well, you have a damned poor way of showing it."

"Can't argue with you on that score," Nathan said, taking the needle. He took a deep breath to steady his hands and pushed it through Emily's skin with as much care and precision as he could manage.

Emily reared up in pain and George pressed her back onto the settee. "Keep still. This won't take long."

Through tightly clenched teeth, she said, "My aunt told me that stitching someone whom you care about is difficult. She forgot to mention how painful it is for the person being stitched up."

"Well, that's because she's never been stupid enough to get herself shot, so she wouldn't know," George said pointedly.

"Oh George, I'm in enough pain as it is without a reprimand from you," she said, sucking in air through her tight lips.

"I'm sorry. Not long now, I promise."

Nathan drew the thread through one more time. "All done."

George stood up. "You'll understand that I never want to

see you anywhere near my sister again."

Nathan nodded, his throat too dry to speak. He pointed to the bedroom to indicate that he wanted to talk to Peter.

"We'll wait," George said. "Lord Brakenhale should be here soon."

Nathan unlocked the door and handed George the key to lock the door behind him.

"Get up," Nathan snarled at Peter, who was sitting on the edge of the bed, his head in his hands.

"How is Miss Ellerton?"

"You're not worthy of speaking her name," Nathan said, pacing the room in front of him.

"I'm sorry, I'm sorry. I never thought she would do something like that."

Nathan let out a disbelieving huff. "Then you truly don't know her. If you'd have had an ounce of her loyalty, you'd have known exactly what she would do."

"How can you say that of me?" He gave his brother a pleading look.

"You really want me to answer that?"

He gripped the edge of the bed. "Please tell me she will recover."

"She'll live. Which is more than I can say for you."

"But I've done nothing wrong."

"You deny your actions even now?" Nathan seethed. Emily had come close to getting killed all because of his despicable, traitorous brother.

"I have nothing to admit to," Peter said.

Nathan grabbed Peter by the lapels of his coat and shoved him against the wall, ignoring the searing pain streaking through his ribs.

"I ought to strangle you with my bare hands." He held back only in deference to the sacrifice Emily had made to save Peter's skin, and all for his sake. It would be an insult to her if he killed him now, regardless of how much he wanted to.

Peter tried to pry Nathan's hands from his collar, but his grip was too strong. "You wouldn't kill me; think what it would do to mother and Dorothy."

"Oh, we've already mourned you and a lot more that you deserved," Nathan said, letting go of him, unable to bear to touch him. He picked up a blue ceramic wash bowl and smashed it against the wall before swinging back to face Peter. "Your fate will be decided by a court of law. Though it grieves me to think that Emily harmed herself trying to protect your worthless hide. Come tomorrow morning, you will be swinging from the yardarm."

"No! I'm no traitor."

"Give it up Peter; Robert's man of affairs reported that you withdrew a large sum of unauthorised funds."

"I didn't."

"Not only have you betrayed your king and country, you've embezzled funds from our mission."

"But I've not been anywhere near him," Peter said, shaking his head.

"I have a letter from him that says different, so don't deny it."

"It wouldn't do me any good if I did. You've already convicted me."

"You convicted yourself the day you betrayed us."

"And you've let a woman fool you again. You're so besotted you cannot see the truth."

Nathan's jaw clenched. "Don't you dare accuse me of that!"

"Why not? It's true."

"She risked her life to protect you and now you try to use her as an scape-goat." Nathan stared at his brother with incredulity.

"You're the one who's completely blinded, so much so you'll watch me swing from the gallows and all for some light skirt with sultry green eyes."

Nathan thumped him, hitting him squarely on his cheekbone. He stood over his brother's slumped form, breathing heavily, a deep sense of satisfaction coursing through him. "Tell it to Lord Brakenhale. I believe he has arrived." He stepped over him and knocked on the door and, once through, he locked it behind him.

He greeted Lord Brakenhale, who was accompanied by Edward Clarrington and Simon Pykett.

"My God. What has happened?" Robert said as he saw Emily's bandaged arm. "Is Miss Ellerton hurt?"

George stood up. "She's been shot, but it's not serious. I need to get her home, though."

"Of course, take Edward's coach," Robert said. "Edward will assist you both."

"By all means." Edward walked forwards and helped George to assist Emily up.

"Myself and Simon will take Peter into custody. As for you, Nathan, I want you to go home. You still need to get yourself seen to."

"But —"

"I said go home. Leave Peter to me. I'll not decide his fate until we've spoken tomorrow. For now, get some rest. You look as though you need it," Robert said.

Nathan gave one last glance towards the room he'd locked

Peter in, then looked at Emily being carried down the stairs by George. He couldn't help her at present, but he needed to talk to her, to tell her — to tell her what? That risking her life to save his brother was still not worthy of a marriage proposal from him. He shook his head. George was right, he was a bastard, and he didn't deserve to be anywhere near her.

And as for Peter, the last thing he needed was to be anywhere near him, either. With a curt nod to Robert, he turned and left.

* * *

Emily laid nestled against her brother in the carriage, with a concerned Edward opposite her. Her head pounded, and the rocking of the carriage only added to her disorientation. She tentatively touched her arm, the pain slicing through her befuddlement.

Snippets of the recent events swam through her mind. A picture of Nathan's face; full of fear and affection for her. The tenderness of his ministrations as he stitched her arm. George's words to Nathan. '*I never want to see you anywhere near my sister again.*'

No! She couldn't let that happen. She tried to push herself up, but dizziness overwhelmed her. She'd wanted to know if Nathan loved her. After his actions and behaviour when he was treating her, she had her answer. She had to see him again, but for now, she needed to rest. Closing her eyes, she tried valiantly to keep the picture of his beloved face in her mind.

Chapter Thirty-Five

Pain throbbed through Nathan with renewed vigour now the adrenalin from the turmoil was receding.

He climbed the stairs of his London town house, intending to head straight to his room, but his mother came into the hall and caught him.

"Oh my goodness, what happened to you?" She ran gentle fingers along his bruised cheek and winced at the cut on his lip.

He shook his head. "Not now, mother. I'm in no mood for questions."

His mother glanced at a house maid making her way across the hall and, ignoring Nathan's words, ushered him into her withdrawing room. "And I'm in no mood to be fobbed off, not after recent events. Tell me, who did this to you?" She stood before him with the regal bearing of a queen whom one does not ignore.

Nathan released a heavy sigh. "George Ellerton."

"But how? I thought he'd been arrested."

"Lord Brakenhale has released him as he's not the traitor," Nathan said with a shake of his head.

"I do not understand. What about Peter's murder?"

"George did not kill Peter."

His mother's gaze flew to him and in the depths of her grey eyes, he saw hope and uncertainty. He released a shattered breath. He owed her the truth, regardless of how much it would hurt her.

Taking his mother's hands in his, he sat on the settee and pulled his mother to sit down next to him and said simply, "Peter is not dead."

"Thank God," his mother said, her hand flying to her chest.

"Do not thank Him yet," Nathan said in a quiet voice.

"What are you saying?"

He dropped her hands and, standing up, walked around the settee, rubbing his aching ribs before he turned to face her. "Peter is the traitor."

His mother rose to her feet, shaking her head. "No, you must be mistaken."

"Believe me. I wish it were so." His own brother; a traitor. How could this have happened?

"It's not possible," she said, her voice shaking. "Where is he now?"

"In Lord Brakenhale's custody."

"Then we must go and see him."

Nathan hesitated. It would do no good, but he could not deny his mother the chance to try. "You can visit him tomorrow, after I have spoken to Lord Brakenhale."

"Very well." She stared at the fire before lifting her speculative grey gaze to him. "So George Ellerton is innocent. That is good, is it not?"

"Good? What is there of good?" The events of the last few hours must be addling his mind, for he could find no good in any of this.

"Because now you can repair Miss Ellerton's reputation."

Nathan twisted away, balling his hands into fists. If only it was that simple. "I'm not worthy of her."

"How can you say that?"

"She risked her life to protect Peter, knowing he was the traitor to spare me further pain."

"She did that for you?"

Nathan released a bitter laugh. "Yes, because of me, she put herself in harm's way."

"Then now is your chance to protect her and repair her reputation in return."

"Do you not see? Even her own brother has forbidden me from marrying her as he knows how unworthy I am." He touched his cut lip. George had made his sentiments very clear.

"It is not his reputation that has been ruined. His reticence must be obstinate male pride instead of brotherly care, so pay it no heed."

Nathan let out a sharp breath and pinned his mother with a pained look. "Even if I were to ignore him, it would make no difference — you know my vow. I'll not betray those whose memory I have sworn to honour."

"You betray them by using those you claim to respect as an excuse not to remedy the ruined reputation of a young lady who loves you?" she said with equal determination. "You make me ashamed of you. More so than Peter at present."

"How can you say that?" Her love and unshakable faith in him had kept him going all these years. She had given him the strength to continue when his guilt for the lives he had cost had overwhelmed him. She had shown him that he could still do something worthwhile. He couldn't bear it if she disowned him.

"Forsaking marriage in memory of those whose lost lives you feel responsible for is honourable." She walked over to him and placed her hand on his bruised cheek. "But to refuse to repair a young lady's reputation that you have ruined because of your oath is a dishonour to those whose memory you claim to protect."

"You know my vow has nothing to do with marriage but with everything that comes with it. I cannot allow myself those things, not after what I did." Nathan yanked his cuff and noticed the missing ribbon. He was bereft without its reassuring presence and reminder of Emily's faith in him.

"Then find a way to put things right for Miss Ellerton and keep your vow in other ways."

Nathan slumped against the windowsill, his shoulders shuddering as he breathed a heavy sigh. "If I marry her, it would be in name only. I cannot give her the things that should come with marriage."

"Her reputation must come first."

"It would deny her the very things she should gain by marriage. It seems a poor rescue, even by my paltry standards," he said, with self-loathing.

"Without her reputation being repaired, she will never experience those things either and it may leave her with an even worse alternative."

Nathan bowed his head. How could he reconcile what he owed to those whose deaths he'd caused with the need to repair Miss Ellerton's reputation? To repay her compassion by denying her what marriage should bring her? He threw his head back and squeezed his eyes shut. Marriage to Emily was the one thing he'd ever truly wanted, though his heart squeezed at the knowledge he did not deserve it. Now he was forced to marry her to save her reputation and in the process destroy what chance she had of a future life and family. God certainly knew how to punish him; he just wished he did not have to punish Emily into the bargain too.

Chapter Thirty-Six

"Stop fussing, George. I'm fine." Emily waved his solicitations away as she lay on a daybed in her aunt's drawing room, a shawl draped artfully over her legs and a bowl of fruit resting on a table by her side.

He ruffled her hair. "Very well. Will you manage on your own while I visit Lord Brakenhale and find out what has happened with Peter?"

"As long as you promise to tell me exactly what has happened."

He paused and let out a long breath. "Very well, but I suspect it may not be good news."

"I understand," she said, giving a sad nod.

He gave her a peck on her cheek and left her in his aunt's care.

Emily dropped her gaze from her aunt and stared at her closed hand. Her mind reeled with the enormity of recent events. George had proven his innocence, but for Nathan, discovering his brother was the traitor must be past bearing. It was difficult enough for him when he'd thought his beloved brother had died, but to know he was alive and had betrayed him and everything he believed in must be excruciating.

The butler entered and announced Lord Thornburn wished to visit her. Emily glanced at her aunt. "I assumed George had kept the ban against Lord Thornburn."

"He did," her aunt said with an innocent smile. "I told the butler to disregard it if George was not here."

"Oh." Emily was not sure if she was ready to talk to Nathan, and she certainly did not want him to see her reclining on the daybed as though she were an invalid. Hearing his confident footsteps nearing, she threw the shawl aside as she prepared to stand.

"Please do not get up. I would not wish to disturb your recovery," he said, bowing to her and her aunt.

Emily hesitated, uncertain how to react. They had experienced and shared so much. Most of it in the last few days. She indicated the chair opposite her and waited while he seated himself with deliberate care. How much that was to do with the situation and how much to do with the pummelling her brother had given him she did not know. She gave him a tumultuous smile by way of apology for his current discomfiture.

Her aunt stood up. "If you'll excuse me a moment, I have something important I must attend to."

He stood and bowed as she left, then with a grunt of pain which he tried to hide, he sat down again. His concerned gaze returned to Emily and her skin prickled as he searched her face before flicking to her bandaged arm and then to the bowl of fruit. His brow puckered as he looked at it.

"I remember saying to you how every family tree had one bad apple." He indicated the fruit with a wry smile.

Emily was transported back to the green salon, standing before him in angry defiance, defending her family from him.

Her cheeks flared in embarrassment at her words. She'd never intended for them to cause him pain, just to show her support for her brother. How he must feel the contradictory position they were now in.

"My words have certainly come back to haunt me." He lifted his slate grey gaze to her. It held no malice toward her for her actions that day. "You and your defence of your family have proven to be true, whilst it was my own brother who was the bad apple, growing up beside me, and I never suspected a thing."

"Don't blame yourself for your brother's failings." She hated the self-recrimination he was heaping on himself. "Your mother certainly would not allow you to."

"No, she would tell me I had to stand on my own merits and not be brought down by the actions of others."

"Your mother is a very wise woman."

He nodded. "She is indeed. But I did not come here to talk about Peter. I came to see how you are faring?"

Emily took in his black eye and scarred lip and thought she should be asking him the same question, but she suspected his pride would prevent him from wishing to admit to being hurt. She gave him a reassuring smile. "I am well. My arm is sore, but that is to be expected."

"Have you had it seen to?"

"Yes, the doctor came earlier. He commended you on your stitches, by the way, but I will still have a scar."

"I'm truly sorry," he said, with a catch in his throat.

"Don't be. I shall just have to invent a new fashion for longer sleeves."

He half smiled at her words and her heart swelled with pleasure before being pierced by a stab of longing for what they had lost.

"An excellent solution. You will need to inform your seamstress of your requirements for your wedding dress."

Emily sat bolt upright. "My wedding dress? Is that a proposal?"

"Yes." But his cloud grey gaze slid away from her.

"Oh." Emily could not express any words. This was what she wanted. But she could not endure the life she had led with her parents and George. Waiting for their return. Especially waiting for Nathan. But he'd had his own reasons for not marrying her. She gave him a quizzical look. "What about your oath never to marry?"

He stood and walked over to the window, bracing one arm against the frame. "I have decided that under the circumstances, I owe it to you to provide you with the protection of my name."

Hope fluttered in her heart. With a choked voice, she asked. "Will you be giving up your role in the diplomatic service?"

"No, I will continue working as before. We will marry, you will stay here with my mother, and I will not be returning home thereafter."

"Oh, I see." Emily slid her legs off the daybed and stood. "In that case, I'm afraid that I have to decline your offer."

He spun around and stared at her with a flummoxed expression. "You're declining my offer? On what grounds?"

"I do not think we would suit." She shook as she raised her chin and she prayed Nathan would not notice and know how much it hurt her to say this.

"Not suit! We are way past not suiting. You could be carrying my child," he said, gesturing wildly towards her midriff. "Therefore, you do not have any choice in the matter."

"Is that so?" Now she was shaking with rage. "At your mother's house, you made it abundantly clear you could never marry me, even though I could still have been carrying your child."

"I would have ensured you and any child were well taken care of. Anyway, that was before—"

"Before what? Before I risked my life to save your brother," she said, with a huff. "If I'd known then that was all it would take to evoke a marriage proposal from you, I would have done it sooner."

"Ah, so you admit you do want to marry me."

"No more than *you* want to marry me." She gave a haughty raise of her chin and folded her arms across her chest.

"What is that supposed to mean?"

"It means I am aware that you would rather let me be ruined than forsake your oath. Whilst it never occurred to you, I would never accept a marriage proposal from you, anyway."

"And why not?"

"Because you never believed I was good enough." Not enough to give up his role, her heart whispered. Not enough to stay in England with her, so she need never suffer the way she had when her parents left her.

"How can you believe such a thing?" he said, stepping closer to her.

Emily held up her hand to stop him, her other hand she held clenched at her side.

"You know how my parents died." He flinched at her words. "And yet, this is what you offer me."

"I have forsaken my oath for you by offering you marriage."

"You are not offering me marriage, you are only offering the protection of your name and nothing more."

He had the decency to look away as he said, "That I cannot deny."

"Why will you not stay with me?" Emily hated the plaintive sound of her voice.

He twisted away from her and ran his hand through his hair. He put his head back, and for a while, he did not move.

Emily waited, her chest rising in rapid gasps, hoping he would give up the service for her, and in doing so, prove to her that he truly wanted to marry her for her sake and because he loved her.

He turned and shook his head. "I made an oath to forgo the pleasures of a family after my mistake led to the loss of my friend's family. I swore then to continue their work and I cannot give that up, not after breaking my first oath to them for you. I will not taint their memory so."

"No, but you happily tainted my reputation, knowing full well you would do nothing to remedy it."

"With the way things were, we both knew marriage was out of the question. You understood that as well as I, and as you are also fully aware, I have broken no promise to you."

Emily looked down at her clenched fist, clamping her trembling lip between her teeth. He was a man of his word, once given he would not break it; she had the strength of his convictions to thank for his restraint against George. How could she force him to break his long-held oath to those that had lost their lives when she owed him her gratitude for sparing George's life and against such extreme provocation? But she could accept nothing less and his oath prevented him from offering her anything more.

She pressed her jaw together, trying valiantly not to cry, not to hurt him more with her tears. This was worse, so much worse than when he had called to say that Peter had been killed. She'd known then that there could never be anything between them, but now that he knew Peter wasn't dead, he still intended to leave her. Marry her first and then leave her. The humiliation would be a pain beyond enduring. But she would not beg. She lifted her head and looked him straight in his steel-hardened eyes and said, "Good day to you, Lord Thornburn."

His face dropped and Emily's gut twisted at the hurt she had inflicted on him with her words, but she would not take them back. She could not accept his proposal of half a marriage, spent in the turmoil of uncertainty.

Nathan slapped his gloves against his thigh, ignoring the sharp sting, as he looked at her, standing brave and defiant before him, refusing to be bullied by him or the emotions consuming her. So reminiscent of the first time he'd met her. How he had admired her then, and that was before all the loyalty and faith she had shown in him. She was indeed a remarkable woman. But she was wrong about one thing; it was not Emily who was unworthy, it was him. It had always been him who was not worthy, ever since that fateful night, and Emily's injury was confirmation of his unworthiness.

Seeing the bandage wrapped around her arm brought back the vivid memory of how Emily had looked him in the eye after she had been shot and said her actions had been for him. Did that not prove how unworthy he was whilst proclaiming her worth? She deserved to know how much he admired her, but words would be hollow when he could not offer her what she needed.

He straightened, preparing to bow to her, but Emily put a hand against his chest to prevent him.

He understood. Oh God, how he understood. Thirty years of having good manners drummed into him warred with the need to allow Emily this one concession. She did not want his respect when he was not prepared to give up his role for her. If she could not have that, then she didn't want anything else from him. It was a sacrifice he understood.

He clenched his jaw, a muscle twitching with the strain of his restraint. He couldn't leave her without demonstrating his respect for her, and he couldn't stay if he was unwilling to forsake his oath for her. It was his mistakes of the past that had cost the lives of good, honourable people. He could not forget what he owed them, not for anything, not even for Emily. Though his heart twisted in defiance of his decision.

His eyes roved over her, memorising every curve and slant of her heart-shaped face, settling on a loose tendril of titian hair laying against her delicate cheek. Her chin raised in its stubborn jut, but he did not miss the quiver as she tried valiantly to hold on to her composure. Finally, his gaze returned to her malachite eyes shimmering with unshed tears. He'd caused this loyal, courageous young lady pain. This was why he could not stay with her.

With the bitter taste of regret burning the back of his throat, he ignored the dictates of his upbringing and, without uttering a single word, turned on his heel and left.

Emily waited until the sound of his footsteps had faded, dropped her head and opened her hand; curled in the centre lay the blood-stained ribbon.

Chapter Thirty-Seven

Emily stared at the ribbon through a blur of tears. How could Nathan keep such a difficult promise to her and then refuse to give up his role? She needed to talk to George. To understand why he had pledged such a heartfelt oath. Impatient for him to return, she slipped into the library, which her brother used as a study when he was in London. As he worked away so much, it was pointless for him to rent his own apartment.

With the fireplace empty, the curtains drawn to hide the late morning sun and no candles lit; she found the room comforting in its darkness. Sitting down, she placed her arms on the desk in front of her and rested her head on them, blinking back her tears. She would not cry.

As George strode into the room, she lifted her head up, trying to search his shadowed face. "What's happened with Peter?"

"Nothing yet. Lord Brakenhale is waiting to speak to Lord Thornburn before deciding his fate."

Emily put her head on one side. "Lord Brakenhale holds Lord Thornburn's opinion in high esteem. This is the second time he has waited for him before deciding on someone's future." Proof again of how highly he was respected. Her chest tightened; she'd made her decision, painful though it was, she had no other choice. She couldn't accept his half marriage proposal.

"True, but Lord Brakenhale always prefers to have all the facts before acting. It is the reason he is so well-respected himself."

"I see."

"Was that Lord Thornburn I saw leaving?"

Emily shielded her eyes as George pulled the curtains open. Lying to him was futile. "Yes."

He swung to face her, silhouetted against the window. "Did he make an offer of marriage to you?"

"Well yes, but—"

"I forbid you to marry him."

She stared at her brother. How could he say that after what had happened? "He ruined me, if you remember. I would have thought you would have insisted he marry me."

"There are things which make that impossible."

"You mean his oath?" Although she was uncertain that was what he meant at all.

"Yes, that and the reasons behind his oath."

"What reasons?"

George heaved a heavy sigh and ran his hand along the inside of his collar. "I should not be the one telling you this."

"Please George, I need answers. I will not rest until I know what happened in his past to make him act the way he has."

"Very well, but it is not a pleasant story."

She nodded. "I am prepared for whatever you have to tell me."

"So be it." He braced his arm against the bookshelves lining one side of his study. He stared past her as though looking into the distance. It was a moment before he continued.

Desperate for the truth, she prodded, "Go on."

He cleared his throat. "Nathan was once betrothed."

"Was betrothed?" Emily said, the full import of the past tense striking her like a blow. Nathan was too honourable not to have married her once he'd promised. There was only one conclusion she could draw. She glanced at George and saw him struggling to maintain his own composure. "Did you know her?"

"No, she died before I joined the diplomatic service."

"But you've heard mention of her."

He glanced down at his boots, nudging at the wooden plinth that ran along the bottom of the shelves. He cleared his throat, but even so, she had to strain to hear his words.

"Yes, those that knew her said she was beautiful, courageous, brave and, most importantly, loyal. Many I now work with owe their lives to her. Nathan included, along with Edward and Robert, of course. She could be trusted completely. She never let anyone down."

"What happened?"

George swallowed and took a deep breath. "Nathan met a French woman, the Comtesse de Alessandro. She had information that England required, but she was too terrified to help. She needed gentle coaxing and persuading before finally agreeing to assist. It was Nathan who succeeded in battering down her resistance."

"How did he manage that?"

"In the time-honoured fashion," he said, giving her an unflinchingly steady look.

"You mean he seduced her?"

He looked away from her, but the deep lines of his face revealed the truth. "She was one of the many women he seduced in the name of duty, was she not?" she said, remembering what George had told her before.

"Yes, but unbeknownst to everyone, she was also a French spy."

Her stomach tightened. "When did Nathan find out?"

"Several weeks later when she turned up on his doorstep, extremely upset; she could not stop crying. She told him that Fouche's men were after her. In order to protect her, Nathan gave her the address of one of our safe houses."

Emily trembled with trepidation. "What happened then?"

"Shortly afterwards, he received a tip-off about her true allegiance and he raced after her. He was too late. She'd already reached the house."

"And the Comtesse de Alessandro killed his betrothed," Emily said, the truth dawning on her with painful clarity.

"Yes, she and a group of Fouche's men she had in tow. Nathan never forgave himself for falling for the Comtesse's false tears and lies." The bitterness at what had happened vibrated through his words. "He held himself accountable for her death and that of her mother and others who were killed as well."

"But what was his betrothed doing at the safe house?"

"She ran it, along with her family."

Emily's heart constricted in sympathy for the pain Nathan must have suffered and the guilt he carried around with him. She understood the enormity of his culpability and his need to assuage his guilt through his vow. Her own demands from him were selfish and pitiful in comparison. She'd thrown his marriage proposal back in his face because it had been only half a marriage, and now she realised how much he was forsaking of his oath to offer her that much in order to remedy her ruined reputation, a reputation she'd been equally responsible for ruining. She'd expected him to give everything up for her when she was not willing to give up anything for him in return.

The night at Lady Eubank's party when she'd tricked him with her tears came back to her. Contrition gnawed at her for her deception. It must have taken a great deal for him to trust her after what had happened and all along she'd been lying to him. How could she have done that to him? She closed her eyes against an onslaught of guilt and wrapped her arms around herself, trying to imbue some sense of comfort, but there was none. What she had done was unforgivable. No wonder he could not bear to be around her anymore.

"Everyone he comes into contact with gets hurt," George said, squeezing the spine of a book between his fingers.

"He didn't hurt you, even with great provocation." His restraint against George had been admirable.

"But you cannot deny he has hurt you."

Not as much as I have hurt him. The guilt of her actions and words to him pierced her heart.

George came around his desk and stood in front of her. "This is why I cannot allow you to marry him."

Emily gnawed on her lip. She understood what her brother was saying, but he was wrong. She was the one who'd caused Nathan hurt by refusing his marriage proposal, a proposal that he had given to her in despite of his oath to those he had failed.

She owed it to him to accept his proposal and the life he offered her. It may not be the life she wanted, but it behoved her to acknowledge the sacrifice he had made to placate her.

She needed to see him, but she could not let George know what she was planning. "I had already refused him."

George sagged with relief and placed his hand on her shoulder, giving it a firm squeeze. "You did the right thing."

Emily could not bring herself to look at him. "It may take me some time to truly accept that. If you do not mind, I will return to my room."

"It's not even midday."

"I need to be alone."

George nodded. "I'll come by later to see how you are."

"No," Emily burst out. She gave him a quick smile to hide her blunder. "I would rather not be disturbed. Please make my excuses to Aunt Amelia and Uncle Charles."

"Of course." George leaned forwards and kissed her cheek.

"Thank you," Emily said, standing up and hurrying from the room.

First she had lied to Nathan with her tears and now she had thrown his marriage proposal back in his face after he'd broken his solemn oath for her. She had to make him understand that she was sorry for her lies and to convince him she was still worthy of him breaking his oath for, and there was only one honourable way for her to do that.

Chapter Thirty-Eight

Nathan was disgusted at his own asininity. Of course Emily would see straight through him to his contemptible soul and the degrading marriage offer he'd made her. What had he been thinking?

He shrugged out of his green superfine jacket. He could not attend an interview regarding Peter's future wearing the same jacket he had worn to propose to Emily in. It would be disrespectful. He pulled on a dark blue jacket instead.

Now his cuff links were wrong. He'd worn his emerald ones as they matched Emily's eyes. He switched them for onyx ones.

He'd been a fool to imagine he deserved marriage to someone as exceptional as Emily. He should have accepted the truth and not broken his own promise by offering for her. Thinking he was doing right by her when instead he was forcing her to live a life that would have destroyed her.

"My lord, you have a visitor."

"Who is it?" Nathan said, yanking his cuff as he tried to force his cufflink through.

"Miss Ellerton."

Nathan stilled. Apprehension coursed through him. Was she here to give him more bad news?

"I'll be down presently. Show her into the white drawing room."

"Very good, my lord."

Nathan looked in the mirror and frowned. What could she want? She was better off without him. Who had he been fooling to think he was worthy of marriage to her, even in name only? He did not deserve her, and she certainly did not deserve him and his half proposal.

A few minutes later, Nathan entered the drawing room to find Emily with her back to him, scrutinising a painting depicting a battle scene. He took in the graceful arch of her neck as she tilted her head to one side, a few strands of wispy titian hair escaping her coiffure. She was still wearing her cream pelisse, so she did not intend on staying long, although she had removed her gloves and bonnet, which were laying on a side table.

"Miss Ellerton. I thought you'd never want to see me again." He did not miss her wince at the use of her formal name as she turned to face him.

She took a step towards him and then stopped, her movements uncertain, so uncharacteristic of her usual fearless demeanour. It made his insides twist to see that he'd caused her to lose a part of herself, a part he'd so admired.

"I feel I may have spoken too hastily earlier," she said in a rush.

His heart thumped into his chest. Could she be saying what his heart hoped she was? Nathan gave a determined shake of his head. She didn't deserve an unworthy man like him. "No, you were perfectly correct in your reaction. It is I who should be apologising. What I offered you was an insult to you and your sensibilities."

"No Nathan, you are incapable of insulting anyone."

His chest swelled at her use of his name and her defence of him, but it did not make him worthy. "My actions towards you prove otherwise."

"I know about your betrothed," she said, her voice soft. She took a resolute step towards him.

Nathan's throat tightened. What had happened to his betrothed was a reminder of why he couldn't marry her. "Then you understand why you would be better off without me; I'm not safe to be around."

"I love you." She tilted her head up.

Nathan caught the unguarded honesty of her words in the glint of her green eyes, and he nearly stumbled to his knees. He did not deserve her love. "You mustn't. I don't deserve it." He dropped his gaze from her.

"It's too late, for I have loved you since the day you held me in Lady Eubank's garden — when I lied to you about George's whereabouts and tricked you with my tears. You cradled me in your arms and comforted me because I was worried about him, even though you desperately wanted to arrest him. You should have hated me that day, and you could have used my tears against me, but you didn't."

He'd loved her from that moment, too. Her bravery and courage, her damnable stalwart stubbornness. Her loyalty even in the face of his overwhelming prejudice. He'd known she was rare even then. A true diamond amongst women. He'd been both lost and found in that moment. "You remind me of her," he said, his voice gruff.

"Your betrothed?"

"Yes, she had your courage and loyalty. You are so similar to her in that regard."

"I'm glad. It pleases me to know her good qualities live on in me."

His chest squeezed. "Which is why I cannot marry you. I don't deserve you, and more importantly, you don't deserve the life I offered you."

She shook her head. "Losing my parents when they were so far away was the worst thing to happen to me. I thought I could not bear to live like that again. But knowing I would be making that sacrifice so you could keep your oath would be my compensation."

Nathan stared at her, unable to believe she was prepared to give into her fears so he could keep his integrity. "No, I cannot let you. I know how much your parents' deaths and their way of life hurt you. I cannot allow you to suffer that way for me."

"And I will not let you taint your reputation by leaving mine in tatters when you have condescended to remedy the fact by forsaking part of your oath for me. It would be dishonourable of me to do so and you know I could never act dishonourably."

Nathan's heart lurched in his chest. He couldn't believe she was willing to do this for him. He was aware how much it would pain her, but he could not disrespect her wishes. "Do you understand what you are agreeing to?"

"Yes. I'm agreeing to marry a man of consummate integrity and honour," she said, her face glowing with pride for him.

Oh lord, she was magnificent. "I wish I could give you the marriage you deserve."

"You are. Now hold me like you did in Lady Eubank's garden."

Nathan's lips curved up into a deep smile as he reached out

and wrapped his arms around her. He dipped his head and kissed her with all the joy and disbelief that she loved him as much as he did her.

He crushed her to him as his lips moved over hers, devouring her softness. A warm glow spreading through him.

"There is just one thing," she said, pulling out of his embrace. "George is against the marriage, so we will have to go to Scotland."

Nathan nodded. "Leave the arrangements to me. We will have to leave quite late. Lord Brakenhale has requested I appear before him at four o'clock to discuss what is to become of Peter."

He glanced at the marquetry clock on the mantel. It was twelve noon.

Chapter Thirty-Nine

Opening up her valise, Emily began packing her clothes and essentials that she would need for her journey to Scotland. She could not risk enlisting the aid of her maid and so she was only taking things her maid would not miss at first glance.

Hearing a knock on her bedroom door, she hurriedly shut the valise and shoved it under her bed. "Come in."

The butler entered. "Mr Ellerton requests your presence in his study, miss."

Her stomach clenched. Did George suspect? "I'll be down presently."

She took a deep breath and steeled herself as she headed to George's study. A footman held the door open for her and, lifting her head, she swept into the room. "You wished to speak with me."

George regarded her with barely contained anger from behind his desk. "I think the correct question should be, is there something you wish to tell me?"

She chewed on her lower lip and shook her head.

"Do you think me a fool?" he said.

"No, of course not."

"I intercepted this." He held up a letter with Nathan's seal on it. "So I will ask you again. Is there something you wish to tell me?"

Emily swallowed. Why was he so angry? If Nathan was willing to forgo part of his oath to repair her reputation, then that should be a good thing. "Please believe me, I did not want to disobey your wishes. But when you explained about Nathan's past, I realised I had been wrong to turn down his offer of marriage."

Shaking his head, George pushed himself up. "You cannot marry him. Please, no one knows you spent the night with him, so there is no scandal and we can find you a decent husband who will not mind your lack of virginity. Someone better than Lord Thornburn."

"There is no one better than Nathan. I love him. Can you not see that?"

"Please Emily. I beg of you, call off this marriage."

"No, I will not," she said, stamping her foot. "You do not understand what he is forsaking for me."

"And you do not understand what he has already cost you," George said, as his hands formed fists on his desk.

She scrunched her brow. "What are you talking about?"

"I cannot tell you," he said in an anguished voice.

"And I cannot go back on my promise to Nathan."

"Emily, please do not make me do this," he said, as he slumped into his chair.

"Do what?"

"Tell you the whole of what happened."

Emily gripped the back of the chair in front of her, her voice a hoarse whisper, "There's more?"

"Yes," George said, his face taking on a bleak edge.

"Tell me. I'll not break my betrothal otherwise."

He dropped his head, and it was a long moment before he lifted his gaze to her, and what she saw in the depth of his eyes nearly sent her to her knees.

In an emotionless tone, he began, "There were a couple at the house, whom Nathan's betrothed and mother were trying to help."

"Why?"

"They worked for the foreign office."

A horrible, sick feeling spread through Emily's stomach. "What happened?"

"They had important papers with them; papers that if they fell into French hands would have destroyed everything they and the British government had worked for." George ran his hand along the edge of his desk, his eyes downcast as he strove to hold on to his composure.

His struggle was palpable and Emily leaned forwards, gripping the stiff leather of the chair. "Go on," she prompted when she feared he would say no more.

"Instead of escaping, they stayed to destroy the papers." He swallowed. "Nathan's betrothed and her mother died trying to give them the time to achieve their task."

"What happened to them?"

"They were killed protecting our country's secrets."

"Who were they?" Emily asked, her voice wavering.

"They were known to the diplomatic world as Lord and Lady Oakley."

"Known as? You mean Oakley were not their real names?" She began to shake as fearful suspicions built in her mind.

"They took the name from their family home."

A strangled numbness descended on Emily, robbing her voice of emotion as she said with absolute conviction, "Oakleaf Manor; father's ancestral home."

"Yes."

The numbness erupted into a furnace of pain. "Mama, papa, that's how they died?"

"Yes."

Emily covered her face with her hands as hot tears dripped through her fingers. It was Nathan's fault that her parents were dead. How could this be possible?

Through the pain came one thought. Emily dropped her hands and lifted her gaze to George. "Does Nathan know that Lord and Lady Oakley were our parents?"

"No. I only recently put the pieces together. Edward Clarrington confirmed it."

"You never told Nathan?"

George shook his head. "What good would it have done? We needed to work together. His knowing could have jeopardised our safety. I couldn't risk that, and I owed him too much to put that burden on him. Now, do you understand why I cannot let you marry him?"

Twisting her fingers into the folds of her skirts, Emily fled from the room.

Chapter Forty

Staring past her reflection in the mirror, Emily gripped the pendant her parents had given her. Nathan was to blame for her parent's death. The thought was incomprehensible. She loved him, had given herself to him, but because of him, her parents were dead.

Because he seduced the Comtesse de Alessandro, her parents were dead.

Now she understood why George had refused to allow her to marry him. George was right; she couldn't marry him.

She lifted her writing box out of her drawer and unfolded the lid. Pulling out paper, ink and quill, she dashed off a hurried note to say she could no longer marry him and that she absolved him of any responsibility towards her.

She signed her name across the bottom and, bowing her head, she let the tears fall. They fell for her parents' preventable deaths, for Nathan's involvement in their deaths, and finally they fell for what she had lost and could never regain with Nathan.

A few minutes later, she lifted her head, folded the paper, stamped her seal and sprinkled it with sand.

She stood and pulled her bell-pull and when her maid arrived, asked that she send the letter forthwith.

As soon as her maid shut the door behind her, Emily sank onto her bed and curled up into a ball as sobs racked her body.

* * *

Joining his mother, Nathan told her about Emily agreeing to marry him. His mother had clapped her hands and spun around in an undignified manner.

He was almost tempted to do the same. It was unbelievable that Emily had agreed most magnanimously to his rather disagreeable terms.

With a spring in his step, he planned their travel. His mother was happy to prepare his country seat, ready for Emily's arrival, after they returned from Gretna Green. Then he'd written a letter to confirm the details to Emily and asked his footman to give it to Emily's maid along with a guinea and the express instructions that it was to be given to Emily and no one else.

He returned to his study and poured himself a whisky. Today was a day of mixed events, one of happiness and one of extreme difficulty. He wished there could be a better resolution to Peter's predicament, but he had brought it on himself and all Nathan and his family could do was to bear it as best they could.

He pulled out his pocket watch and glanced at the time. It was nearing three; time to get ready to call on Lord Brakenhale. He headed to his room and tugged the bell-pull. A moment later, the butler entered.

"That was quick," Nathan said with a smile.

The butler raised his eyebrows. "This arrived for you just now."

He handed him a letter written in a rushed hand.

Flipping it over, Nathan recognised Emily's seal and tore the letter open, expecting her to be confirming his arrangements. But instead she wrote that she no longer wished to marry him and absolved him of any responsibility towards her. He slumped against the mantelpiece, not believing the words she had written.

His first impulse was to call on her and demand she change her mind, but she was right; what he'd offered her was no life. She'd done her duty by acknowledging his reasons for his half marriage and now she was doing what was best for her; getting as far away from him and his destructive influence as she could. She was better off without him; he'd known it all along. Why had he let himself believe otherwise? Because when Emily looked at him, he truly believed that he was the great and honourable man she saw. And he so wanted to be that man. They'd both been fooling themselves.

He took one last look at her signature scrawled almost illegibly and slung the letter into the fire along with all his sense of worthiness.

Grabbing a cravat, he began tying it into an intricate knot, but his fingers wouldn't obey his instructions. He pulled the cravat free and picked up another, this time tying a simple knot.

His thoughts returned to Emily's refusal. It was just as well George had not discovered their plans, as he could not withstand another beating at the moment. Unless this was

George's doing. He glanced at the letter, now little more than cinders in the fire. He had to make certain this was Emily's choice, and that she was not being forced into it by George. He could not bear the thought of her living with this decision if she had made it against her wishes.

Chapter Forty-One

At the fierce banging on the front door, Emily curled into a tight ball. She had hoped to avoid a confrontation with Nathan. She'd been fooling herself. He was a man who needed answers. Of course, he would demand an explanation, but it was an explanation she could not give.

She crept onto the landing and watched Nathan stride into George's study. Gulping down a lungful of air, she decided she should at least tell him her decision in person and headed to the stairs.

Nathan's voice echoed up to her, "This is your doing."

"It's nothing of the sort," George said. "Emily no longer wishes to marry you and, as her legal guardian, I also withhold my consent, as you were already very much aware of."

"I'm not leaving until I have seen her." His voice was resolute. He would wait all day if needed.

"If you care about her as much as you claim to, then I suggest you avoid causing her any more pain and leave."

Trust her brother to be so protective of her, but she had to do this herself.

"I need to know this is her decision and not yours."

Stepping into the doorway, Emily said, "It's my decision." Her voice held steady even though her emotions were in tatters.

He swung around to face her, his silver eyes full of concern and her heart screamed a denial; he could not have been to blame for her parents' deaths. But when he came towards her, she involuntarily flinched away from him. Confusion marred his brow beneath his unruly lock. She had to make him understand that she could no longer marry him, but she didn't want to cause him more distress and recrimination by informing him of the real reason. "George speaks the truth when he says I no longer wish to marry you."

"But why?"

She shook her head. "Please, I must ask you not to question me further on this matter. I have made up my mind."

He spun around to face George. "You bastard. You've pressured her into refusing my suit against her sense of honour. You know it will destroy her in the long run."

"I've done nothing to dissuade her. This is all her own decision. Until you arrived, I was not even aware she had called it off."

"Liar," he said, as he made a grab for George across the table.

George leaned back out of his reach. "It's time he knew," he said, looking past Nathan to Emily.

"Please George, no." She hurried into the room. Nathan did not deserve that burden.

"Knew what?" Nathan demanded.

"The full extent of your wrongs against Emily," George said, standing up.

"I've acknowledged them all, and she has accepted them."

"Not all of them," George shot back.

Emily threw herself between George and Nathan, her arms outstretched to both. "Enough. I will countenance no further discussion on this matter. This is my decision and it is final."

Nathan grabbed her hand, and Emily's stomach lurched at the revulsion that coursed through her. This was the man she loved. Yet he was responsible for her parents' deaths. She tried to tug her hand free, but he would not let go.

"Emily, tell me why you no longer wish to wed me."

She lifted her gaze to his, pleading curled in the centre of his storm grey eyes. "I cannot," she said, fighting the tears that threatened to fall.

"I will not rest until I find out," he said in his gentle, caring voice.

It was her undoing. She could not let him find out from someone else. If he was to hear the truth, it would be from her.

She nodded and guided Nathan to a chair and sat opposite him. She held his hands in hers. Such strong and capable hands; she rubbed them as though trying to comfort him when in truth she was the one seeking comfort from the man who had destroyed her childhood.

Lifting her gaze to his, she traced the contours of his beloved face, then with a squeeze of his hands, she said, "Your betrothed died trying to protect my parents."

"I do not understand," Nathan said, his mind unable to process her words.

"My parents were at the house when Fouche's men arrived." Her voice cracked as she forced the words through her tight throat. "They worked for the diplomatic service under the names of Lord and Lady Oakley."

Nathan snatched the back of the chair as he lurched unsteadily to his feet. Understanding dawning in horrifying clarity. He was not only to blame for the deaths of his betrothed and her mother, but also for Emily and George's parents. He shoved his hand through his hair. How could this be possible? He'd held Emily and comforted her while she cried for the loss of her parents, and all the while, he'd been the one responsible.

He looked down at Emily with her head tilted up to him, and her moss green eyes only held sorrow for him. He sank onto the chair in front of her and wrapped his arms around her. "I'm sorry, I'm so sorry."

She stiffened in his embrace and he released her immediately. Of course, she would want nothing more to do with him; this wass why she could no longer marry him. He was not worthy of being in the same room as her. He pushed himself to his feet. He'd outstayed his welcome. "I will trespass on you no longer."

The clock on the mantel chimed the hour of four. Oh God, he was meant to be meeting with Lord Brakenhale to discuss Peter's fate. He snatched his hat off the desk and, unable to formulate any further words, he left.

Chapter Forty-two

Nathan, incapable of dwelling on the unexpected news of his involvement in the death of Emily's parents, now had to face the arduous interview with Lord Brakenhale concerning the future of his brother. How had his life come to this?

He arrived at Robert's office, strode over to his sideboard, yanked the stopper off a decanter and poured himself a liberal shot of brandy. He knocked the contents back and poured himself another. Then, without preamble, he demanded, "What's the status with Peter?"

"He still lives, for now at least," Robert said, giving him a concerned look.

Nathan ignored his astute gaze. "Has he told you where the documents are that he claims prove his innocence?"

"No, he refuses to do so until we release him without charge."

"So he's still protesting his innocence." He sank into a chair.

"Yes, he's sticking to his story, interesting is it not?"

"How so?" Nathan said incredulously at Robert's remark. He could not take any more revelations at present.

"All these stories make little sense." The leather of his chair creaked as he leaned back. "Interestingly, though, you take out one variable and suddenly everything becomes clear."

"What variable?"

"Dubeck."

"What about him?" Nathan was not ready to hear any more aspersions regarding his comrade, but a trickle of suspicion began to build pace.

Robert leaned forwards. "You take away what everyone says Dubeck said to them and the rest of their stories all tally. As soon as you add him back in, everyone is accusing everyone else. Plus, there is one other missing piece."

"What piece?" Nathan said, but he suspected he already knew.

"In all the time you have been back, been to Jersey and returned home, Dubeck has not made it here. Strange, do you not think?"

"Maybe he didn't know who to trust."

"Or maybe we've been waiting so long for him to arrive we did not consider one other option."

"What opt...? Oh, he's been here all the time." Nathan twisted his gloves between his hands. Why had he not seen this before? But his loyalty to his friend rose to the surface. No, Dubeck would not have betrayed them. It made no sense for him to defile what his family had died for. But Robert's tone suggested his absolute conviction in his words, and he was rarely wrong.

"Who else could have written that supposed letter from me to George?" Robert asked.

"He trained in the field," Nathan said in a huff of self-disgust as he realised he'd not considered the fact Dubeck knew all the tricks taught at the Bureau Noir. Another sickening realisation hit him. "Oh good God, if so, then that wasn't the only letter he forged."

Robert gave Nathan a curious look.

"The letters he showed to George to imply one of us had betrayed our country; that started this witch hunt. And not forgetting the letter from your French agent – the one which implied Peter had withdrawn unauthorised funds."

"Ah."

"Take that letter out and Peter's account of his stay in gaol and the time taken to return home all match up. Dubeck forged that letter, sending it here before he helped *rescue* Peter. So by the time he got home, we would have received the letter and assumed he was the traitor," Nathan said, the pieces falling into place. Triumph swelled through him before the elation skittered to a sickening halt. Oh God, he'd nearly killed Peter, believing him to be a traitor and for putting Emily in danger, and he'd so wanted to kill George for what he believed he'd done to Peter. He'd nearly committed the unforgiveable. Only Emily and her faith in him had stopped him.

He closed his eyes as a conflicting wave of relief and horror at what he would have done if Emily had not prevented him washed through him. Thank goodness she had placed her faith in him and made him make that promise, for if she hadn't, the consequences would have been devastating. He had so much to thank her for.

Another wave of nausea swept over him. She'd done all that for him when he'd been the one responsible for her parents' deaths. The irony was almost past bearing.

Robert's brow creased. "But that still leaves one question. Why?"

But Nathan knew the answer. "Because he'd discovered the same thing George has," Nathan said, throwing back his head.

"And what is that?"

"That I am to blame for the deaths of his loved ones."

Chapter Forty-Three

Emily had to get away. Pushing herself up, she fled to her aunt's room. "Aunt Amelia, I do not mean to distress you, but I have to leave town."

"Did Lord Thornburn upset you while I was gone?" Her expression was fierce, as though she was ready to go into battle for her.

Emily shook her head. "I cannot explain. Please understand that I must leave now."

"But we cannot get everything organised until at least tomorrow morning."

"That's too long. I will take my maid and a few necessities. You can bring everything else back tomorrow. If I leave now and order the driver to hurry and reduce the stops, I can be home by nightfall. It will be too arduous a journey for you." She gave her aunt a beseeching look.

"But I cannot let you travel on your own. You must take George with you."

She could not sit in a coach with George. She needed solitude to get her thoughts in order. "I would rather he did not know I was going."

"But why?"

"Either you allow me to go now or I will make my own way." She was in no mood to brook any argument. She needed to get away from George, as his presence would remind her of the devastating truth he had told her.

"If it means that much to you, then I will make the arrangements."

"Thank you." Emily gave her aunt a kiss on her cheek.

Twenty minutes later, she stood at the front door and waved goodbye to her aunt in a blur of tears. Turning, she hurried down the steps and into the waiting coach.

Once inside, she opened her hand; inside lay her blood-stained ribbon. How could the man who had kept his promise to her against such provocation be responsible for her parents' deaths? It did not seem possible, yet it was true.

Lost in her worries, she did not notice her maid was not in the coach. It was only when the coach took an unexpected sharp turn her senses registered that something was wrong. She glanced out of the window; they were headed in the wrong direction.

She pounded on the roof to gain the driver's attention. The hatch opened and a man she did not recognise, even though he wore her uncle's livery, looked through.

"You be quiet and behave yourself and no-one will be harmed," the big, bearded coachman said in a stern voice.

"Where are you taking me?"

"To visit my master. It won't take long," he said, slamming the hatch shut.

Fear coiled in her throat. The coach took another sharp turn, and she fell back against the seat. She scanned the street and houses passing by. Should she scream? Should she try to jump from the coach? On the one side was the traffic travelling the other way; she would be trampled by the horses or crushed under the wheels if she tried it. On the other side lay the pavement and pedestrians.

Before she could even formulate a plan, the carriage pulled to a stop. She pressed against the squabs as the steps were lowered and a meaty arm reached in and dragged her out.

She blinked against the harsh afternoon sunlight that reflected off the pale stone wall of a smart town house, stifling a scream as the door burst open and a burly footman pulled her inside.

He led her up a flight of stairs and into a small, well-appointed drawing room. The only door was the one she had been ushered through. Opposite were two long windows with the heavy red damask curtains drawn back. They faced the rear of the house and not the road. She would be unlikely to gain help if she shouted from them.

A slim gentleman of advancing years stood up as she entered. "Welcome, Miss Ellerton."

"You have the advantage over me, Sir, as you know who I am, but I do not believe we have been introduced."

The gentleman indicated the cream and red striped settee facing the crackling fire and waited until she reluctantly took the proffered seat.

"You are quite correct. We have not, but your reputation precedes you."

"I'm not sure that I follow," Emily said, the hackles rising on her neck.

"I have it on good authority that you are good friends with Lord Thornburn."

"I do not think you could class us as good friends."

"My information is rarely incorrect."

Emily eyed him with speculation. She should not tip her hand and decided to agree with his assumptions for now. "If you say so."

"An interesting response, not a denial or an admission, but it does suggest that your previous relationship with him was of an intimate nature." His voice had an unsettling drawl.

Emily stood up. "I request you do not subject me to any more of your conjecture. Especially when you have not had the decency to inform me as to whom you are."

"I am Thomas Dubeck, at your service," he said, with a sweeping bow.

Emily's brow furrowed. This was the man George had risked his life to protect. What would he want with her? "Why did you bring me here?"

"Just to talk. I wanted to get to know you." The corner of his lip lifted in an unnerving manner.

Her lungs constricted; she had to get out of here. "I'm afraid I'm not very good company at present. So if you could arrange for me to be returned home, it would be very much appreciated."

Dubeck shook his head as he took a step towards her. "I dislike people who insult my hospitality."

"In as much as your hospitality so far has extended to you offering me a seat which I have accepted, then I feel that my leaving now has not afforded you any offence."

"I'm not done talking with you." His dark eyes formed tight slits.

Fear inched its way down her spine. "Is there something specific you wished to discuss?"

"Yes, your current relationship with Lord Thornburn."

"There isn't one and there never will be."

"Hmm, which one of you decided that?"

"It was mutual."

"Hold out your hand," he said, as his gaze bored into her tightly fisted right hand.

Emily debated the wisdom of refusing. But suspecting he would only force her if she did not obey, she thrust her hand out with a haughty lift of her head.

"Open it."

She uncurled her gloved hand.

"What is that?" he asked, taking the ribbon and holding it up.

"It's just a piece of ribbon."

"Is this blood?"

Emily refused to answer, staring resolutely at a point above his left shoulder.

"Yours or Nathan's?"

She flinched as she remembered the beating George had given to Nathan.

Dubeck chuckled. "Nathan's it is then. Well, well, well. It seems he is prepared to be injured for you. Now that works out very good for me."

"No," Emily said, before she could stop herself.

Dubeck merely smiled more and stepped over to the bell-pull. He wrote a quick missive and slid the ribbon inside. When the butler arrived, he handed him the letter. "Give this to Lord Thornburn. Make sure he comes alone." His voice was gruff with hatred.

"Your driver said you promised no one would be harmed."

"I lied."

"Not your first, I suspect."

"I just wanted the opportunity of getting to know you. Please sit, you will be more comfortable."

Contemplating her options, she pursed her lips. Making Dubeck think he was in control seemed the best way to proceed, so with a slowly released breath, she retook her seat.

Dubeck nodded with pleasure at her obedience and took the seat opposite her that afforded a view of the door. He stroked the wispy beard on his chin. "So Miss Ellerton, why don't you tell me how you met Lord Thornburn, and just so you are aware, I will know if you are lying."

Emily swallowed and glanced at the clock sat on a side table, trying to judge how long she was going to need to keep him occupied before Nathan arrived.

* * *

Marching along the marbled corridor of the foreign office, Nathan's mind reeled from all he'd learned. Dubeck; a man he'd admired and respected and had pledged an oath in deference to his loss, had betrayed them. But what did he hope to achieve with his lies? His behaviour made no sense. Was this a personal vendetta against him?

He'd left Peter locked up. It wasn't fair, but until things could be sorted out it seemed the most logical decision to ensure he knew where he was.

On entering his home, his harassed butler greeted him.

"A letter came for you, my lord. Delivered by a footman unlike any footman I have ever seen."

With trepidation, Nathan took the letter and flipped it over.

His heart stopped; the seal was Dubeck's. He tore the letter open and out fell Emily's ribbon.

Blood pumping, he stooped to pick it up as he read the missive.

'We're waiting for you. Come alone.'

Nathan scanned the address. It was two streets away. He hollered for the butler, "Get someone to take this to George Ellerton and then on to Lord Brakenhale. Hurry, man. Now." Nathan thrust the envelope at the butler. The ribbon he tucked into his pocket.

He rushed out into the street, barging past pedestrians and knocking street vendors out of his way. On reaching the house, he thumped the knocker.

Chapter Forty-Four

Hands folded in her lap, Emily sat next to Dubeck and tried to keep calm as she watched the clock on the side table slowly tick the passage of time.

At the loud banging reverberating through the house, Emily twisted her fingers into the folds of her skirt, fighting to show no outward reaction to the noise, whilst hot blood pumped through her veins.

The door swung open as an enraged Nathan strode into the room. Her heart sang as she twisted in her seat. He'd come to save her.

"Thank you for keeping Miss Ellerton company," Nathan said, as he stalked towards her. "I'll escort her home now."

A hand clamped around her arm and dragged her up.

"You'll stay where you are if you don't want the little lady to get hurt."

A wince escaped her as Dubeck grabbed her wounded arm. He gave her a curious look as he slid his fingers under the sleeve of her dress to the bandage. Smiling, he looked at Nathan as his thumb squeezed against her wound.

Emily pressed her lips together. She would not cry out and

give him the triumph of using her against Nathan. But his thumb dug in harder and a small cry escaped her as blood seeped free to mar her sleeve.

"There, you see, Thornburn," Dubeck spat. "You're a danger to every young woman you interact with, causing them nothing but heartache, pain, and death."

Nathan's face grew white hot with fury. "Let her go. She has nothing to do with this."

"You think not? Because of you, I lost my loved ones. Now it's your turn."

"No!" Nathan shouted, stepping forwards.

Dubeck pulled Emily against him. "One more step and you'll regret it."

Nathan took a step back, keeping his arms by his side.

"That's better," Dubeck said.

"Why are you doing this?" Nathan asked, keeping his eyes levelled on Dubeck. "Your wife and daughter died six years ago. Why turn on me now?"

Emily's head swung around to face Dubeck. His wife and daughter were dead, but that meant only one thing. His daughter had been Nathan's betrothed, and it was her parents she had died to protect.

Dubeck's face contorted and Emily tried to pull away from him, but his incensed grip only tightened. "Why now?" he sneered. "Because until recently I didn't realise you caused their deaths. I always knew you'd taken it hard, but I thought that was purely because you'd been too late to save them and had felt it keenly. I thought you had loved my daughter. By your example, you gave me the strength to carry on, to continue the fight they had died for. Then I learned the ugly truth; that your regret was not for the loss of my family but because of your guilt for your part in their deaths.

"All because you fell for some misty-eyed girl with lies hidden behind her tears," he said, his voice becoming high pitched. "Those false tears became my real tears."

Nathan took a slow, steady step towards them, his hands held up in supplication. "I'll accept that I made a mistake. And I know what that mistake cost you, but I tried to save them and when I couldn't, I pledged to make it up to them."

His overcast grey eyes flickered to Emily and her heart flipped over. He was referring to her parents as well. She bit her bottom lip to stop herself from shaking.

"How dare you say that to me?" Dubeck said, as his hand dug painfully into Emily's arm. "You worked alongside me for all those years and you never said a word. You weren't trying to help me through that difficult time, you were trying to assuage your own guilt. Your compassion for me was nothing more than the desperate need to achieve atonement for what you had done."

"That's not true." He took another careful step closer.

"If you didn't feel guilty, then why did you never tell me it was you who led that murderous bitch to my door?"

"I was trying to spare you pain."

"You were trying to protect your own pitiful hide."

Too scared to move, Emily stood next to Dubeck as his hand squeezed agonisingly around her wounded arm. She was caught between two combatants. She didn't dare whimper or make a sound.

"Yes, maybe you're right," Nathan said, as he sidestepped a rosewood table. "But I am truly sorry for the loss of Valerie and Susan, and Lord and Lady Oakley; they were brave and honourable people. They would not have wanted this."

"Don't you dare tell me what they would have wanted or otherwise, that is not your place."

"Then tell me truthfully if Valerie would have wanted this?" Nathan said, indicating Emily. "What would she say if she could see you now?"

"Do not bring my wife into this."

"Why not? You did."

"This isn't about her. It's about you and your betrayal of me," Dubeck screamed.

"I made an error in judgement."

"It wasn't your mind that was making the decisions. They died because you couldn't resist the charms of a traitorous light-skirt. I thought you'd at least have had more respect for my daughter after your betrothal, but that meant nothing to you. I have thought long and hard about how I wanted to punish you," Dubeck said, dragging Emily back a step as he increased the distance between them and Nathan.

"I wanted you to lose the trust of everyone around you, for you to exact revenge against them, only to learn later that they were innocent. I even tried to slow George down, so you'd have a chance of catching up with him."

"You shot George!" Emily swung around to face Dubeck. "But he didn't do anything to you."

"You think not?" Dubeck said. "When I first discovered Nathan's treachery, I tried to have him killed, but George saved him."

George's fevered dream; he'd cried out a heartfelt warning to Nathan. She closed her eyes in relief that he'd succeeded. Her eyes flew open. George must have saved Nathan after he'd found out about his involvement in their parents' deaths. She whispered a quick thank you to George for his loyalty to

Nathan, even after he'd discovered the truth.

"When that failed, I decided to hurt Nathan like he'd hurt me. So I tried to make him believe George was a traitor, in the hopes he would kill him, but the coward couldn't bring himself to do it. So I gave him more incentive and made him believe George had killed Peter. That didn't work either, so I returned Peter to him whilst making it look like Peter was the traitor," Dubeck said, turning to Nathan.

"I did it in the hopes you'd kill him yourself before I revealed the truth. I wanted you to know what it was like to lose a loved one and then to realise you'd been working alongside the person who was responsible."

Emily attempted to yank her arm free of his grasp. "I cannot let you dishonour your wife and daughter's sacrifice in this way."

"This has nothing to do with you," Dubeck said, twisting her arm behind her back and pulling her hard against him.

"Yes, it does," Emily said, looking Dubeck straight in his coal-black eyes. "Because it was my parents your wife and daughter died trying to protect."

Dubeck stared at her and then lifted his gaze to Nathan. "See, there is no end to the anguish you have caused." His gaze dropped back to Emily and her skin crawled at the hatred burning in his eyes. "You must despise him as much as I."

How could she despise Nathan? He'd regretted what had happened and through his strength of character he'd kept his promise to her against great provocation and he'd honoured those he'd failed by pledging to dedicate his life to their cause. How could she hate a man who made such a sacrifice for something he was not to blame for? It was not Nathan's fault the Comtesse de Alessandro had been a traitor. Therefore, it was not his fault her parents had been killed. She no longer held him to blame. Her heart swelled at everything he'd done in her parents' memory. She stared at Dubeck's contorted face, and her limbs stopped shaking. Dubeck was hurt and angry, but he was also wrong. She uttered one word. "No."

"How can you not hate him after everything he has done to you?" Dubeck cried, wet spittle spraying over Emily's face.

"Because I know how deeply he regrets what happened and how he has tried to atone for it by forsaking his own happiness and pledging himself to the cause they died for. I know what he has denied himself in honour of them and I forgive him," Emily said, as the tight band that had been constricting her chest fell away, letting her breathe fully since she'd first discovered the truth about her parents' deaths.

"No!" Dubeck screamed, thrusting Emily away from him as though she were repugnant. He glared at Nathan. "Your debt to me can never be repaid, not to me. I'm the one who lost everything."

Nathan reached out and pulled Emily to him, but when she threaded her slender fingers through his in a symbol of trust and solidarity, his knees nearly buckled beneath him. She should hate him. She had every right to hate him, for he hated himself for the pain he had caused. He'd held her as she cried for the loss of her parents. They'd been on their last assignment and he had let them get killed. He'd taken so much away from her and yet she forgave him. The enormity of her compassion pulsated through his veins. And in that moment, he understood that she would not allow him to carry his guilt anymore. He had to forgive himself.

He turned to Dubeck. "For years I have carried the guilt of Valerie, Susan and Lord and Lady Oakley's deaths. I vowed my punishment would be to deny myself a wife and family of my own, and even after all the sacrifices Emily has made for me," he said, squeezing her hand in gratitude, "And even with her complete trust and faith in me, I still denied myself what my heart most desired. I turned her away."

Emily nodded to show he spoke the truth. "He left me, in deference to you, your wife and daughter, and unbeknownst to him at the time, my parents."

"I did that for you, Dubeck," Nathan said, staring at the dilapidated shell of his former friend. A man he had such sympathy and admiration for. "In penitence for my mistake, for not being able to save your family, I vowed to forgo the pleasure of a family of my own. I gave up my chance of happiness, but not anymore. My debt to you is paid, and it is you I am to thank for showing me that. Now I can love Emily without guilt. For that, I shall be eternally grateful to you, Dubeck."

"No!" Dubeck shouted, as he snatched up a fire iron and lunged at Nathan.

Emily stepped between them and grabbed his arm. "Let it go," she said, keeping her eyes level with his. "It's time to let it go." Her voice was gentle and compassionate.

He sank to the ground. "They're gone, and they're never coming back," he sobbed.

Crouching down, Emily wrapped her arms around his gaunt body. "I know. I miss my parents, too." She cradled him while he cried.

Nathan came over and pulled her up. "That's enough now."

A commotion ensued in the hallway, followed by Robert Darnell, George Ellerton and Simon Pykett bursting through the door.

George hurried over to Emily and engulfed her in a hug.

Simon hauled Dubeck to his feet.

"Go easy on him," Nathan said.

"I'll not die a traitor for the cause my Valerie and Susan gave their lives for," Dubeck said, struggling to pull out of Simon's grip.

"Well, that's rather difficult under the circumstances." Robert shook his head at him. "You've jeopardised our mission."

"I just wanted Nathan to suffer."

"And he has," Robert said.

"But not enough," Dubeck said, crumpling into a heap.

"We'll take it from here," Robert said to Nathan. "You take Miss Ellerton home."

Robert was trying once again to force him into close quarters with Emily in the hopes he would give up his oath. Nathan smiled, for he had decided to do just that and was eternally grateful to Robert for giving him the opportunity to be alone with her.

He led her out and waved down a hackney carriage. Once inside, he pulled her ribbon out of his pocket and wrapped it solemnly around her ring finger as a declaration of his intentions.

Without a word, he lifted her chin up and slanted his lips over hers. Tracing the contours of her lips with the tip of his tongue, his hands wrapped around her, pulling her to him as he savoured the feeling of holding a loved one in his arms. This is what he had been denying himself all these years; the simple pleasure of being able to love without recrimination.

And he'd been wrong. He did not have Dubeck to thank; he had Emily for showing him he was worthy of this and all the things that came with a wife and children. She had given him a future and for that, he would give her his heart.

He pulled back, but kept her ensconced in his arms. "Emily, will you do me the greatest honour and agree to be my wife?"

She rested her hand against his face. "I will, and I will happily live here while you continue your work."

He shook his head. "No, I want a full life with you and lots of children. As Robert said, it is time I started living the life I have been so diligently protecting."

"But what about the cause my parents died for?"

"Your parents died trying to safeguard this way of life for you and the best way for us to honour them is to live the life they died protecting."

A teary smile broke across Emily's face, and she threw her arms around him. She kissed his bruised eye, the cut on his nose and finally his swollen lip. "I think, as well as long sleeves, I need to tell my seamstress to add a blue ribbon to my wedding dress."

THE END.

Afterword

If you enjoyed reading The Earl's Dangerous Secret, please leave a review. This helps new readers find my books.

You can find me on social media:
Facebook: @EllieHenshawAuthor
Twitter: @EllieHenshaw
Instagram: @EllieHenshaw

Printed in Dunstable, United Kingdom

63681757R00194